The pilot must have felt me watching him.

He looked up as he neared the building, saw me, and smiled.

My heart stuttered.

This particular pilot had that handsome pilot look. The look that could have easily put him on the cover of a men's magazine.

I looked away.

Just because a man was handsome didn't mean I had to be attracted to him.

Besides, I wasn't looking for a boyfriend.

FIRST TIME CHARM

FIRST TIME CHARM

THE WORTHINGTONS

KATHRYN KALEIGH

FIRST TIME CHARM

PREVIEW: THREE BROKEN RULES

To learn more about Kathryn Kaleigh, visit

www.kathrynkaleigh.com

Kathryn Kaleigh

1

BRIANNA WORTHINGTON

*A*fter zipping up the side of my lipstick red pencil skirt, I stepped into my black red-bottomed heels.

I pulled a black cashmere sweater from a shelf in my walk-in closet and pulled it on over my white silk button down blouse.

I turned this way and that in front of the full-length mirror propped on the floor of one end of my closet.

At five seven, I was the tallest of my four sisters. Two older sisters and one younger sister in my immediate family and one much older half-sister who already had kids of her own.

In fact, the half-sister, Danielle, was the only one of us who had any children and she lived in California. My oldest sister Madison was married and my next oldest sister, Ainsley, was engaged.

Ainsley lived here in Houston, but Madison had moved to Denver for a university professor job.

Madison took after Momma. Both of them were psychologists.

Ainsley took after Daddy. They were both airplane pilots for Daddy's company Skye Travels.

Then there was me.

I was an odd combination of both Daddy and Momma.

I had Daddy's passion, but I preferred to keep both feet literally on the ground. Daddy lived and breathed aviation. Me. I didn't fly simply because I had no reason to.

I was quite content driving around Houston in my 2022 fire-engine red Maserati Quattroporte.

Yes. Daddy bought it for me.

And anyone who had a problem with that could take it up with somebody who cared. Because I didn't.

I didn't have time in my life for judgmental people.

Besides, I had a thick skin.

I'd been dissed by the best of them. Perfect strangers felt compelled to give me their opinions of everything from my lifestyle to my career choice to the color of my lipstick.

So I went with what made me happy.

I had Momma's fashion sense and breezy personality.

Momma could walk into a room and charm anyone.

She was a drug representative turned psychologist.

From what I'd heard Daddy say, never in a critical way, the psychology training had taken some of the natural shine off that innate charm.

What he actually said was that she was a lot more serious now than she had been before.

But after giving birth to five children, all after the age of thirty, she'd earned the right to be as serious as she wanted.

I walked through my living room, stylishly furnished in neutral tones and turned on all the lights as I went.

I straightened the blue vase filled with pale pink roses and dark pink daisies on the table in my foyer.

Stepping into my home office, I pulled my MacBook from the desk draw, powered it on, and logged in.

I quickly opened my template, typed in the date and a working title.

Then I hit record and sat on a little stool in front of my desk.

"Hello lovelies," I said into the camera. "Welcome back to my channel. If this is your first time here, my name is Brianna Worthington and I'm going to talk to you today about creating your very own capsule wardrobe. It's not hard. And there are two important things I want you to take away from today's video. One is that a capsule wardrobe does not have to be boring."

I stepped away from the camera to show off my red pencil skirt and high heels.

"Seriously?" I asked with an impish grin. "Does this look boring?"

I turned this way and that so the camera could capture my full outfit.

"And second, a capsule wardrobe doesn't have to last forever. The guideline is that it lasts for about three months. For those of us who love shopping, that's awesome news."

"But…" I held up a finger and sat back down on my stool so I could look directly into my camera.

"You can start anywhere and your capsule wardrobe can last as long as you want it to. In fact, when I started my capsule wardrobe, I started simple. I started with this shirt I'm wearing. And guess where I bought it?"

I paused for effect.

"No. Not Nordstrom's. I bought this blouse from Target. And two years later I'm still wearing it. I wear it all the time. With everything.

"And it's so basic, no one even notices. Then I built around it."

I swept a hand down my skirt.

"A year later I bought this skirt at Nordstrom's. It was on sale. I admit. But it's good quality. I'll put the link below so you can look it up if you want to. And, yes, it's so basic and not trendy that they still sell it after almost a year."

I leaned forward into the camera.

"But… and this is very important. If you're going to buy new pieces for your wardrobe, buy things that fit you perfectly on the day you walk out of the store with them. Do not buy something that you hope will fit in a few months when you lose ten pounds. And another thing."

I paused again for effect.

"Buy things that you feel comfortable wearing. Something that is you. Not something that your fantasy you would wear. You know. The one where you're outgoing and carefree. Trendy.

"If the thought of wearing a tight red skirt sets your nerves on edge and you know you'd never put it on and walk out your front door, pick something more basic and add something like a scarf for color."

My phone chimed and a text message popped up on my screen.

I hit pause on my recording.

Editing was part of the process and was to be expected.

I didn't even mind editing.

But I rarely shot a video more than one time.

If I got interrupted. Like right now. I'd just edit out the interruption and keep going.

MOMMA: *Good morning.*

It was funny because not even having five children had gotten Momma out of the habit of thinking she had to communicate a normal conversation through text messaging.

She didn't seem to understand that greetings weren't required.

You could simply pick up a conversation you'd been having days ago as though no time at all had passed.

But I'd given up on trying to change that about her. I was just happy she texted at all at the ripe old age of fifty-five.

ME: *Hi.*

MOMMA: *Don't forget. Dinner on Sunday.*

ME: *I know. It's in my phone.*

MOMMA: *You should keep a paper calendar, too. It's easier to maintain. And keep up with.*

ME: *Okay.*

Another thing I'd given up on. Making Momma go digital was a lost cause. Not worth the fight.

But even though I left her alone about her paper calendars, there was no way I was going to start writing my appointments down on paper and Momma knew it.

There was no sense in reminding her, though, of the many ways the two of us were different. There were far too many ways that we were alike.

And those things were what mattered.

I didn't have to be a psychologist like her and my oldest sister to know these things.

Thinking that Momma was finished with the current conversation, I played back the last of my recording to orient myself back to what I'd been talking about.

MOMMA: Did you remember that you're picking your sister up from the airport today?

Damn. Damn. Damn.

I unlocked my phone and checked my calendar. I'd forgotten to set an alert and it had completely gotten overlooked.

ME: Of course not. I'm on my way out the door now.

Damn it. I hated it when Momma was right about her paper calendars.

I logged out and closed my computer. Tucked it back into the drawer and slid the stool back under the desk.

In my defense, picking my sister up from the airport was a most unusual request.

She was flying in on one of Daddy's planes. By one of Daddy's pilots. Probably Madison's husband if he was available. And I couldn't imagine why he wouldn't be. The two of them were stuck like glue.

Most people would just get an Uber or in my family's case, they'd schedule a car to pick them up.

But this was Madison's first time home since her wedding to her college sweetheart Kade. You'd think she was freaking royalty the way everyone was acting.

Madison and Kade had been college sweethearts only to break up for several years before they finally got back together, apparently by accident, and finally got married.

Anyway, apparently, I was the only person available to pick up my sister from the airport.

They would go down the list. Daddy had a flight. Ainsley had a flight. Momma had a patient. Quinn had a meeting. My younger sister was in class or whatever she did.

So that left me. The one who worked at home.

Somehow the *worked* part of the phrase *worked at home* was silent.

Like the P in psychology.

And, like always, I told myself it was okay. Because I was happy to see my sister and we could have lunch together before she was swept up in everyone else's activities.

I grabbed my charcoal wool coat, shrugged into it, and dragged my hair out of the collar.

I'd pull it back, but there wasn't time.

I was seriously late.

Next time, maybe, my sister would schedule a driver to pick her up.

A real driver.

2

JACKSON FLEMING

*S*eeing the skyline of Houston again brought back a lot of memories.

I'd grown up in Houston, but college had taken me away.

I always figured I'd find my way back there some day.

And I'd always thought of Houston as home even though I hadn't lived there in twelve years.

I was what people called an easy-going person.

I liked flying. And as long as I was flying, I was content.

My buddy, Daniel, had been the one who convinced me to join him in Denver after college.

We'd progressed from college roommates to apartment roommates and we'd lived together for the sum total of two months before he'd moved in with a new girlfriend.

To his credit, they were still together, though, for the life of me, I didn't know how a man could meet a girl and move in with her in just two months.

There were too many variables.

Anybody could be on their good behavior for two months.

Hell, I'd known people who could hold it together for over a year before they showed their true colors.

But I was glad my buddy had had good luck with his whirlwind romance.

I still lived in the same apartment we'd moved into back then.

Occasionally I considered looking for something else, but then I'd get a call for a flight and that would go out of my mind for the unforeseeable future.

As I approached the runway of the Houston airport, it occurred to me that I probably saw Denver as a temporary stopover. One that had lasted seven years.

The problem was I had established connections in Denver. I didn't work for any particular airline.

I did private contracting.

And damn if it didn't keep me busy.

More business than any regular job.

They said sitting was the new smoking. Well, I might as well hang it up. I kept waiting for somebody to make an airplane with room for pilots to stand up while they navigated the plane.

Surely someone out there was working on that.

I heard my passenger, Madison Worthington, talking on her cell. Technically she was Mrs. Kade Johnson, but since she was Dr. Worthington, she'd kept her own last name.

I didn't much see the point in that.

But I was an old-fashioned guy.

I figured that if two people were going to get married and become a family, the least they could do was to share a name.

I didn't even care if I had to be the one to change my name.

Kade could have changed his name to Kade Worthington.

There would have been nothing wrong with that, at least not in my book.

Unfortunately, that was one of those things that could get a man-card revoked.

So they kept their own names.

Not my problem.

And the whole thing was more than I needed to know.

I just needed to know when to pick her up and where to drop her off.

All the other personal stuff really wasn't my business.

I also knew that this week was Madison's birthday and that her husband was going to be flying in later in the day.

They had a whole family thing planned for Sunday.

Just knowing all this information made me uncomfortable.

The more I knew, the more I had to interact and the more I had to keep up with.

I didn't have to have the plane back until tomorrow so instead of flying straight back like I normally would—just so I could take another flight job, I was planning to spend the night in Houston.

Drive around a bit and see how things were holding up.

Maybe revisit some of my old stomping grounds.

I didn't really know anyone from here anymore, so I didn't have any plans past that.

That suited me just fine.

Other than planning my work flights, I preferred to let things happen as they fell.

Life seemed to move a whole lot smoother when a man didn't jerk on the steering wheel too much.

3

———

BRIANNA

*W*hy was it that anytime I was late, there was a traffic jam?

By the time I pulled up to the private terminal, I was ten minutes late.

I parked and stepped out of the car.

I didn't see any of Daddy's planes on the tarmac.

What a relief.

I wasn't so worried about making Madison wait as I was hearing about how my digital calendar had tripped me up.

Being the most modern member of the Worthington family, I had a reputation to maintain.

It was especially important since no one in my family seemed to understand what it was exactly that I did.

When I said YouTuber, I got blank looks. Going on to say that I had over one hundred thousand followers didn't do anything to help.

Talking about fashion and minimalism and organization didn't help either.

Yet, when one of my sisters had an event, I was the one they called for fashion advice.

Since the plane wasn't there yet, I went to the terminal and went upstairs to the third floor where the Skye Travels offices were housed.

To say that Skye Travels was a closely held corporation was an understatement.

My father, Noah, had an office. My brother, Quinn, who was the CEO of the Houston office had an office. And my sister, Ainsley, had a small office there, too.

Ainsley was the newest Skye Travels pilot.

She'd been flying for years, but Daddy wouldn't hire her until she had enough experience.

Personally, I thought Daddy had been too hard on her. Ainsley was a good pilot. As good as any of the guys he hired.

Although she was the only female pilot working for Skye Travels right now, I didn't think that her being a girl had anything to do with his reluctance to hire her right out of school.

I think it was because he only hired the best.

And even if Ainsley was already good, he made her wait. Daddy was a fair man and he didn't want anyone to think he'd showed favoritism to his own daughter.

He could have, though, and no one would have said a word to him.

He was, after all, Noah Worthington.

I think Ainsley deserved special consideration.

What was the point of owning your own company if you couldn't hire whoever you wanted to?

The elevator door opened and I stepped into the lobby of Skye Travels.

It was always quiet. And spacious.

It had a good feel to it.

Maybe one day I'd shoot a video here. Think about setting up an office space.

Or not.

My brand was working from home.

I wasn't about to break what was working.

It was an idea, though, so I tucked it into the back of my mind.

I went to the window and watched as one of Daddy's planes touched down on the runway outside.

Skye Travels scrawled in red across the plane looked edgy and modern.

Daddy had recently redesigned his logo and I'd helped him with that.

At least someone in my family appreciated my skills.

A few minutes later, my sister stepped out of the plane.

She looked good. As always.

Glowing.

One of the local guys unloaded her luggage.

My sister did not know how to travel light.

The pilot stepped out and spoke to one of the mechanics.

I didn't recognize the pilot, but that wasn't surprising. Unlike the rest of the family, I didn't spend a lot of time at the airport.

I watched as the pilot walked across the tarmac.

He wasn't wearing the Skye Travels uniform, and most noticeably, he wasn't wearing a cap.

Daddy insisted that all his pilots wear a cap.

So this guy didn't work for Daddy.

He walked with a self-assured confidence that seemed to come with the job.

I'd observed over the years that pilots were a self-assured lot.

My sister Ainsley, a pilot herself, refused to date pilots. She claimed she knew too much about their lifestyle.

Ironically she was engaged to a pilot, but he was only a pilot for himself. Well, for them.

He actually owned his own video game creation company.

I put one hand on my hip. No one questioned the status of his job.

I didn't see how creating video games was all that far from making videos about minimalism and fashion.

The pilot must have felt me watching him.

He looked up as he neared the building, saw me, and smiled.

My heart stuttered.

This particular pilot had that handsome pilot look. The look that could have easily put him on the cover of a men's magazine.

I looked away.

Just because a man was handsome didn't mean I had to be attracted to him.

Besides, I wasn't looking for a boyfriend.

4

JACKSON

I needed to go inside. Do some paperwork.

Just part of the job.

I hadn't thought to reserve a car.

The airports almost always provided one.

I hadn't taken into account, though, that this time I was planning on staying a couple of days.

I should have rented a car so I didn't have to count on anyone here to provide me with transportation.

After I took care of my business here, I'd walk over to the main airport and rent a car.

I looked up toward the window of the lobby and nearly missed a step.

I was used to people watching me.

Women liked a man in uniform.

I usually paid them no attention.

I didn't have time for a relationship and hooking up just made me tired.

Turns out I wasn't built for it.

I had five fingers and a palm that were a lot less emotionally draining than involving someone else in my private life.

Besides, I was funny about touching people I didn't know.

I didn't just dip my wick anywhere.

But the woman looking at me from the window nearly took my breath away.

Maybe it was the way the sunlight struck her through the glass window.

Or maybe it was the way her hair fell softly over her right shoulder.

Or maybe it was the way her lips curved into a perfect bow.

Or maybe it was just that she was the most beautiful woman I'd ever seen.

Whatever it was about her, I knew that no matter what else I did, I had to talk to her.

After the near misstep, I started walking faster.

Knowing airports like I did, I knew a person could disappear in a heartbeat, never to be seen again.

She could get onto a plane to absolutely anywhere and it would be impossible for me to ever see her again.

As I pushed the elevator button, I reminded myself that this was a private terminal.

She wasn't likely to just disappear onto an airplane to one of a million places.

Nonetheless, I tapped my fingers against the iPad bag I carried over my right shoulder.

I needed to be cool.

I didn't need the most beautiful girl I'd ever seen to think I was a freak. I needed an excuse to talk to her.

I'd think of something.

The elevator dinged and I stepped off into the Skye Travels lobby.

This was the opposite of a busy airport terminal.

So much so, I almost thought I'd gotten off on the wrong floor.

But private terminals were calm by nature.

People who flew privately did so with the expectation that they would avoid the chaos of the typical airport.

Besides, Skye Travels was tastefully scripted on the wall just outside the elevator.

I turned the corner and the first thing I saw was the reception desk.

A young lady sat there, wearing a headset, typing on a keyboard. Nothing unusual.

Then I saw the young lady I'd seen from below.

She was talking with my passenger—Madison Worthington.

I stood and watched them for a moment while I tried to sort out this situation.

Madison had been only a few minutes ahead of me.

I watched as the two women hugged, then I realized that they had an uncanny resemblance, though Madison wasn't quite as tall as the other girl.

Sisters.

They were sisters.

I was certain of it.

In sync, they turned and went off down the hallway. Into the offices of Skye Travels.

Offices that were off-limits to me.

Not surprising since this was a family held corporation.

I'd just wait for her to come back out into the lobby.

And while I waited, I'd take care of my business.

5

____

BRIANNA

"I want to go see Daddy," Madison said after giving me a quick hug.

"He's on a flight," I said. "That's why I was elected to pick you up, remember?"

"Right," Madison said. "And so we can have lunch."

"Exactly," I said with a quick smile, feeling guilty for implying that I hadn't wanted to see her.

"I'll just say hi to Quinn then," she said. "If he's in."

"He's probably there," I said.

"Who's your pilot?" I asked, as the man I watched from the window stepped into the lobby.

Madison was cool enough to not look in the guy's direction.

"Jackson Fleming," she said as we headed toward our brother's office.

"I haven't seen him before."

And he was definitely someone I'd remember.

I considered myself immune to the whole man in a uniform thing. But Jackson had looked at me different than most.

For one, he didn't know who I was.

"You wouldn't," Madison said. "He's contract."

"That's different. Daddy needs to hire more people."

Madison laughed. "Hardly." Then she shrugged. "Maybe."

I looked at her sideways.

Madison shrugged. "Denver is new turf for Skye Travels. It's okay, though, he was good. And he left me alone. Gave me time to do some work."

I nodded in understanding.

Our brother Quinn was the only one of the siblings who didn't seem to have inherited our parents' drive to succeed.

Sure. Quinn was the CEO of this office. But he spent his days working deals.

Maybe to him that was work just like making videos was work to me.

I tried not to judge.

Still. It just seemed like Quinn wasn't as driven as the rest of us.

We reached Quinn's office.

"Hold on," he said then covered the receiver. "Hey Madison. Glad you made it." He pointed to the phone. "Can we catch up later? This is kind of important."

"No problem," Madison said.

Again, I tried not to judge my brother.

He was good at keeping this place running smoothly as Daddy took more and more steps away from the day-to-day hands on workings.

Daddy pretty much did what he wanted to do these days.

And some of those days involved doing nothing more than convincing our mother to get away from her own work and do something fun with him.

In the last year, they'd taken a cruise and had gone on several trips.

They'd been going through a lot together. And although I didn't think our mother was ready to go into any kind of semi-retirement, Daddy's situation had kind of forced her to get there sooner rather than later.

"Well," Madison said. "Shall we go across the street for lunch?"

"Sounds good."

One of the valets had already taken my keys and put Madison's luggage in my car.

The Skyhouse club across the street was our typical meeting place whenever we were around the airport. It was a rather convenient marketing thing that it had a similar name to our company, yet there was no relationship whatsoever.

At least nothing that any of us knew about.

During the day, it was frequented by pilots and passengers alike.

And in the evenings was just a general hangout place.

But it was convenient and close to our terminal.

And had the best martinis.

We went back through the lobby.

I didn't see Jackson anywhere.

He had paperwork to do, so he should have been around.

I didn't ask.

The last thing I needed to do was to hook up with a contract pilot out of Denver.

Life was already far too complicated to add any kind of attraction to… well… anyone.

I hadn't declared a moratorium on men like my sister Ainsley had done before she'd met her fiancé Wyatt. But I hadn't had a serious relationship since college.

I'd found that life was so much simpler that way.

6

JACKSON

The receptionist, Helen, had let me set up on a table in the back to work. It looked like something of a supply room/workroom. Big table. Shelves on one side loaded with printer paper and other office supplies.

From here I could hear her talking on the phone. It wasn't distracting at all. Just part of the work life of being a contract pilot. No real office.

Often times I sat in the lobby of various private terminals and completed my paperwork, so noise and activity didn't bother me one bit.

Though I appreciated her generous offer, I would have preferred to have been somewhere closer where I could watch for Madison's sister.

Though no one had confirmed my suspicion about who she was, I had no doubt.

In fact, thinking back, I remembered Madison saying something about her sister picking her up from the airport.

I'd thought it was a little bit strange, since the daughter of the owner of Skye Travels would no doubt have access to all sorts of transportation.

Had Madison mentioned the name of her sister?

This was one of those rare occasions where my efforts to avoid getting into the personal business of my passengers backfired.

Just as I was finishing up my paperwork, a man walked into my little workspace.

"Hello," he said. "Are you Jackson?"

"Yes." Closing my iPad, I stood up.

"I'm Noah Worthington," the man said, holding out a hand.

"It's a pleasure to meet you," I said. A pleasure and very much unexpected.

"I just wanted to thank you for getting my daughter here safely."

"Of course, Sir," I said. "It's my job."

Noah leaned a hip against the table.

"If you're like the rest of us," he said. "it's more than a job."

I leaned back in my chair. I'd heard about Noah Worthington. He was a legend in the aviation world.

He'd started as a commercial pilot. Bought himself a plane and in just a few short years created an empire.

No one questioned his decisions and I personally knew of several pilots who wanted to fly for him.

Working for Skye Travels was considered one of those almost unattainable jobs that somehow had become more coveted than flying for the commercial airlines.

It wasn't surprising. The big airlines had gotten too big to care about anything other than the bottom line.

But Noah was still small enough and hands-on enough to provide personal attention to his pilots and he even took some passengers up himself.

Or so I'd heard.

"Actually right now, I'm so busy with contract work that I barely have time to think about anything other than getting from one airport to the next."

"My son-in-law, Kade Johnson, said you're one of the best."

Kade. That would be Madison's husband. I'd met him and we'd even had drinks one evening.

I guess that was how I pulled this job.

"That's quite the compliment," I said. "but I just do the best job I can."

"I like modesty in a competent man," Noah said. "Can I take you to dinner? Maybe discuss some possibilities?"

There was a time when I would have jumped at the opportunity to take on more work.

But right now I was so busy the thought of adding even more work to my life made me almost nauseated.

"I was actually going to take a couple of days. Look around." I shrugged. "I grew up in Houston."

"I know," Noah said.

Ah. Noah had checked into my background. Now I was a little off-balance. Whatever the man had to discuss, it was serious enough that he'd taken the time to check into my background. To go far enough back to see that I grew up in Houston. Few people bothered to go that far back.

Once they got back to my college years, they had everything they needed to know about me.

I'd been considered the top student in my class. I'd ridden on that reputation until I'd made a new reputation as a contractor.

"I'd like to talk with you," Noah said. "And I happen to be free tonight."

"Alright," I said. I wouldn't mind having company for dinner. Besides curiosity got the best of me. What could Noah Worthington possibly want with me? He had a string of pilots coming right out of school with the sole goal of being hired on with him.

It wasn't like he was short on pilots.

But he had been short in Denver. That was how I ended up here.

"Good," he said. "We can take my car. There's a place called the Skyhouse across the street. Good food and good martinis."

"Skyhouse," I said. "Yours?"

Noah straightened.

"Unfortunately, no. Though at times I wish I'd thought of it first. It's actually good advertising for the both of us. Fortunately, the fellow who owns it is a good man."

Together Noah and I walked through the lobby of Skye Travels.

And although I looked around for Madison's sister, I didn't see her anywhere.

In fact, I didn't see anyone else other than Helen sitting at the desk.

"See you tomorrow, Helen," Noah said as we walked past.

Individual attention. That, I decided was Noah's secret to success.

How many owners of successful companies knew all the names of their employees?

"Did you happen to meet my other daughter?" Noah asked, catching me off guard.

I hoped my expression didn't betray the level of guilt that I felt for thinking about the man's daughter.

"No," I said. "She's the one picking Madison up?

"Yeah," he said. "Brianna. They're probably at the Skyhouse now. I'll introduce you."

"Sure," I said, trying to act nonchalant. But somehow I felt like Noah was setting me up with his own daughter.

Wishful thinking. That's all that was.

No man in his right mind would set his daughter up with a man, much less a contract pilot from out of state.

7

BRIANNA

*W*e sat in a booth in the bar section of the restaurant. It was that time of day when people started to spill in. Not just passengers, flight staff, and pilots, but people off the street who purposely came here for the food and the good drinks, especially the martinis.

My sister Madison was the oldest in the family so she was four years older than I was.

And on top of that, our other sister Ainsley had been born right between us.

So Madison and Ainsley had always been close. Then my younger sister Wynter was close to the youngest in the family, Quinn.

So that made me literally the middle child in a family with five children.

I wasn't the typical middle child, though. I didn't act out or work hard to get attention.

Instead, I just sort of did my own thing.

But Madison was easy to be around and easy to talk to.

Probably had something to do with her being a psychologist.

She was a good listener.

But tonight she seemed a little distracted.

Yet… she had a happy glow about her.

"You look happy," I said. "Marriage must agree with you."

"It does," she said. "Kade and I are quite content."

"What can I get you two lovely ladies to drink?" John, a fairly new server stopped by our booth. John's hair was just on the verge of being too long and he had a goatee.

But the ladies seemed to like him, so apparently management hadn't insisted that he change his appearance.

Personally, I liked my men clean-shaven.

And with that, my thoughts flashed to the handsome pilot who had flown my sister here.

"The usual martini for you?" John asked.

I wasn't sure if he actually remembered that I like a martini. If he did, he had an excellent memory because I only came here every few weeks at most.

Maybe it was just a ploy to make me think he remembered.

"Yes please," I said, idly picking up a menu. Not that I needed to even look at it. I always ordered one of two things and nothing on the menu ever changed. Why mess with perfection?

"And for the other beautiful lady?" he asked Madison.

"I'll have a ginger ale with orange juice," she said.

Actually, I thought, maybe I would get something different tonight. Maybe I'd have the tuna sandwich.

A ginger ale with orange juice.

John had walked off before my sister's words registered.

"Ginger ale?" I asked, looking at her sideways. "You never…"

Madison was grinning.

I put both my hands flat on the table and leaned forward.

"Madison," I said. "Are you…?"

"Yes," Madison said. "Kade and I are going to have a baby."

"Oh. My. God. Momma is going to flip."

That explained why she was freaking glowing.

My sister had gone and gotten herself pregnant.

Momma and Daddy were going to go through the roof with excitement.

Daddy had grandchildren from my half-sister Danielle, but this would be Momma's first.

In a way, I kinda felt sorry for Madison.

Giving my parents their first grandchild together was going to give her a whole heck of a lot of attention. At least she lived in Denver. That would help.

"I'm kinda flipping, too," Madison said. "It's amazingly exciting."

"Have you told anybody?" I asked.

"Actually, you're the first," she said. "It's the real reason Kade and I wanted to come down this weekend. To tell everyone."

"Wow." Everything was changing. First Madison had gotten married. Now Ainsley was engaged. And we were about to have babies.

"There's Daddy now," Madison said, sliding out of the booth.

She was across the restaurant before I barely had time to register that Daddy was coming in through the door.

Daddy grabbed Madison up in a big hug.

And then I saw him.

Daddy had brought the pilot with him. Jackson.

My gaze locked with his and I felt my face flushing.

I was already grinning with Madison's exciting news.

Now I found myself smiling at Jackson.

And he was smiling back.

Madison looked over her shoulder at me and then all three of them were coming this way.

So much for our quiet sisterly dinner out.

Daddy and the handsome pilot were coming to sit with us.

8

JACKSON

What I'd expected to be a quiet business dinner had suddenly become a family dinner.

After quick introductions, Madison and Brianna sat on one side of the booth and I slid in with Noah sitting beside me.

This setup put me directly across from Brianna.

As everyone settled in, I studied Brianna.

Her features were similar, but softer than her sister's.

The girls must look like their mother, because I honestly didn't see Noah in either of them. Except maybe the eyes. Could be that I was just seeing what I wanted to see though.

Altogether, they were a good-looking group.

And this was only part of the family. I couldn't help but wonder how the rest of the family fit in.

Brianna and Madison exchanged a look. One of those private looks that only sisters could share.

The server brought their drinks and Noah ordered two martinis for us. I'd mentioned on the ride over that the martini was my drink of choice and he'd assured me that this place had the best.

Brianna was having a martini, but Madison was having a mimosa. That didn't go unnoticed by Noah.

"You didn't want a martini?" Noah asked.

Madison shrugged. "This is my new favorite," she said.

Noah grinned. "Already, living out in the west is changing you."

"A little maybe," Madison said, with a small smile.

And there was that look between sisters again.

That was the instant I knew. To be so brilliant, Noah was clueless.

His daughter was pregnant. And he didn't even suspect a thing.

It was impossible to tell a mimosa that had alcohol from one that had ginger ale—at least just by looking at them. But if I were a betting man, I'd bet Madison was avoiding alcohol.

My gaze met Brianna's again.

Noah and Madison had moved on and were talking about Kade.

They didn't seem to notice that Brianna and I weren't saying anything.

Brianna had caught my attention from a distance, but she was even more beautiful up close.

Her skin looked impossibly smooth and her eyes were clear and deep. She watched me with a depth I rarely saw.

And those lips. Those lips that curved into a perfect bow had me thinking about things that would have Noah tossing me out on my ear.

I shifted in my seat and pulled my gaze away from Brianna's. If Noah had any inkling where my thoughts were headed, he wouldn't be so generously allowing me to be a part of his unexpected family reunion.

The server brought our martinis and Noah lifted a glass.

"To family and new friends," he said.

With one sip, I knew Noah was right. The Skyhouse

bartender knew what he was doing. This was one of the best martinis I'd ever had. Hands down.

"I thought you had a flight today," Madison said to Noah. "Are you just getting back?"

"I had to dash up to the Dallas office. One of the pilots up there is having some personal problems."

"What kind of personal problems?" Madison asked.

Noah leaned back in his chair. "Nothing that couldn't be worked out."

As the small talk continued, I watched Brianna.

When her gaze darted back to mine, I smiled.

Her eyes widened and her lips curved up at the edges.

I still didn't know what Noah had wanted to talk with me about.

And right now I wasn't sure it mattered.

I'd spend an evening looking at his daughter, Brianna, any night of the week.

9

BRIANNA

The restaurant was crowded now. More so than usual.

Daddy wasn't supposed to be back until later. If I'd known he was going to be here, he could have picked Madison up.

It worked out, though, because I was the only one who knew Madison's secret. I was going to be an aunt.

Daddy had noted that her drink was different, but he had no way of knowing that it was just ginger ale.

My gaze snapped back to Jackson. It was hard to not look at him, especially when he was looking at me like he wanted to eat me right up.

Still… I found myself wondering why Daddy had brought him to dinner. It wasn't really surprising. Daddy was that way.

It was part of why he always had a stack of resumes on his desk.

Jackson had been the pilot who flew Madison in from Denver, so naturally Daddy would befriend him. It was what Momma would call southern hospitality.

My sister Ainsley said she never dated pilots. I happened to know that she'd made that decision only after dating one. I didn't know what happened, only that it had ended badly.

Now she was engaged to a pilot. Sort of. Not sort of engaged, but sort of a pilot.

He owned his own company with several locations and had his own airplane that he flew for himself.

Actually Wyatt, as an entrepreneur, fit right in with my family. Like Daddy, Wyatt had successfully started his own company. Wyatt's had something to do with creating or producing video games. Both, I think.

Holding his drink with both hands, Jackson narrowed his eyes and looked at me with sudden recognition.

"Wait," he said. "I know you."

I shook my head. "I don't think so."

I had over one million YouTube followers, but there was no way Jackson Fleming was one of them.

I made videos about fashion and living a minimalistic life.

Sure I posted at least twice a week, so there were a lot of them out there.

No one in my own family watched all my videos.

There was no way a pilot from Colorado watched my videos. Not enough to recognize me. In fact, I'd never been recognized in public.

"You make those videos," he said.

My eyes widened and my fingers tightened on the stem of my glass.

Madison and Daddy were looking at us now.

"The ones about fashion and such."

"Look at that, Brianna," Madison said with an amused grin. "And you didn't think you were famous."

"I'm not famous," I said, looking at Jackson sideways. Surely he had me confused with someone else.

"My little sister watches all your videos."

I glanced at Madison, then back at Jackson.

"You just did one on… throwing out the blue jean jacket look and wearing a leather jacket instead."

I just gaped at him.

He had seen my channel.

And he recognized me.

He just scored so many points in my book.

Just like that.

10

JACKSON

There were a lot of unspoken advantages to being a contract pilot.

Not only did I get to choose which flight I took, but I was able to take my sister with me.

That had ended up being an unanticipated game changer for me.

By having the freedom to take my sister with me, I'd kept her out of more trouble than anyone could imagine.

After our parents got divorced, my sister had taken it hard.

She'd been going down a troubled path. The whole thing had started when she was fifteen.

That was when I'd moved to Denver and started working with Daniel. My sister had actually spent a lot of time with me.

And I'd taken her on countless flights.

Tiffany was twenty-one now and she was a college student in Denver.

She still traveled with me on occasion.

Most times I passed her off as my flight attendant.

But during the actual flights, she sat in the passenger seat and hung out. She spent a lot of time studying, but a girl couldn't study all the time.

And right now she was addicted to YouTube. And one of her favorites was Brianna Worthington.

I didn't set out to watch Brianna. After all, I was a guy and guys weren't supposed to be interested in fashion. But Brianna engaged with her audience with smooth skill. And she was funny.

I ignored most of Tiffany's videos, but anytime she turned on Brianna, I found myself paying attention. Even if Tiffany was wearing her air pods, I would watch her.

Sometimes Tiffany would turn the volume up so I could hear if she thought I might be interested.

And here she was. Sitting right here in front of me.

I would never ever have guessed that Brianna was Noah's daughter.

It was unexpected.

And I had to say delightful.

Tiffany was going to flip when I told her that I'd met Briana.

But it wasn't just her videos that had my attention.

She was even more lovely in person than on camera.

And when she smiled, my heart went into loop the loops.

"Jackson," Noah asked. "which part of Houston are you from?"

One look from Noah and my heart settled down. It was almost like he knew I was thinking about his daughter.

I shoved my menu aside.

"River Oaks, I said. "near Rice."

Noah nodded. "Ever think about moving back?" he asked.

His gaze locked onto mine and I had a glimpse of the formidable side of Noah Worthington.

I swallowed hard. This was not a man to be lied to.

"I have thought about it," I said. "but to be honest, I've been too busy to think about much of anything."

Noah's gaze pierced mine.

"A man shouldn't work all the time," he said. "And I'm speaking from my own experience."

"Yes sir," I said, "I agree completely. That's why I'm taking the next few days off to roam around Houston a bit."

"It's changed a lot since you were here," Noah said. "Do you have someone to show you around?"

"No," I said. "I'll manage."

Noah looked over at Brianna. "Brianna, why don't you give Jackson a tour?"

Brianna's expression mimicked the way I felt. Deer in the headlights.

"Oh," she said. "I'm sure Jackson already has things planned."

I looked over, snagging her gaze, a little smile playing about my lips.

"Actually," I said. "I'm not much of a planner."

Brianna and Madison exchanged a look. I could only imagine what meaning lay hidden behind that glance.

11

BRIANNA

*A*nd once again the work-from-home thing came around and bit me in the butt.

Though I had to admit that I wasn't so sure I minded as much as I thought I should.

After dinner, Madison and Daddy shifted her luggage over from my car to Daddy's.

Madison had decided that instead of coming home with me, she wanted to go with Daddy to see Momma.

I didn't blame her. But still, I'd stopped what I was working on and had come all this way to get her.

"I'm sorry," Madison said to me. "You don't mind, do you?"

"Of course not," I said. "I'll see you this weekend."

"Okay," Madison said, giving me a quick hug. "Thanks for keeping my secret," she whispered.

"Thanks for sharing," I said.

I stood next to my car and watched as Daddy spoke with Jackson while Madison got inside his car.

Daddy walked over to me, bringing Jackson with him.

"Good to see you," Daddy said, giving me a quick hug.

"You, too, Daddy."

"Would you mind giving Jackson a ride to his hotel? He's staying down your way."

"Sure," I said. "I can do that."

I guess.

It wasn't what I had planned. But Daddy lived in the opposite direction from me and apparently from Jackson's hotel.

Daddy clapped Jackson on the shoulder.

"I'll see you tomorrow," he said.

"Sure thing," Jackson said and Daddy walked away, leaving us standing there in the parking lot next to my Maserati.

"Nice car," he said.

"Thanks. So where are you staying exactly?"

Holding up a finger, he tapped on his phone.

I just put my hands on my hips.

Seriously? Was he going to just stand there in front of me and use his phone?

It took him all of about two minutes, but those two minutes seemed to drag.

A couple left the restaurant, got into their car, and drove off while I waited.

"Looks like I'll be staying at the Post Oak Hotel."

"Did you just make that reservation?" I asked.

"Yes," he said, having the decency to look at bit sheepish.

"Wow. When you said you weren't much of a planner, you really meant it, didn't you?"

"I guess so," he said. "Can I put this in the trunk?"

I clicked open the trunk of my impeccably clean car and Jackson set his leather bag inside.

"Thanks for giving me a ride," he said. "But I can get a taxi."

I shrugged. "Daddy seemed to think you needed a ride."

Then before he could ask, I added, "I've never known him to ask anything unreasonable."

Jackson just grinned. "He's a persistent man, your father."

I opened my door and dropped into the driver's seat. Jackson could come along if he wanted to.

And he did. He opened the passenger door and climbed inside.

With the door closed, it was quiet inside the car.

Quiet and it suddenly felt intimate.

"You still use taxis?" I asked.

He put his phone in his jacket pocket. I was impressed. Nothing worse than a passenger who stared at his phone.

"Bad experience with Ubers," he said.

"I see," I said, backing out of the parking space. I couldn't help but wonder if his bad experience with anything had something to do with his lack of planning.

I didn't understand people who didn't plan.

How did they get anything done without planning? Especially a pilot.

I wanted to ask, but decided against it.

"You're meeting with my father," I said as I pulled out onto the road.

"So it seems."

"What's that about?" Traffic was heavy tonight, so I had to pay attention.

"I was hoping you could tell me."

I put the car in self-driving mode and glanced over at him. "You don't know?"

Jackson shook his head.

"No clue."

I put on my blinker and moved into the middle lane. We had about a twenty minute ride.

"Maybe he's trying to recruit you."

Jackson scoffed.

"Why would he do that? From what I hear, he's got people lined up down the street to go to work for him. Besides, I like to be in charge of my own schedule."

I smiled to myself. An interesting comment coming from a man who didn't plan. How could a person who didn't plan not have a schedule.

He seemed to read my mind.

"Yes," he said. "I do have a schedule. I just don't plan my free time."

That made a little more sense, but I didn't tell him so.

I concentrated on the drive. Even with the car in self-drive mode, I had to keep my hands on the wheel and my eyes on the road.

"Have you always lived here?" he asked.

"Born and raised," I said.

"So was I, but I've lived other places. But you haven't?"

I looked at him sideways. "Why would I want to live anywhere else?"

"College?"

"The University of Houston is a perfectly good university."

"I would have figured you more for Rice University girl."

I changed lanes again as we neared my exit.

"Really? Rice didn't suit me."

"Hmm," he said.

"Where did you go to school?" I asked.

"Auburn," he said. "They have a great aviation program."

"So I've heard. And now you live in Denver."

He nodded.

"And yet you're from Houston."

"Funny that you'd be judgmental since your sister lives in Denver."

I took the exit and moved into the right lane.

"I never said I was judging."

He shrugged.

"Where are you meeting my father?" I asked as we neared the hotel.

The drive suddenly seemed to have gone far too quickly.

"He said he'd find me."

I laughed. "Sounds like my father. Sometimes he likes to fly by the seat of his pants."

"Sounds like a kindred spirit."

"I didn't say he doesn't plan. He plans all the time. He just doesn't necessarily plan *how* he's going to get there."

Wyatt was looking at me with a confused expression.

I just smiled to myself.

Sometimes I turned things around to my advantage on purpose, even if they didn't make all that much sense.

"We're here," I said, driving up to the front door and waving off the valet who rushed to take care of parking my car.

Instead of jumping out, Wyatt also waved off the valet who came to open his own door.

"Looks like a nice choice," I said. "even if it was last minute."

Jackson grinned. "I never said it was last minute."

He tapped his fingers against the door knob.

"Want to let these guys park the car? Come inside for a drink?"

I had to catch myself.

The offer threw me completely off guard.

Jackson had just flown into town. Didn't have any plans. Invites the first girl he comes across inside.

Classic move.

"I have work to do," I said.

"Now?" he asked.

"My sister pulled me away so, yeah, I have some work to catch up on."

"Too bad," he said. "Maybe next time."

I didn't answer. I popped the trunk, but didn't say anything as he climbed out of the car.

I waited while he pulled his bag out of my trunk, tossed it over his shoulder, and came back to the door.

"Thanks again for the ride," he said as he closed the passenger door and strode up to the front doors of the hotel.

I let out the breath I hadn't realized I'd been holding.

My sister Ainsley was rubbing off on me.

Ainsley didn't date pilots. And I could see her point.

Pilots could be dangerous.

Especially when they came Daddy approved.

As he disappeared inside the front doors of the hotel, I put my car in drive and headed the few blocks to my high-rise condo.

I really did have work to do.

And I really didn't have time to be thinking about Jackson Fleming.

A pilot who'd just flown in from Denver.

Even if he was from Houston, he hadn't lived here in over ten years and a lot of the Houston had rubbed off of him.

What was wrong with Daddy anyway?

Since he'd gotten sick, he wasn't quite like he'd used to be.

He was getting older. That was all.

I blew out a breath and pulled into my parking spot.

As hard as that was to accept, I knew it had to happen at some time in the future. I'd just always thought that day was so far in the future that I'd be ready when it happened.

But even more concerning, at least at the moment, was that Jackson had invited me for a drink.

And I'd almost accepted.

12

JACKSON

I stood in the otherwise empty elevator as it climbed high and higher with one hand against the wall.

Idiot.

I was an absolute idiot.

Want to come inside for a drink?

My own words echoed in my head like a bad song.

And now that I'd heard it, I couldn't unhear it.

Now that I'd asked her, I couldn't unask her.

Brianna was Noah Worthington's daughter.

A man I was having a business meeting with tomorrow, though that was a whole other story.

First of all, I didn't have any reason to meet with him, business or otherwise.

I had more jobs than I could possibly do. I certainly couldn't add anything more to my load.

But at any rate, the aviation world was a small world.

I could have walked into the restaurant's bar and found at least one Houston woman to talk to for a few minutes or even hours.

I didn't need to blur the lines with Noah's daughter.

Besides, I actually *liked* Brianna Worthington. And my sister liked her.

Tiffany would laugh at me for trying to get Brianna to have a drink with me.

Brianna the YouTube celebrity.

It wasn't that I had a self-esteem problem.

It wasn't that at all.

It was just that I knew when to leave things alone. I knew how quickly things could go south. So I had a rule to never mix business with pleasure.

I wasn't one of those pilots who dated flight attendants.

I could safely say that I had never even kissed a flight attendant. And I personally didn't know another pilot who could say the same.

So I had a lot of self-restraint.

Or so I had thought.

But apparently there was something about Brianna that had just burned that rule to the ground.

I stepped off the elevator and turned right toward my room.

Though I hadn't told Brianna, I had reserved this room before I left Denver, but I hadn't remembered the name of it until I looked it up.

It had been amusing to let her think that I was making a reservation at the last minute.

I hadn't lied though when I said I didn't plan my free time.

Sometimes I let Tiffany plan it.

She loved finding things for us to do when I took her on trips with me. And if that's what it took to keep my little sister happy and out of trouble, I was more than happy to let her drag me to a museum or even an opera, though for the life of me, I couldn't see what she got out of opera.

I used my phone to unlock my door and stepped inside my room.

It was roomy and elegant. Just the way I liked it.

There was even a chilled bottle of champagne waiting for me. But I didn't touch it.

Instead I loosened my tie and tossed my leather bag on the desk.

Flipping open my iPad, I grabbed a bottle of water, and went to work on Google.

It took half an hour, but persistence paid off and I found what I was looking for.

Now. Now I was ready for my meeting with Noah tomorrow.

And in the process, some of the pain of being rejected by Brianna had faded.

Unfortunately, I liked her even more. She had a good head on her shoulders and that was something I admired.

All I had to do was to tread carefully.

And make sure I kept my own head straight.

13

BRIANNA

My alarm went off at five a.m.

Slapping at my phone to make it stop, I asked why, and buried my head under my pillow.

Why was my alarm going off at five o'clock in the morning?

It was an ungodly time to have to wake up so rudely.

But unfortunately, the damage was done and my mind was waking.

It was Ainsley's fault I was awake in the middle of the night.

I'd promised to help her out with something today.

When I'd agreed, five o'clock had seemed doable.

Well, I'd agreed and now I was awake, so I might as well get the day started.

With a groan, I tossed the pillow aside, sat up, and crossed my legs. I was wearing my favorite heathered gray cotton pajamas.

At one point, when I'd first gotten them, I had actually done a video wearing these pajamas.

Had Jackson seen that video? Had he seen me in my pajamas?

I had never worried about what anyone thought about my videos. I got as many thumbs down as the next girl, but that was just human nature. I had never posted anything that I thought was inappropriate.

Yet the thought of Jackson seeing me in my pajamas put a whole new spin on things.

My God.

I was attracted to him.

And not just a little.

Enough that I'd fallen asleep thinking about him and now I was waking up thinking about him.

This was not good.

I climbed out of bed and padded into my kitchen. I pulled my latte maker out of one of the lower cabinets and made myself a latte.

I took the coffee cup to the window and looked out over the city.

Damn it.

I sat on the window seat and pulled a pillow into my lap. The only decorative pillow I owned.

From here, I could see the front of the Post Oak Hotel.

Jackson was somewhere inside. Probably sleeping. Lucky devil.

And I knew, in a way that only a woman could know, that if I'd wanted to I could be there with him right now.

That would not have been a good choice for me, everything considered, but it didn't keep me from thinking about it and knowing that it could have happened.

It was probably fortuitous that I was spending some time with Ainsley today.

She had a good perspective on pilots and on the many reasons to not date them.

And I used the term date loosely.

Having a one-night stand with Jackson Fleming was not what I considered dating.

I wasn't even sure he was dating material.

First of all, he lived in Denver.

And second of all, he was just overall disagreeable in a subtle way that got under my skin.

Daddy should never have put me in that position.

Now that I thought about it, I think he'd just been so happy to see Madison that he'd just thrown me out there without thinking.

Nah. Daddy wouldn't do that.

My second alarm went off. Then one that told me it was time for me to take a shower and get dressed.

I had just enough time before Ainsley would be here to pick me up.

This was one time when I was glad I had streamlined my closet. There was a time when I wouldn't have known what to wear, but today was different.

Today I knew exactly what to wear.

The upside of having fewer clothes was having fewer choices.

And fewer choices made life so much easier.

I'd have to script something out about that. Something more coherent than my early morning rambling thoughts, and do a video.

I made a quick note in my idea notebook and headed to the shower.

As the hot water ran over my head, I wondered if Ainsley would be willing to let me video her today.

My family may not understand what I did for a living, but they could not escape being part of it.

Just wasn't possible.

I smiled to myself as I pulled on a loose dress, then pulled a matching camel-colored sweater on over it.

Then I put on a pair of flat ankle boots and went to work on drying my hair.

Today was going to be a good day.

All I had to do was to keep reminding myself that Jackson Fleming was not and should not be part of my life.

14

―――――

JACKSON

This was the first time I'd slept late since… I couldn't even remember when.

The room was on a high enough level that there weren't even any traffic noises to wake me.

And since I'd put my phone on do-not-disturb and I had purposely not set an alarm, my body had taken complete advantage of the situation.

I rolled over and checked my phone.

Noah had messaged me two hours ago.

He wanted me to meet him at the Skye Travels office.

Not a surprise.

I'd have to get a taxi to get back to the airport.

It was for the best.

The further I stayed away from Brianna the better.

I doubted she spent much time around the airport.

She probably didn't have much of a need to.

I could only guess at the huge amount of work that must go into making her videos.

And she had over a million followers.

Impressive to say the least.

Taking a long hot shower helped to clear my head.

I would do the business meeting with Noah, then I'd rent a car at the airport and do some driving around.

Noah had tried to volunteer Brianna to show me around.

Fortunately that had been left hanging and seemed to have been forgotten.

I turned off the water and toweled off.

Maybe I should have pursued that angle instead of trying to get her to have a drink with me.

The long-term outcome on a tour around the city was far better than the short-term possibility of a drink.

Especially since the tour had been her father's idea.

Although his daughters, at least the ones I'd met so far, seemed to be successful in their own rights, Noah still seemed to run things.

He was a formidable presence, I mused as I ran a razor over my cheeks.

I was glad I wasn't going for an interview with the man. I'd be nervous as hell.

Even meeting him at all had me admittedly a little apprehensive.

It was probably a good thing Brianna hadn't had a drink with me last night.

Damn. The girl was way smarter than I was acting.

That's what happened when I thought with the wrong head, I thought as I rinsed off my razor.

Then I smiled to myself as I ran a comb through my hair.

I didn't judge myself for being interested.

I'd been drawn to her from the moment I'd seen her watching me.

She had the look of a fairy princess and now that I knew who she was, it was more than just her looks that I was drawn to.

It was everything about her.

Even though I was trying to tell myself it was bad idea to see her again, I knew it was exactly what I wanted to do.

But first I had to deal with her father.

15

———

BRIANNA

"I can't believe you're doing this," I said as Ainsley and I taxied along the runway in Teterboro Airport just outside of Manhattan.

Ainsley glanced over at me.

"You have Wyatt to blame for this," she said. "He insisted."

I didn't say anything, but I shot her a look.

"Okay," she said, bringing the plane to a stop. "I am curious. I mean. Think about it. His cousin owns a bridal store in Manhattan. How can I not at least go take a look?"

"You have to," I said, agreeing with her. "And you know you'll have to buy your dress here."

Ainsley made a face. "You think so?"

I shrugged.

"You can't start off a marriage with bad blood. Besides. If she doesn't have anything you like, just find it somewhere else and get her to order it for you. Best for all."

"You're a wise woman," Ainsley said. "It must be all that decluttering."

I laughed. "I told you. Decluttering frees up the mind."

Ainsley unhooked her four-point harness.

"Maybe so. For you anyway. I use flying to clear mind out."

I unhooked my own harness.

"Speaking of," I said, pulling my cell phone out of my purse. "How do you feel about me documenting this?"

Ainsley looked at me like I'd lost my mind.

It was a look I wasn't unfamiliar with.

"You are not putting me in one of your videos," she said.

"Okay. But how about if I just record it. And I promise I won't use it without your permission."

She looked at me sideways.

"If you weren't my sister," she said.

I grinned. "But I am."

We grabbed our bags and climbed out of the plane.

As expected, there was a limo waiting.

"Was this Wyatt's idea, too?" I asked.

"Of course."

We climbed into the limo. There was a chilled bottle of champagne waiting.

"Is this for us?" I asked.

"I'm sure," she said.

"Come on Ainsley," I said. "You have to let me film it. If nothing else for you to show your children."

"Children. You're getting a little ahead of yourself, don't you think?"

I'd been thinking about Madison and her pregnancy, but I was sworn to secrecy.

"You never know," I said. "It's something that tends to happen after a girl gets married."

We settled into the limo and changed into our high heels.

Ainsley let the subject drop.

"So I was wondering if I could maybe talk to you about something personal," I asked.

"Personal? What do we not talk about?"

I looked out the window at the New York skyline,

wondering how it was that I was the only member of my immediate family who had never been to New York. And I was the one interested in fashion. It made no sense.

Taking a deep breath, I looked back at Ainsley. The difference was this question wasn't so much about her and as it was me.

"What made you change your mind?"

"About what?" she asked, her brow furrowed.

"About marrying a pilot."

She looked blankly at me for a moment.

"Let's open this champagne."

"It's not even noon," I said.

"So?" Ainsley pulled out the champagne and deftly popped the cork.

After pouring two glasses of champagne and handing one to me, she smiled.

"I just want a sip," she said. "Bottle to throttle and all." She took a tiny sip and closed her eyes. "Should have had Wyatt fly us."

I shrugged. "Next time."

"I didn't change my mind," Ainsley said. "Wyatt isn't technically a pilot. He just flies planes."

"That sounds like a justification."

"No, really," Ainsley insisted. "His job isn't flying. He just uses flying to get to his job."

Ainsley leaned forward, warming to the topic.

"Besides," she said. "It wouldn't matter."

"So you did change your mind."

"Sort of," she said. "I think it doesn't really matter. Every man is different. Look at Daddy. He loves Momma more than anything in the world." She paused. "Except maybe me."

I laughed, nearly spilling my drink.

Us girls had a running joke about which one of us Daddy loved the most. We all claimed to be his favorite.

He'd never shown favoritism, of course, which made the whole running topic all the more interesting.

"So you're saying that if Wyatt was a pilot… Making a living at it, it wouldn't change how you felt about him?"

"Of course it wouldn't," she said.

I turned and watched as we crossed the bridge into Manhattan.

My heart was beating a little bit faster.

New York was one of those places I'd always wanted to visit.

Too bad we were just going to a bridal shop, then going home.

There were so many things to see and do here.

It was absolutely amazing.

And I was barely thinking about Jackson at all.

Just once every New York minute.

16

JACKSON

$\mathcal{S}$ince a taxi wasn't available, I had to take an Uber.

Fortunately, this time, everything went smoothly. The driver was quick to get there, didn't try to make small talk, and was a decent driver.

The Skye Travels office wasn't much to look at from the outside. It was a nondescript office building with an understated sign out front.

There was long-term parking and short-term parking.

Needing neither, I parked out front, strode inside, and pressed the elevator button.

I glanced at my watch, then put my hands behind my back.

I'd been in terminals like this a hundred times over.

Yet this time, I felt my nerves fraying on the ends.

And it was for no reason.

I wasn't here for any official purpose.

Maybe Noah was just being hospitable, though I couldn't see why a busy man like himself would donate his valuable time to being hospitable.

The elevator opened up and I stepped inside. Pushed the button taking me to the third and top floor of the building.

I wondered what was on the second floor, if anything.

My guess was that the floor was probably vacant.

I stepped off the elevator into the Skye Travels lobby.

The décor was understated. As I walked through to the receptionist desk, I found myself wondering if Brianna had anything to do with the clean lines and understated elegance of the lobby.

It seemed to reflect her style.

Helen, the receptionist was sitting at her desk.

"I'll let Noah know that you're here," she said before I could say anything.

Efficient and professional. I liked it.

I'd heard somewhere that Madison, Noah's oldest daughter had worked here during her college years, answering the phones and doing scheduling.

But now she was a psychologist in Denver.

She'd taken everything she'd learned here and now ran her own private practice.

No doubt, she'd taken the experience she'd gained here from working with her father and applied it to her own business.

She was fortunate.

I hadn't had anyone to show me the ropes.

Coming from a broken home, I'd just had to figure things out for myself.

And I hadn't done half bad.

I'd lived simply and banked my money.

So much so that I was thinking about buying an airplane of my own.

It would take my business up a notch. The only thing keeping me down was not having enough time to execute the idea.

I figured the time would come eventually. Just like I'd eventually move out of the one- bedroom apartment where I'd lived since moving to Denver right after college.

Helen covered the microphone of her headset with one hand.

"You can go on back," she said.

Helen seemed to assume that I knew where I was going.

It wasn't hard to locate Noah's office overlooking the tarmac.

He was standing in front of the floor to ceiling window, hands behind his back, looking toward the sky.

"It's a beautiful day for flying," he said.

"Agreed," I said.

That was the good thing about Texas weather. There were very few weather delays, at least not in Houston.

Noah turned around and gestured toward the two chairs sitting in the corner of the room.

There was a little table between them with two unopened bottles of water.

"To what do I owe the pleasure?" I asked as we sat across from one another.

Noah picked up a bottle of water. Handed it to me. Then picked up the other for himself.

"My wife, Savannah," he said. "insists that I stay hydrated. Sometimes I feel a bit overwatered, but it makes her happy."

"Sounds like she does a good job of looking out for you," I said, turning the cap on my water and drinking soundly.

"She does," he said. "Very much so. I couldn't have done what I've done without her."

I nodded, but refrained from commenting since I didn't know where he was headed with this conversation.

"That's the thing about women," he said. "they can really get under your skin." He balanced the bottle of water on one knee. "But that's not why I wanted to meet with you."

"I'm curious why," I said.

"You have an exemplary flight record," he said.

"Thank you." I already knew that Noah had checked into my background. It wasn't something that bothered me. It was just the nature of what he did.

"You like flying the Denver area?" he asked.

"Hard to dislike such beautiful scenery," I said.

"My wife and I have a cabin up near Estes Park," he said. "We don't get to spend much time there though."

"Nice area," I said. "growing."

"Sounds like you don't have much time to do much more than enjoy the scenery."

"I stay busy," I said.

"Jackson," Noah said. "A man can be too busy."

I didn't say anything. It seemed an odd statement coming from the successful founder of a successful company.

"Ever think about slowing down? Going in a different direction?"

"At times," I admitted. "but change takes time."

"Uh huh," Noah said, studying me.

"What if you could change that in one fell swoop? Would you?"

"I don't know," I said, honestly. "I guess that depends on what that change is."

Noah sat back in his chair and straightened his pants legs.

He was trying to seem relaxed and casual.

Yet the more relaxed and casual he became, the more I went on alert. I was schooled in power plays.

Noah might be making idle conversation, but I didn't know him well enough to know.

"Jackson," he said. "I'd like to make you a job offer."

17

BRIANNA

The sun was setting by the time the Houston airport came back into view.

It had been a busy day. Busy and productive.

The back seat of the airplane was full of packages, some in shiny white boxes, others in shiny white bags. All with the understated silver heart logo of the bridal shop.

Ainsley, my practical, no nonsense sister had gone into a bridal shop in New York and had come out with a wedding dress and all the accoutrements. Shoes. Garter. A tiara.

I'd told her three times that she could order something.

But she insisted that this dress was the one. And I had to admit that the dress she'd chosen was absolutely stunning.

Really. I didn't have a lot of experience with weddings, but I was pretty sure it wasn't supposed to be this easy to find THE perfect dress.

If I hadn't seen the dress on Ainsley, I would have accused her of just picking something to have it done.

She wasn't exactly the most intentional shopper. Her closet was full of clothes she'd bought and never even worn.

The only clothes she really cared about had the Skye Travels logo imprinted on them.

I'd had a lot of time to think on the flight.

Pleasantly exhausted, I'd just let my mind wander where it would.

And my thoughts kept winding back around to Jackson.

Even when I intentionally tried to think about other things, like videos for my channel, my thoughts didn't cooperate.

He was handsome, there was no doubt about that.

And it was his eyes that haunted me the most.

Clear blue eyes that seemed to see me for who I was.

In that short time I'd been around him, I had seen a lot in those eyes.

Acceptance. Admiration. Attraction.

All things I saw in him. So Madison would say I was projecting my own feelings onto him.

Sometimes psychologists had a propensity to take all the fun out of things, especially things like romance.

But seeing her with Kade told a completely different story.

Their happily ever after was chock full of romance.

Then there was my sister Ainsley. I'd never seen her so full of life.

She had her dream job flying for Skye Travels and she had her dream guy, Wyatt. Wyatt pushed her out of her comfort zone.

Pushed her to enjoy more than just flying.

I'd never have believed that my practical sister would fly all the way from Houston to New York to look at wedding dresses, much less buy everything she needed right there on the spot.

I looked over at her as she spoke into the microphone, preparing to land the airplane.

Ainsley had everything she wanted. The universe had truly aligned for her.

And even though I clearly remembered, not so long ago, her insisting that a man wasn't necessary for happiness, I saw none of that in her now.

I had wanted to talk to her more about her decision to be with Wyatt, but I was pretty sure it was a decision of the heart and not her head.

Jackson had invited me to have a drink with him last night.

I'd panicked.

Jackson made me nervous.

Any guy who made my heart race like that would make me nervous.

It didn't help that Jackson was the first man who'd had such a profound and immediate effect on my senses.

To say that I was unprepared was an understatement.

My life was orderly and planned.

I had a vision board, for God's sake.

And even though I wanted a husband and family someday, it wasn't something I'd included on my vision board.

I planned to put that on there in a couple of years. After I had my career firmly stabilized.

As a firm believer in the law of attraction, I hadn't planned on attracting more than I'd put out there.

And Jackson was most definitely more. More of everything.

I bit my lip and stared down at the stores and freeways that were coming into view below.

I wasn't a nervous flyer, exactly, but I was always relieved when the plane was low enough that I could see trees and cars and familiar buildings below.

After being so high in the sky, seeing things on the ground clearly gave me a false sense of security that we were almost back on the ground.

That was probably one of the many reasons why Ainsley was Noah's one child who became a pilot. That and her brain worked that way.

I looked at all the gauges and got totally over my head.

I knew that I could figure out how to fly a plane if I wanted to. The problem was I just didn't want to.

I was more interested in fashion and helping people make their homes more comfortable.

Those things were my passion.

As the wheels touched down on the runaway, my thoughts returned to Jackson.

Being around him would no doubt require a lot more flying than I was used to.

I was the least frequent flyer in the family. Even less than my younger sister Wynter.

And my brother Quinn didn't count one way or the other.

Father had made him CEO of the Houston office and no one had quite figured out why. He wasn't a pilot and couldn't fly a plane if his life depended on it.

But he could convince a person to do just about anything.

He should really be in politics.

Daddy had asked me to show Jackson around town. I'd sidestepped the request.

So I'd essentially rejected him twice over.

Maybe I'd been adopted. I didn't have my Father's love of flying. And I didn't have my mother's southern hospitality gene.

I was my own person, content to just be.

Maybe it was because I was the middle child, but I'd learned to entertain myself.

And I was quite content with my life.

Jackson Fleming would do nothing but turn my life upside down.

As we taxied toward the Skye Travels terminal, I knew I'd made the right decision.

Keeping my distance from Jackson Fleming had been the right thing to do.

The safe thing to do.
Why was it that it felt so wrong?

18

JACKSON

A job offer.

I hadn't seen that one coming.

Not even a little bit.

Noah and I had talked about how busy I was. How I had no time to do anything other than work and couldn't possibly squeeze anything else into my life.

It seemed like the more we talked about that, the more determined Noah became to get me to consider working for him.

I stood up and went to his office window overlooking the tarmac.

I spotted a plane coming in from the east, just a speck. I watched it until the wheels touched down in a perfect landing.

The red Skye Travels logo splashed across the tail of the aircraft told me it was one of Noah's planes.

Not surprising.

Skye Travels pilots had a reputation for being the best.

As the plane came to a stop, the early evening sunlight glinted off the windshield.

I heard Noah walk over to his little refrigerator.

He handed me another bottle of water and went back to his chair.

For such a successful, busy man, he was incredibly patient.

I twisted the cap off the water and drank deeply. He wasn't kidding about drinking a lot of water.

I couldn't figure out why Noah was offering me a job out of the blue.

His desk had nothing on it other than an Apple computer and the credenza behind it had a healthy green ivy.

No personal items.

But somewhere there was a stack of applications from pilots all over the country at all stages of their careers.

Surely he wasn't at a loss for applicants.

After a black sedan pulled up next to the plane, the driver stepped out and waited.

The plane's door opened and the steps came down.

A young lady wearing a Skye Travel's uniform stepped out and said something to the driver before she ducked back inside the plane.

The pilot wore dark shades and had a long ponytail secured beneath her cap.

A minute later, she handed a large shiny white box to the driver.

After the box was safely stashed in the trunk, the pilot handed him several other bags.

Then stepped aside for someone else to come out.

I recognized her immediately.

It was Brianna.

Unlike the pilot, she wore her long hair down, currently pulled over her left shoulder and no shades.

I immediately saw the resemblance.

The female pilot was Ainsley Worthington, Brianna's sister.

Brianna, wearing white canvas sneakers, carefully made her way down the steps. The driver took her oversized bag and held out a hand to help her to the ground.

The bold Texas wind tousled her hair as she turned and walked toward the terminal.

I took a deep breath and held my ground.

As I expected, she looked up toward her father's window.

She missed a step as she saw me standing there watching her.

I smiled a slow smile that she didn't return.

Instead, she hiked the handbag more securely on her shoulder and looked away.

Some men might be offended, but I was even more intrigued.

I wanted to know more about Brianna Worthington.

I wanted to know what made her tick. I wanted to know everything.

I had several flights on my calendar for the next couple of weeks, but nothing I couldn't cancel.

After all, I wasn't the only contract pilot in Denver. I could give them all a good referral.

Turning back around to face Noah, I looked him dead in the eye.

I didn't know if Noah was getting dementia or just what he had up his sleeve in asking me to work for him.

But whatever it was, didn't matter so much right now. The offer was out there. And the pay he was offering matched everything I was making myself. Only I didn't have to keep up with the billing or the payments or anything else involved in being a contract worker.

Maybe Noah was right. Maybe by offering me a job, he was giving me new lease on life. Freedom that I'd never had in my career.

Since I couldn't see a right or wrong answer, I went with my gut.

"Alright," I said. "I'll take the job."

19

———

BRIANNA

*A*insley was taking a car back to her condo.

I would have gone with her, but I wanted to see Daddy first. Needed to talk with him.

And according to the text message I'd just gotten, he was in his office.

I had not expected to see Jackson standing in Daddy's office looking down at me.

It was like the first time we'd met, only reversed.

This time he was watching me walk across the tarmac to the terminal.

And this time I knew who he was.

He wasn't just a random pilot who'd flown my sister down from Denver while her husband took a later flight.

He was Jackson Fleming.

I still didn't know much about him other than he was charming and came Daddy-approved.

I was actually here to ask Daddy for an explanation.

But now that wasn't going to happen.

I couldn't very well ask about Jackson when he was standing right there.

Stepping inside the building, I pressed the elevator button.

I wiped my hands along my simple dress. I was nervous about seeing Jackson again.

And I wasn't sure how he was going react to seeing me again.

I'd sort of rejected him and I'd ignored Daddy's request to show him around.

If pressed though, I had a good reason.

I'd had this day scheduled with Ainsley for two weeks.

And it had been a good day.

She'd managed to get just about everything she needed for her wedding.

Oddly enough, what she didn't have was a venue.

When I'd asked her about it, she'd just smiled and said it would all come together.

I didn't know how she thought that was going to happen, especially not when they didn't even have a date. Or if they did, they hadn't told anyone yet.

I made a mental note to ask her about that. With a big family like ours, she needed to do a save-the-date announcement. Surely Ainsley wasn't planning an elopement.

But she had the dress and that was quite honestly the most important part. Other than the groom, of course. And she had that taken care of, too.

Wyatt had literally moved his home and office to Houston in order to be with her.

Just like Kade had moved to Denver to be with Madison.

My two older sisters had hit the jackpot on men.

They didn't know how lucky they were.

Men didn't come along like that every day.

Men who loved their women enough to give up everything for them.

The elevator dinged and I stepped out into the Skye Travels lobby.

I needed to pull myself together.

Though I'd spent a lot of time thinking about Jackson since we'd met, he wasn't that kind of guy.

Jackson was focused on his own career.

His own life.

And guys like that didn't have the time or inclination to blow up their lives for a woman.

I stepped off the elevator and went straight back to Daddy's office.

No one was at the receptionist desk. Helen must have left early for the day.

As I went down the hallway, I heard Quinn talking on his phone. Quinn was always talking to somebody.

I stopped at Daddy's door and took in the situation.

Jackson was still standing at the window, though now his back was to it.

Daddy was sitting in his chair.

And they were both looking at me.

It was a little disconcerting.

I was used to having people looking at me, but on video, not live.

So I forced a smile onto my lips.

"You two look like you're up to something," I said.

20

———

JACKSON

*B*rianna had to be one of the most perceptive women I'd ever met.

But Noah and I weren't up to anything.

Not really.

Except for the fact that he'd just managed to convince me to leave my contract job and take a job working for Skye Travels.

What the hell was I thinking?

I had at least half a dozen flights to cancel, which all in all, wasn't that much.

The odd thing was that most of my flights were scheduled last minute. Like my flight here to Houston.

Kade had been delayed, but Madison had wanted to go ahead.

That's where I came in. I was the last minute guy.

I had a strong network and was the first person a lot of people called.

But there were a lot of us out there.

It wasn't like I was leaving anyone in a lurch. There were a lot of people who could fill my shoes. And wanted jobs. Young, hungry pilots.

On the other side, I didn't live in Houston. Sure, I'd grown up here, but I didn't have family here anymore. And I'd lost touch with the friends I'd had before I left for college.

Then there was my sister.

Tiffany was doing her college thing.

As a matter of fact, she hadn't flown with me in over a month.

"Did you have a good trip with Ainsley?" Noah asked her, interrupting my realization that I'd pretty much just jumped off the deep end.

"We did," Brianna said, going over to give Noah a quick hug. "She got a lot of things crossed off her list."

Brianna glanced at me before leaning against Noah's desk.

I smiled to myself.

Noah had raised some confident women, for sure.

She just assumed that she was welcome to jump right into our conversation.

Of course, I reminded myself, Noah had left the door open. That must have been some kind of code in the family.

An open door must mean that they're welcome.

"Did she say anything to you about setting a date?" Noah asked.

"No," Brianna said, brow creased. "I was just wondering about that. She hasn't said anything to anyone?"

Noah shook his head. "I was hoping she'd tell you something today."

"Not a word," Brianna said. "And it didn't occur to me to ask her about it until I was on my way up here."

"Well, at any rate," Noah said, looking at me. "Jackson has just agreed to come to work here at Skye Travels."

Brianna dropped into the chair behind her and looked from Noah to me and back again.

"How did you manage that?" she asked.

I wasn't sure whether she was asking Noah or me.

Neither one of us answered right away.

I was still stuck back there, wondering how she was so certain that chair would be behind her.

"Well," she said, looking at me. "Welcome aboard. When do you start?"

"I don't know," I said. "We haven't gotten that far."

Noah leaned forward, tapped on his computer and looked up at me.

"I have a quick flight you can take in the morning," he said. "Just up to Dallas and back."

"I thought you told me I should work less."

Noah just grinned. "Did I? But flying is flying, right?"

I knew exactly what he meant.

Even though I'd planned a couple of days off, the thought of getting back in the air was irresistible.

Noah would know that.

And if I'd refused without a good reason, he'd probably have taken his offer off the table.

"I'll go with you," Noah said. "Meet me here at eight in the morning."

"Sure," I said. And although I said it with nonchalance and ease, I had a gut feeling that my life had somehow just flipped upside down.

21

———

BRIANNA

I left Daddy's office feeling off-balance.

I hadn't gotten to ask him about Jackson. About why he was so insistent that Jackson not only come to work at Skye Travels, but he had wanted me to show him around.

He hadn't said anything about it tonight, though.

Instead, he'd told me that he was going to show Jackson some of the computer program. I was welcome to wait if I wanted to.

I'd claimed to be tired from my trip.

It was partly true.

I also wanted to get home and look at the video footage I'd taken of Ainsley's day at the bridal shop. See if any kind of inspiration struck.

Then, if it did, I'd have to figure out how to talk Ainsley, the private one in the family, into giving me permission to use it.

But my real reason for calling an Uber and heading home was that I had a lot to process.

Jackson was coming to work at Skye Travels.

How Daddy had managed that, practically overnight, I'd never know.

They said Daddy was a legend. I didn't know about that, but he did pull off some things that were a mystery to me.

Just as I stepped out of the Uber and reached the elevator, my phone chimed with a text message.

I didn't recognize the number.

409-753-7593: *Want to celebrate with me?*

A little shiver went up my spine. Although I didn't recognize the number, something told me it wasn't spam.

ME: *Who is this?*

409-753-7593: *Jackson*

I lowered the phone and stepped onto the elevator. Took a deep breath and waited while the elevator went up to my twenty-seventh-floor condo.

I stepped off the private elevator into my living room.

And immediately felt a sense of calm envelope me.

I took my handbag to my closet and set it on its shelf.

I kicked off my shoes, and went to my living room, pressed a button to raise the shades, and stretched out on my sofa.

Then I unlocked my phone and stared at the text message.

Jackson.

Why did he have this effect on me?

I instinctively knew that this was one of those key moments in life when what seemed like a minor decision could turn out to have a major outcome.

I could ignore the text and turn in early.

There were no outside commitments on my calendar tomorrow. I was free to stay home and work.

A perfect day in my mind.

Or I could respond.

If I responded, I couldn't predict anything after that.

Except maybe one thing.

A broken heart.

My fingers hovered over the keys.

Was it worth it?

22

JACKSON

BRIANNA: *What did you have in mind?*

I stepped onto the elevator and pressed the button to take me to the ground floor.

I grinned all the way down.

It had taken her long enough to answer. She'd had me thinking she was going to blow me off.

I got into the back seat of the Uber and sent back a response.

ME: *Headed back to the hotel. Dinner?*

Silence again. I pictured her staring at her phone, trying to decided what she wanted to do.

Brianna seemed to have such an orderly life. She was so put together.

But somehow I was able to unbalance her.

I took that as a good sign.

Especially since she unbalanced me.

She was ultimately the reason I'd agreed to go to work for Skye Travels.

I was not an impulsive person.

I'd lived in the same apartment for seven years. I'd done the same kind of work since college.

I was the least impulsive person I knew.

Yet I'd just upended my life one hundred percent.

I had to get an apartment. I had to reschedule all my flights and let my regulars know that I wouldn't be back to Denver. Get a Texas driver's license, for God's sake.

A person like me didn't do that.

It wasn't like Noah had offered me that much money. It was about the same as I was making now. Minus the paperwork and billing. All he required was putting some information into a computer program before and after a flight.

What he offered me, though, that had sealed the deal was less work.

Less work AND a chance to get to know his daughter, Brianna. An actual use for the extra time.

I checked my phone again and saw a reply from Brianna. Finally.

BRIANNA: *Ok*

It wasn't much, but it was more than I had expected.

It was enough that I was cautiously encouraged.

But I wanted her to feel comfortable. In control and on her own turf.

ME: *You name the place.*

ME: *And Time.*

More silence on her end.

It was fifteen minutes later and we were stuck in traffic when I got a response this time.

BRIANNA: *Restaurant at your hotel. 7.*

ME: *See you there.*

I had exactly one hour and five minutes to get back to my hotel, shower, change, and meet her downstairs.

I checked GPS to see how far out we were from the hotel.

Twenty-five minutes with traffic.

It was going to be close.

Leaning forward, I spoke to the driver.

"Is there any way to get there faster? To get out of this traffic?"

"I can take the next exit," the driver said. "Try the back roads, but no guarantee, this time of day."

"I understand," I said. "Let's do it."

That was the great thing about flying. Other than the occasional airport congestion, there were no traffic jams.

And even then, the airplane was always moving. Not just sitting and idling like we were doing now. We might not get there any quicker, but at least there was movement.

I settled back in the seat and let my thoughts race with all the things I had to do.

I'd actually let Noah talk me into taking a flight tomorrow, so I didn't have much time to take care of any of my personal business.

But right now, I didn't care.

It was going to be a good night.

23

BRIANNA

Something had gotten into me.

Maybe I'd caught a bug or something.

Stepping out of the shower, I went into my closet, and pulled out my one go-out dress.

It was a plain black dress that I could wear to any black-tie event.

To change it up, I put on my deep red leather jacket and black red bottomed shoes.

I grabbed up my clutch and keys and headed for the door.

I had just enough time to make it to the Blow Dry Salon, then makeup. I had a girl there, Zoe, who would do my hair and makeup.

It was a treat that I sometimes took advantage of before I did one of my special videos.

This was the first time I'd ever gone to the Blow Dry Salon before a date.

A date.

I couldn't even say how long it had been since I'd even been on a date.

Was meeting a new Skye Travels employee considered a date or a business dinner?

Either way, it was an outing.

And it was Jackson.

So it might not be a date, but it felt like a date.

I told myself I needed to get out of the house once in a while so I'd know what I was talking about when I did my videos.

That was the reason I'd said yes.

At least that's what I told myself.

I couldn't pretend to know what was going on in popular culture if I never left my condo.

Besides, maybe I would pick some new piece of information for my videos.

The scent of shampoo and hair products soothed my thoughts and while I sat getting my hair dried, I let them wander.

Zoe knew I liked to close my eyes and sit quietly while she did my hair. I wasn't one of those girls who liked to talk to the stylist. Zoe didn't seem to mind. Besides, the loud dryer was prohibitive for conversation.

I'd had a good day with Ainsley. I'd never seen her have so much fun in a clothing store.

I'd taken some good video footage and if I decided any of it was relevant to my channel, I had a good feeling she might give me permission to use it.

Seeing Jackson there in Daddy's office was completely unexpected.

I thought Jackson would be off doing some sight-seeing. Or something. Anything other than being there at Skye Travels.

I couldn't help thinking that Jackson and Daddy must have already known each other.

The whole thing was bizarre.

It wasn't like Daddy was short on pilots here in Houston.

If he'd hired him for the new office in Denver, I could have understood that. But Daddy had recruited him for here. In Houston.

And for some reason Jackson kept asking me out.

Zoe turned off the hair dryer and set it aside.

I opened my eyes and looked in the mirror. As I always did after Zoe worked her magic, I felt hundred percent better.

"Good?" Zoe asked.

I smiled. "As always."

"Want the usual makeup?" she asked.

"I'm thinking a little more eye makeup," I said.

Zoe grinned. "You have a date?"

"No. Just going out."

As Zoe smoothed eye shadow over my lids, I wondered if I was lying to her about having a date.

And even more importantly, I wondered if I was lying to myself.

If I were going to go on a date, Jackson would definitely be a good choice.

He was handsome, charming, and successful.

Besides those basic characteristics, he had just enough persistence to keep me off-balanced without feeling pressured.

The bottom line was I liked him.

But I wasn't in the market for a boyfriend.

Life was keeping me far too busy.

24

JACKSON

The bar was loud and although all the tables were taken, it didn't feel crowded. It was a large space with lots of room between tables.

I had actually made it ten minutes early. My hair was still damp from the shower, but it wasn't noticeable. And it would dry quickly.

I wore my dark gray suit. The one I kept in my travel bag for those occasions when I got asked to accompany people to various events.

Being a private pilot often meant invitations to all sorts of events like parties that required black tie dress.

I had a bourbon in front of me, but it was just a prop. I had a flight in the morning, so my twenty-four-hour bottle to throttle rule was in full force.

When I'd asked Brianna to dinner, I really had meant dinner. Unlike last night, when I'd asked her to have a drink.

My buddies said I was too honest with women. Frankly I saw nothing wrong with saying what I meant and meaning what I said.

Games had their place in life, but not in relationships.

Some women at a table nearby burst into laughter. They appeared to be having a baby shower since the woman at the head of the table was obviously very pregnant and was receiving all sorts of baby gifts.

I wondered when Madison was planning to tell Noah that she was expecting a baby.

They seemed to be a close family and I felt a little tinge of jealousy when I compared my own broken family to theirs.

I unlocked my phone and sent my sister a text.

ME: *Everything going ok up there?*

TIFFANY: *Going great. Studying for test.*

ME: *Talk tomorrow?*

TIFFANY: *Sure.*

My sister was doing well. She had friends now and seemed to be having her own normal college life. Without me.

I would still see her. That was just one of the great things about being a pilot.

I almost didn't recognize Brianna when she walked through the door.

She looked different somehow. More confident. She was wearing a black dress with a red jacket.

When I raised a hand, she smiled and walked toward me.

Not only was her hair more bouncy and smooth, but she also had an air of glamour about her. And she looked more confident.

More in her element.

Standing up, I pulled out a chair for her.

"You look beautiful," I said.

Actually I was rather honored that she'd fixed up for me.

I sat back down and looked into her stunning green eyes.

"I'm glad you could make it," I said.

She shrugged. "Hated the thought of you celebrating alone."

But there was something about the way she smiled when she said it that told me all I needed to know.

This was a date.

I'd heard that a lot of the pilots who worked at Skye Travels had met their spouses through work.

But meeting someone through work was a lot different from dating the boss's daughter.

Too bad.

I'd come too far to turn back now.

25

BRIANNA

"Would you like a drink?" Jackson asked as the server stopped at our table.

"Just a sparkling water." I smiled at the server. I'd had champagne at the wedding boutique and that was more than I was accustomed to drinking.

Besides, I wanted to be on top of my game with Jackson.

Even without a drink, he made it hard for me to think clearly.

"So," I said, as the server left. "Welcome to Skye Travels."

"Thank you," he said, with a little lopsided grin.

The server brought my water and I watched him over my glass as I took a sip.

Jackson Fleming was a mysterious man.

I wanted to know what had compelled him to up and take a job in Houston.

And as much as I knew it was probably none of my business, I couldn't keep myself from probing.

"You had plans to move back to Houston?"

He looked at me blankly for a moment.

"No," he said.

That was not the answer I expected.

"So, not at all?"

He shook his head.

"You just flew here, dropped off my sister, and decided to stay?"

"I guess that sums it up," he said.

"Wow." I sat back. "I knew my sister was a compelling woman, but I didn't know she had that kind of effect on people."

I'd started to say on men, but Madison was a happily married woman.

He laughed and picked up his menu.

"Trust me," he said. "Your sister had nothing to do with it. Not that there's anything wrong with Madison. She's a good person. And she's going to be a good mother."

My jaw dropped.

"She said something to you?"

He leaned back, an amused look on his face.

"She didn't have to."

"And I just confirmed it," I said, rolling my eyes at myself.

Jackson laughed. "Don't worry. Her secret is safe with me."

"You just assumed I knew?"

"Of course you knew. You're her sister."

"Our other sisters don't know." I ran a finger along the rim of my water glass.

"She'll tell them."

"She's closer to Ainsley," I said, mostly to myself.

"Maybe," he said. "But she told you."

I tapped my fingers against the table and stared at my blank phone.

"Hey," he said, reaching a hand across the table, almost touching my hand before pulling back.

"You have a big family," he said. "I can't even imagine what that must be like. All I have to worry about is one sister. And I think—hope—that she'd tell me if she got pregnant."

Even though he said the words matter-of-factly, I saw the shadow cross his features. I got the distinct feeling that Jackson may want his sister to tell him if she got pregnant, but he wouldn't be happy about it.

"Can I change the subject?" I asked.

"Okay." He looked a bit perplexed by the question.

"Asking that is a hazard of having a mother and sister who are psychologists."

He smiled. "What's the new subject?"

"I'm just curious how this is supposed to work."

"Well," he said. "I was thinking we'd have dinner, then I'd steal a goodnight kiss. On the cheek maybe. Then I'll text you and we'll do it again."

"What?"

He'd thrown me off-balance again.

"I meant you moving here," I said. "To Houston. Unplanned."

"Oh," he said. "That subject isn't nearly as interesting, but ok."

The server stopped by and took our dinner order.

Afterward, my thoughts were still swirling, but Jackson was grinning.

I narrowed my eyes at him. He'd known exactly what I was talking about.

He was slick.

I'd have to pay more attention to him. Be more careful about how I phrased things.

"So… do you have it figured out?" I asked. "Your move to Houston?"

"I do," he said. "Absolutely."

26

JACKSON

I actually didn't have anything figured out.

But the details of my move to Houston weren't something I wanted to think about right now.

I wanted to focus on this beautiful woman sitting across from me.

To live in this moment and have an intelligent conversation with someone who interested me.

I would be the first to admit that I found very few people that I actually enjoyed talking with.

I'd tried the whole dating app thing. Zoosk. Elite. Tinder.

About ten minutes into that first date, we'd run out of things to talk about.

Or I would. Some of the women I'd gone on dates with could talk for hours about nothing.

I preferred to have some substance to my conversations.

And in all honesty, Brianna and I hadn't had all that much substance to our conversations yet.

But that didn't bother me.

We had two things. First of all, we had a connection.

And second of all, we had the potential of never running out of things to talk about.

In a round about way, we had flying in common. Like most pilots, that was pretty much my favorite conversation.

Not that Brianna was a pilot, but her father owned one of the most successful airlines in the country. Her sister and brother-in-law were pilots. And if I had to guess, there were friends and probably even other family members who fit in this category.

Hell, her brother Quinn ran the Houston office of Skye Travels.

She was enveloped in aviation.

So she could not only talk it, she understood it.

Then there was her You Tube channel.

We hadn't even touched that subject and I had no doubt that it held endless interest.

For both of us.

There was so much to learn about her.

Brianna Worthington ran deep.

And besides that, I just liked looking at her.

So, yes, I'd upended my life.

My sister was probably going to suggest that I have my head examined. I'd never shown any signs of impulsivity.

I had always been the stable one. Always there for her.

But Tiffany had established a life for herself.

My responsibility for her—that I'd willingly taken on—was dissolving.

Tiffany was her own woman now and I no longer had to worry about her falling into the wrong crowd because our parents had split and she was left with a broken home.

"Have you told your sister?" Brianna asked. "About your new job."

"Not yet," I said. And I noticed that she was being a lot more specific in her questions.

She was a fast learner.

I smiled to myself.

"I see," she said. "Are you sure this is something you want to do? Because if you're not, there'll be no hard feelings."

I narrowed my eyes at her. "Did your father put you up to this?"

If he did, that would explain why it had taken her so long to agree to have dinner with me. She was a spy for her father.

"No," she laughed. "Daddy would never do that. He makes his own decisions."

The server brought our plates and we spent a couple of minutes trying out our food.

"Are you a vegetarian?" I asked, just now noticing that she had ordered a salad.

"Pescatarian," she said, holding up a blackened shrimp on her fork.

"Ah. Then I don't suppose you'll be trying my steak."

"Sorry," she said. "Not a chance."

Just more support for my gut instinct that we would never run short of something to talk about.

Brianna had layers to her.

Layers that a man could happily spend a lifetime getting to know.

27

BRIANNA

*J*ackson was surprisingly easy to be with.

We talked, but it didn't seem like forced conversation.

More evidence that this was not a business meeting, no matter how I tried to spin it.

No matter which way I turned it, this was a date.

But not an official date.

He was a new hire for my daddy's company and he'd asked me to help him celebrate.

He didn't know anyone here.

"Have you kept up with any of your friends here?" I asked as I set my napkin next to my plate.

The salad had been good, but I'd only eaten about half of it.

I couldn't eat much at the time. I was like my sister Madison in that way. Madison would take one bite of something and loose interest in it. Ainsley was pretty good about eating and yet she never gained a pound.

Me, I was more careful. I didn't run five miles a day just so I could fill my body with toxins.

Sure, I'd done my share of craziness. Mostly in college.

But once I'd finished the task of decluttering my condo, I'd generalized that to my body.

It hadn't happened overnight and I had certainly never been an athlete, but I'd worked up to five miles a day. And I only ate things that had some nutritional value.

Most of the time.

It wasn't a hard and fast rule. If I was with a group that ordered pizza, then I'd have a slice of pizza.

But if there was a healthy choice, I'd take it.

It just made sense to me.

Jackson made a face and shook his head.

"Nah. I had a group I hung out with, but it wasn't like we were all that close."

"Did you date in high school?"

A little smile crossed his face.

"Of course," he said. "Didn't you?"

"We're talking about you right now," I said, picking up a glass and raising an eyebrow.

He set his own napkin beside his plate.

"I had two girlfriends. Both of them are married now. With children. We didn't stay in touch. So. To answer your question, there's no one that I moved back here for."

A little flush creeped across my cheeks.

I really hadn't been trying to ask him about his dating history. It had just sort of come up. Of course, there were a whole lot of years between high school and now.

There was college. Then there was his time so far as a pilot.

Girls liked a guy in uniform. Especially a guy who looked as good as Jackson did.

He didn't even have to be wearing a uniform to turn heads.

I'd noticed several women looking in our direction and I knew they weren't looking at me.

"I had a high school boyfriend," I said, feeling like I needed to balance the scales. "We didn't stay in touch. I don't even know where he is now."

The server came and took away our plates.

"Would you like a to-go box, ma'am?" he asked me.

"No," I said with a little smile. "but thank you."

That was one of the downsides to not eating much. The servers always seemed to be compelled to point it out to everyone by offering a to-go box.

And I rarely ate left over food.

Not that there was anything wrong with it.

I just didn't eat enough to eat left overs.

I only ate things that tasted good. And it had to be fresh food. Otherwise I considered it wasted calories.

"What about now?" Jackson asked after the server left.

At least Jackson didn't feel the need to point out that I'd barely eaten anything.

"What about now what?"

"Are you seeing anyone?"

Right. We'd been talking about boyfriends.

I shook my head.

"No. No time."

He seemed to study me, one eyebrow lifted.

"No time or no inclination?"

I smiled at him.

Jackson was definitely fun to talk to.

"Actually no inclination to find the time."

"But you wouldn't be opposed to the idea?"

"I guess that depends," I said. "I've never touched a dating app." I wrinkled my nose. "And I'd rather be an old maid than to order a guy off the Internet."

Jackson laughed.

"Good to know," he said, pulled out a credit card, and set it on edge of the table.

I liked his subtleness.

He seemed like the kind of guy who would protect a girl's secrets.

28

JACKSON

"You do know that you just combined slang from two different centuries?" I asked.

"What?" she asked, discreetly checking her phone before she slipped it back into her handbag.

"You said old maid and ordering a date off the Internet. Two different centuries. In the same sentence."

"I guess I did," she said, with a little shrug.

The server picked up my credit card, but instead of taking off with it, he held a little payment machine in his hand while I swiped the card.

I had to remember that I was living in Houston now and most of the restaurants, the upscale ones at least, would have the latest technology.

I traveled all over the place, including some really small towns, so I'd seen everything.

My favorite was paying completely with my phone.

But not too many places had that just yet.

They'd get there.

The future was here. We just had to embrace it.

"Your turn," she said when we were alone again. "A girl in every port?"

"No," I said, cringing. I hated that stereotype.

I was not that kind of guy, despite what so many people expected.

Even if I was so inclined, I often had my little sister with me when I traveled. Or at least I had.

And especially now that she was all grown up, most people assumed that we were together as a couple and left us alone.

I didn't mind.

I found it to be a whole lot easier that way.

"It's good to know that there are still some honorable men out there," she said, running her fingers over the edge of the table.

I wasn't sure whether she believed me or not. If she didn't, it was because she knew as much as I did about the aviation world.

"Let's hope so," I said. "Surely you've met some men who aren't cads."

She smiled.

"I have. But let's just say they're a bit hard to uncover."

"Your sisters seem to have done well," I said.

"They have," she said, leaning back in her chair. "Madison and Kade dated in college, then got back together after a few years. They were always destined to be together. And then Ainsley met Wyatt by accident. I don't know about him, but I know Ainsley wasn't looking for anyone. It just sort of happened."

I grinned. "That's when it's the best, right?"

"Yeah," she said with an absent glance around the restaurant.

She had an odd expression on her face.

"Wait a minute," I said. "You haven't dated since high school?"

"I have, too," she said, then put both palms on the table and leaned forward, looking at me.

"Okay," she said, meeting my gaze. "I haven't had a boyfriend since high school."

"Why not?" I leaned forward. This was getting interesting.

"I've only been out of college for a year."

"You're a youngster," I said. "But no college boyfriend? Really?"

She shook her head.

"Like I said, I didn't have the inclination to make the time."

"Hey," I said. "I'm not judging. Actually it's a good thing."

"How?" she asked, her brows furrowed.

"It means you don't come with a lot of baggage."

And I could think of about a hundred different ways that I could spoil her.

Brianna Worthington was ripe to be charmed.

29

BRIANNA

*M*ost everyone had moved to the bar, clearing out the restaurant. Besides me and Jackson, there was only one other couple sitting at an actual table.

"Do you always close down restaurants," I asked, toying with the little white daisy in a vase on the table.

"It's not my habit," he said.

"What is your habit?" I couldn't say what it was, but I wanted to know everything about Jackson.

"I'm usually an early to bed and early to rise kind of guy."

I shoved the vase back in place and looked into his eyes.

"I'm keeping you up."

He nodded once. "You are." Then he smiled. "And your father has me flying tomorrow."

"Your first flight on the job."

"But I've been in the air for almost every day of my life for the last eight years."

"Everyday?"

I shrugged. "I'm in high demand."

"No wonder you want to work for my daddy. His pilots only fly four days a week. Normally."

"He didn't tell me that."

"Well," I said. "He should have. It's a good selling point."

"I guess he didn't think he had to sell me."

I tilted my head to the side and studied him. I still hadn't figured out why he had suddenly dropped his life in Denver and moved to Houston.

Maybe it wasn't for me to understand.

Or maybe if I saw him again, he would get around to telling me.

Or... maybe he didn't even know.

Sometimes people just wanted to blow up their lives and start over.

I'd actually done a video on that one time.

I hadn't actually known anyone who had done it, but I liked the idea of it.

I figured if life wasn't going the way we wanted to, we needed to change course.

And sometimes the only way to change course was to get off the airplane we were on and get on another. One headed in a completely different direction.

It was quite possible that Jackson had done that.

I rather hoped he hadn't watched that video because it was one of my earlier ones and I wasn't even sure I knew what I was talking about.

But that, I decided, had to be it.

He had returned to his roots to start over again.

He didn't know anyone, so he'd sought me out for some company.

I was good company.

Momma had trained me well.

She hadn't trained me to ask so many personal questions though. I'd figured that one out for myself.

And I would keep it to myself. Momma didn't need to know everything.

Besides, the way I saw it, it was part of the whole dating thing.

Not that I was dating Jackson.

I was merely keeping him company.

"I was in Florida last week to train on a new plane. The Phenom," Jackson was telling me.

"The Phenom. Wyatt has one of those."

"Is that so? Does Noah?"

My phone chimed indicating a text message.

I tried to ignore it.

"Not yet," I said. "I think he's looking into getting one though. He really likes them."

"It's a good plane."

My phone chimed again.

"Sorry," I said. "I have to…"

I stared at the text message.

Then looked up at Jackson.

"I have to go."

Holding my phone in one hand, I grabbed my handbag with the other as I stood up.

I didn't even bother to push the chair in. I just left it sitting there.

And without another word, I raced to the door.

30

JACKSON

I sat at the table, looking across at the empty chair Brianna had just vacated.

She'd left the chair sitting out in the middle of the room. Somehow I had a feeling she didn't normally do that.

She seemed much too orderly to just jump up and leave a chair sitting there without pushing it back up to the table.

Whatever text had been on her phone must have been urgent.

It was one of the fastest exits I'd ever witnessed.

That didn't bother me. Whatever she had to do, she needed to do it.

What bothered me was how much I missed her sitting across from me.

I'd already stayed up far later than I'd intended.

And I could have stayed up all night talking to Brianna about everything and nothing at all.

It's what I had hoped for. I'd hoped that the connection I felt with her was more than just a fleeting attraction. More than just a physical attraction.

And I had been right.

It was physical attraction along with everything else.

We'd stayed too long in the restaurant anyway and I was the last person to leave the tables.

I hadn't realized that Brianna and I had closed down the place.

I smiled to myself as I walked past the bar toward the elevators to my room. Even if I hadn't been flying in the morning, I had no interest in stopping in for a drink.

I'd never had a relationship that started in a bar.

I knew plenty of guys who had, but not me.

I had high standards and wanted not just someone I had a connection with, but someone with substance.

Like Brianna.

Brianna was someone I wouldn't mind closing down a lot of restaurants with.

Tiffany always found my dating habits amusing.

She'd told me more than once. *You don't have to marry someone just because you date them.*

She was right, of course. I just didn't get into casual dating. It seemed like a waste of time to me.

I probably had some kind of attachment issues.

Parents getting divorced could do that, even if I'd already left home. Tiffany and I both agreed that they should have gotten divorced years before they finally did.

But they stayed together for the children.

At least until they couldn't do it any longer.

I stepped into my hotel room and quickly changed out of my clothes.

Tomorrow I'd have to wear this suit again.

I was supposed to meet with the Skye Travels office manager, Helen, in the morning for paperwork and to order my uniform.

This sudden move to Houston should have felt weird. But it didn't. It felt right.

Maybe I was just due for a change.

Or maybe I was doing that thing. Where I jumped to thoughts of getting married before the first date.

I didn't see the problem with thinking ahead. If I couldn't see myself marrying a girl, I didn't see the point of dating her.

If I could, well then, that required some courting.

I just had to tread carefully and keep reminding myself that Brianna was the boss's daughter.

A minor detail.

One that wasn't going to stand in my way.

31

———

BRIANNA

$\mathcal{M}$y heels clicked down the sterile hallway of the hospital.

My heart pounded in my ears drowning out the sound of the monitors as I walked past the patients' rooms.

Almost.

I heard more than I wanted to. But I was focused.

All I had to do was get to my sister's room.

I held my phone and reread her text, even though I had the room number memorized.

One more corner and I reached her room.

With a quick knock, I opened the door and stuck my head inside.

Madison lay in the bed, her eyes closed.

As I slowly approached her bed, her eyes opened.

"Madison," I said. "What's happened?"

"I had some stomach cramping, so I came in to get checked out. I don't think it's a big deal."

"It looks like a big deal," I said. Looking at the monitors she was hooked up to.

"I know," she said. "that's why I didn't tell Momma and Daddy."

I understood completely. Ever since Daddy had been diagnosed with prostate cancer, the five of us siblings made a tacit agreement to involve our parents only when it was absolutely necessary. And the bigger the problem, the more we tried to shield them from it. Especially Daddy, but since Momma told him everything, we kept a lot of stuff from her, too.

"When does Kade get here?" I asked, going to sit on the edge of her bed.

"He's late," she said, worry clouding her features. "His flight was delayed."

"He'll be here," I said, knowing that was what my sister needed right now. Confidence and reassurance that everything would be okay.

"I'm sorry to bother you," she said. "but Ainsley is out of town and…"

I put a hand over hers.

"Please," I said. "you better call me when you need something. I might be your younger sister, but I'll do in a pinch."

"I didn't mean it that way," she said. "You're more than just good in a pinch."

"So what have they said?" I asked, getting back to what was important.

"They want me to stay in bed a few days and rest."

"Seriously?" I said. "Do they know who they're talking to? You don't rest."

"I know, right?" she said.

"Do you have to stay in the hospital for this rest?" I asked, looking at the monitor beeping rhythmically.

It was a sound that struck fear in my heart.

Maybe I'd watched too much TV in my younger years.

Or maybe it was what the sound represented.

"I don't know," Madison said, reaching for a glass of water.

I handed it to her and she drank from the bendy straw.

"They'll let me know tomorrow, I hope."

"That's one thing about hospitals," I said. "they don't get in any hurry."

Madison blew out a breath. "That's for sure."

"Are you sure you don't want me to call Momma?" I asked.

"Not yet," she said. "let me see if I can deal with this myself first. They have enough to worry about."

"Okay," I said. "but I think they're going to be more upset that you didn't tell them."

Madison leaned her head back and closed her eyes.

I took the water glass from her hands and put it back on the bedside table.

"But you're right," I said. "You can tell them after you know more. I'll be here and I won't be leaving your side 'til Kade gets here."

Madison looked at me with grateful eyes that made me feel like a heel for thinking about how the *worked* part of the phrase *worked at home* was silent.

Like the P in psychology.

I was grateful that I had the freedom to be here. And that my older sister had picked me to call.

I loved all my sisters dearly. But Madison was the one I idolized the most.

She was the one with strength.

She'd gone out of state to college. Then another state for internship.

I admired her independence.

And now she was the only one of Noah's children with Momma who lived away.

The rest of us stayed close to family.

Of course, it wasn't just family that kept me in Houston.

I couldn't think of a single place I'd rather live.

Maybe New York. But that would be no more than a fleeting preference.

Houston was home.

Besides having three distinct skylines, it had everything. Temperate winter weather. The best food. The Houston Astros.

Nonetheless, there was something admirable about Madison moving away to pursue her own dreams.

I missed her, of course, but she visited often.

And now that she was going to have a baby, I had a feeling the Worthington family would be burning up the air space between here and Denver.

"I hope I didn't pull you away from anything important," Madison said.

"Of course not," I said.

No wonder they didn't hesitate to call on me. I didn't exactly protest.

Besides, it wasn't worry that flashed through my mind.

It was Jackson.

I hadn't said a word of explanation to him.

He must think me one of the rudest people he'd ever met.

I'd be surprised if I ever even heard from him again.

And I wouldn't blame him in the least. If he'd jumped up and left me sitting at the table like that with no explanation, I didn't know what I'd think.

That was one thing about the Worthington women that wasn't likely to change.

They put family above everything else.

Even Madison had dropped everything when she'd needed to be here for Daddy.

I settled onto the sofa and the nurse brought me a heated blanket.

This is where I'd sleep tonight and then we'd see.

With any luck, Madison would be released in the morning, but I'd stay with her until Kade got here.

It's what we did.

32

———

JACKSON

With a flip of a switch, the wheels came down and I prepared to land at the Houston airport.

My little flight up to Dallas and back had been uneventful.

Unless, of course, you counted having your new boss in the co-pilot's seat.

And not just your new boss. But the legendary Noah Worthington.

Fortunately for me, when I was in the cockpit, I was boss.

Flying was like breathing to me.

So that was the easy part.

The hard part was worrying about how he was going to take the news that I was going to marry his daughter.

There were, of course, about a hundred steps between here and there.

Perhaps with all those steps along the way, he would get used to the idea without putting out a hit on me or give me a good push out the door of one of his airplanes.

I'd been on top of my game today.

The little flight up to Noah's Dallas office had led to a

round of introductions and lunch with Noah and his Dallas office manager.

I still wondered what was behind Noah's sudden job offer and his subsequent introduction to those in his world.

Though no one had said anything, I got the feeling that he didn't do that with all his new hires.

I smiled to myself as I checked the computers and spoke with flight control.

Maybe he already knew about me and Brianna.

In some way, I almost felt like he'd somehow orchestrated it.

That was, of course, wishful thinking and probably fanciful thinking, too.

Although…

I had heard rumors floating about suggesting that Cupid had an affinity for Skye Travels pilots.

And since I was a Skye Travels pilot now…

My landing was perfect.

When we came to a stop, Noah dragged off his headset and looked over at me.

"You seem to be living up to your reputation," he said. "Good flight."

I powered the plane off and glanced absently over at Noah.

"I have a reputation?" I asked. "I didn't know."

Noah shrugged and unbuckled his harness.

"It happens."

"Hm." I unbuckled my own harness. "I hope it isn't too bad."

Reputations were tricky.

They could be legendary like Noah's or, in the case of most people, they carried more bad than good.

It was human nature to want to talk about people's problems rather than the good things they did.

Noah just happened to be the exception.

Noah stood up.

"You don't have anything to worry about," he said. "Seems you keep your head down and do your job."

I nodded.

"That's what I'm supposed to do, right?"

The two of us stepped out of the plane.

"It's what I did," Noah said. "I figured out early on that the only way to be successful was to focus on the process."

As we walked toward the building, I glanced over at Noah.

I had the odd sense that Noah had just given me the secret to his success.

There was more, of course. There was always more.

But he'd just given me the basis for everything.

Or maybe he was just pointing out something that I was already doing.

And he recognized it.

Maybe he saw something of himself in me.

Whatever it was, I felt honored.

And at the same time, I was overcome with guilt.

I liked and admired Noah Worthington.

The fact that I had designs on his daughter left me feeling decidedly uncomfortable and guilty.

I even felt like I was somehow being dishonest by letting him take me under his wing like this while at the same time contemplating how I was going to charm his daughter into my life.

"Come on in to my office," Noah said. "I want to show you something."

Well hell.

If he was going to keep this up, he wasn't going to leave me with any choice.

I was going to have to back off on courting Noah's daughter.

I just wasn't sure I had it in to me.

33

BRIANNA

I stepped off the elevator into my condo at six fifteen the next morning.

Had I ever come home this late from anywhere?

Not that I could remember.

I'd left home at six or even five in the morning, but staying out all night had never been my thing.

Party girl I was not.

Going into my closet, I dropped my handbag on its designated shelf and dropped onto the chaise to pull off my shoes.

I curled up right there on the chaise lounge in my closet and went to sleep.

I'd finally fallen asleep on the couch in Madison's hospital room just after Midnight.

Nurses were in and out checking this and that.

Night and day blurred into one in the hospital.

Then Kade had shown up at three o'clock.

Apparently, he'd had to make a landing in Dallas for some kind of mechanical issue.

But that hadn't stopped him from getting to Madison. He'd rented a car and drove from Dallas to Houston.

The nurses wouldn't let us both stay, but they had taken one look at me and told me to wait until daylight to drive home.

I routinely got my eight hours of sleep every night, so I did not do well in the hospital setting.

The alarm on my cell phone went off, jarring me out of what was about to be my first night's sleep in my closet.

I remembered I needed to charge my phone anyway, so I dragged myself to my bedroom, set the phone on the charger, and climbed into bed.

It would probably take me two days to get myself back to normal.

But Madison was family and I would do it all over again.

I was sound asleep when a text came in on my phone, jarring me awake again.

I didn't know how long I'd been asleep, but I did know that it wasn't long enough.

I almost ignored the message.

Almost.

But worrying that it might be Madison, I pried my eyes open and checked the message.

It wasn't Madison.

It was Momma.

Like everyone else in my family, she knew I got up early.

What was it with my family these last couple of days?

I could go for weeks with hearing nothing from my family outside of our weekly family dinners.

Then all of a sudden, everyone seemed to want something.

MOMMA: *Good morning Brianna. I hope I didn't wake you.*

Momma always started her texts with a formal greeting. She didn't seem to grasp the quick in and out nature of the text message.

I couldn't ignore her either.

It was eight o'clock. Momma must have me confused with someone else. Unless she had one of those gut sense things that I was sleeping.

She had that way about her.

ME: *Not asleep.*

MOMMA: *Good. Have you heard from Madison? We were supposed to have breakfast together.*

Uh oh.

None of us lied to Momma. It just wasn't something we did.

She'd find out and there would be hell to pay.

It didn't even matter that it was to protect her and Daddy.

But torn between Madison's request and not lying to Momma, I skirted the edge.

ME: *Wasn't Kade's flight delayed?*

MOMMA: *He drove in late last night.*

How did Momma know these things? I swear I didn't think Kade had told anyone.

But, of course, he was flying one of Daddy's planes, so Daddy would know.

And if Daddy knew, then Momma knew. They pretty much shared a brain.

ME: *Wouldn't she wait up for him?*

Damn it. Madison had put me in a bad spot.

MOMMA: *You're right. Makes sense.*

I blew out a sigh of relief and laid my head back down on the pillow.

When the phone chimed again, I picked up the phone and read the message.

MOMMA: *She must have forgotten her phone charger. I'll text Kade.*

Good. Let Madison and Kade deal with this. Madison was the one who had decided not to tell them she was in the hospital.

Me? I would have told them.

I'd rather let them worry a bit than have to explain why I kept something like that from them.

That's what happened when you moved away out of state. You started thinking you could handle things without involving your parents.

In the Worthington family, that was just delusional.

34

JACKSON

So much for my plans to slow down and take a week off.

Even though I'd gotten to bed early enough last night and was already awake when Noah called, to say that it was unexpected was an understatement.

So now I was sitting in the back seat of an Uber on my way back to the airport.

Apparently Kade hadn't made it in until the middle of the night.

And he'd driven from Dallas to Houston.

Since he had gotten in so late, Noah was letting him rest.

But he wasn't leaving his airplane stranded in Dallas.

Apparently, there was some mechanical problem that was already fixed.

So Noah asked me to fly to Dallas with him to pick up the stranded airplane.

I didn't mind. I was used to last minute flights.

Last minute flights, had in fact made me successful.

What I couldn't figure out, though, was why Noah was relying on me so much.

Maybe the simplest explanation was the best.

Since I was the new guy, I didn't have a busy schedule yet.

So he knew I was available. And since he was paying me, why not make good use of me as a resource?

When the car pulled up at the terminal, Noah was already there, waiting for me.

He might be sixty years old, but he was still a dashing figure of a man, wearing his uniform and his pilot's cap.

I could only hope to age so well. Both in looks and success.

They had definitely broken the mold with Noah Worthington, as my grandmother used to say.

"Thanks for helping out," Noah said as I reached him on the tarmac.

"Not a problem," I said. "Happy to help."

"I'm flying," he said.

I laughed. Noah said it like a teenager calling shotgun.

And in that moment, I knew exactly why Noah Worthington had been so damned successful.

He loved what he did.

He loved flying. And if I had to guess, he loved Skye Travels.

Even with enough money to pay people to cater to his every whim, he did things for himself.

He didn't need to fly up to Dallas to pick up the airplane Kade had left up there last night.

He just wanted to go.

He wanted to fly.

Noah and I had a lot in common and the more time I spent around him, the more I liked him.

And the more I was conflicted about charming his daughter into dating me.

I wanted to call Noah a friend.

And wasn't sure it was a good idea to date a friend's daughter.

Damn it.

Why couldn't I have talked Brianna into dating me before becoming friends with her father?

Like most things in life, things rarely went in the right order.

It didn't change how I felt.

It just required me to be a bit more creative in how I went about things.

35

BRIANNA

It was two o'clock in the afternoon and I hadn't done my second weekly video.

I'd started out making one a week. I'd been posting one video a week for seventy-eight weeks. That was one and a half years of weekly videos.

I didn't miss.

That was what I thought of as my serious video, though in truth, how serious could fashion be?

Then I'd gone to two.

And I'd been posting two videos a week for three months now.

And somehow that had become a streak as well.

So I currently had two streaks going.

My main video where I talked about fashion and health. That's probably how it had come to be serious. That and I put a lot of preparation into those weekly videos.

Then I had the second video of the week that something of a toss off.

Granted, for me, even a toss off video was usually planned and edited to the max.

But today I was under a time crunch.

So I went outside on my balcony overlooking the city, set my phone up on my tripod and putting the notes I'd quickly scribbled next to me.

Yes, I'd been thinking about this topic for some time, but only in my overnight lack of sleep had it come together in my head.

I clicked record.

"Today I'm going to talk about something that we've all dealt with at one time or another.

"Lack of sleep.

"First of all, know that sleep deprivation can cause a lot of problems. Memory. Aging. Lack of immunity. Increased likelihood of cancer. In fact, night time shift work is now considered a carcinogen."

I took a deep breath and stared into the camera.

"But… don't despair. If you miss a night of sleep now and then, you can recover. And I'm going to talk today about some of the things you can do to ease yourself back into a healthy routine."

I got about halfway down my list that included lots of water for hydration and green tea for antioxidants, when I paused my recording. Before I went any further, I needed to do some more research and follow my own advice with a cup of hot tea and maybe a short nap.

My thoughts running with today's topic, I went inside, turned on the coffee machine that also heated water for tea and, leaning on my kitchen island, went into a deep Google dive.

One thing that was very important to me was making sure I had my facts right.

I might not be a psychologist like my sister, but that didn't give an excuse to get my facts wrong.

In fact, under normal circumstances, I'd probably have Madison review it before posting.

But Madison was in the hospital and I was on a deadline.

So I had to do my own fact checking today.

As I filled my mug with hot water, a text came in on my phone.

CONCIERGE: *You have a delivery. Can I send him up?*

ME: *Yes. Thank you.*

That was just one of the great things about living in a high rise.

Security.

No one just showed up at the door without permission.

In fact, I didn't even have to ask who the delivery person was because even though I wasn't expecting anything, all delivery people were vetted by the concierge on duty.

Taking a break from my research, I took my warm mug and went to wait next to the elevator.

A few minutes later, the elevator dinged and the doors opened.

A delivery guy I didn't recognize stood there holding a bouquet of flowers.

Pink daisies and white lilies arranged with yellow daffodils.

Although pink was my favorite flower color, daffodils were my favorite flower.

It was their strong fresh scent that got me every time.

As I stepped forward to take the bouquet of flowers, my heart did all sorts of summersaults.

An image of Jackson shot though my head.

But there was no way that Jackson would know what kind of flowers I liked.

Except that everyone knew what I liked.

I'd done a video on my favorite flowers.

Now that I thought about it, although I claimed to be a private person, I had very few secrets.

So anyone, with a little research, could figure out what my favorite flowers were.

I thanked the delivery guy and the elevator doors closed.

I set the flowers on the table in the center of my living area and, hands shaking just a bit, located the little envelope, and pulled out the card.

After quickly reading it, I dropped onto my sofa.

The flowers weren't from Jackson.

They were from one of my sponsors. Congratulating me on the new milestone of one million followers.

It was a nice gesture.

But for me it was telling.

I'd been thinking about Jackson a lot.

And I might be in a little bit of trouble where he was concerned.

36

JACKSON

I flew out ahead while Noah stayed in Dallas for a meeting.

Kade's little Cessna handled fine. The mechanical problem had turned out to be minor.

Although I'd enjoyed flying with Noah the last couple of days, I'd missed my time alone with only my own thoughts to keep me company.

I read a lot. And I'd recently read a book by William Glasser. He talked about positive addiction and how things like exercise, meditation, and even music can be addictive. But in a positive way.

Much like negative addictions like drugs and alcohol, people feel a need or urge to do their positive addictions.

I was pretty sure that flying was a positive addiction for me.

And apparently it wasn't just the flying, it was the alone time.

I hadn't really known that until now.

When I was in the air, alone, I could think. Something akin to meditation.

So this was the first time since I'd upended my life that I'd had this space to really think about it.

I still hadn't had the chance to tell Tiffany.

Oddly enough, I considered that to be a good sign.

The fact that she was busy and not dependent on me like she had been when she was a teenager when our parents were getting divorced, supported my decision to move to Houston.

Now that I thought about it, I was pretty sure that I would have already considered leaving Denver if she hadn't been going to school there.

Not that there was anything wrong with Denver, but Houston was home.

I checked the plane's gauges and took a drink of water.

As I leveled off at my highest altitude, my thoughts wandered back to Brianna.

Had I really moved to Houston to be near her?

Considering that we'd only met two days ago, I hoped there was more to it than that.

That would be illogical.

She was just the impetus. The thing that jerked me out of my comfort zone into changing up my life.

I'd need to make a trip up to Denver to pack up my apartment, turn in the keys, and whatnot, but that wouldn't take long. I didn't have a lot in the little apartment. No furniture that was worth bringing with me.

I could even pay someone to go in and do it for me.

Most everything there could simply be donated or tossed.

I had a few clothes and photos and other personal items to pick up, but I could easily do that in a weekend.

Listening to the chatter coming in on the radio, I considered my options.

In the meantime, and more importantly, I needed to find an apartment in Houston.

That would take a little more work, actually, since I'd need to furnish it.

And Houston had not only changed a lot since I'd lived here, but I'd been a kid. Brianna would know which apartments to look at.

And she could certainly help me furnish it.

If she wanted to.

However… that was a job for a girlfriend. Not a potential girlfriend.

There was a huge difference.

Instead of thinking about what she could do to help me, I needed to be thinking about what I could for her.

The first thing I could do was to ask her on a date. A real date.

I needed to do some research. Find out which restaurants were good.

I could ask any of the guys at Skye Travels. They would know.

Noah would definitely know.

But that brought me back to the whole problem of dating his daughter.

I needed to just slow down. Test the waters. See if she even had any interest in dating me.

I was getting ahead of myself.

It was a short flight from Dallas to Houston and by the time I landed in Houston, I still hadn't worked anything out.

And I knew what was going to happen.

It was going to be like my little apartment in Denver. I was going to get busy with work, put it all off, and end up not doing a damn thing.

Not doing a damn thing, though, was not the way to win the heart of a woman like Brianna Worthington.

In order to win her heart, I was going to have to be proactive and force myself to take action.

Doing something was better than doing nothing.

That was something my therapist had taught me.

37

BRIANNA

*S*unday got here sooner than later.

I'd been holed up in my condo, for the most part, recovering from my night spent at the hospital with my sister.

She'd actually been discharged the next morning, so the whole thing had been a false alarm. Better safe than sorry though.

Besides recovering, I'd been working on a couple of videos.

I was just glad my family had decided to give me some space to work. It didn't matter that I was sure it wasn't intentional.

Being the middle child, I was often forgotten about. It worked out well for me because I was self-entertaining and self-sufficient.

I didn't have to be around people all the time to be happy.

But today everyone had to be at Momma and Daddy's house.

It was a family party mostly for Madison.

Of course, I was the only one who knew what the truly important news was.

Madison being pregnant.

I knew that was the real reason she'd come home now.

She wanted to surprise everyone.

My family had no idea what was coming.

I had an appointment at the Blow Dry Salon, so all I had to do was get dressed and head over there.

I had actually darted over to Nordstrom's yesterday. Something I rarely did anymore.

Since going to a minimalistic lifestyle, I had no reason to go shopping.

But I wanted a new dress for today.

Nothing wrong with that.

Except maybe the real reason I wanted a new dress for today.

Jackson was going to be there.

Or at least Daddy had invited him.

Since I hadn't spoken to anyone about it since, I didn't really know what was going to come off.

But with even the remote possibility that Jackson was going to be there, I wanted to look better than ordinary. I wanted to look good. For him.

I wasn't sure how I felt about that.

Trying to look good for a guy was something that I tried to avoid.

I felt like it put me at a disadvantage.

I don't know why I felt that way. I just did.

I spent the next hour having my hair washed, then meticulously blow dried.

There was something soothing about sitting under the hot blow dryer, having my hair painstakingly dried strand by strand.

Some girls went to the spa.

I went to the salon.

It occurred to me as I sat there having my hair dried, that this was something I had never YouTubed about.

My family had known at some point. I'd even come here with Madison once. Not Ainsley. It wasn't Ainsley's thing. I'd definitely brought Wynter here before her prom, but she preferred to do things with her friends, so I didn't know if she even remembered.

This was my own little private thing. The realization made me smile.

I shared my life with the world.

Or... I corrected, I shared a persona of myself with the world.

I occasionally filmed from my balcony, but no one knew if that was a real backdrop or not.

Probably not all that smart on my part, actually.

Nonetheless, I shared very personal things about me with the world.

It felt good to know that there were still some things that were private.

And, I told myself, it didn't matter whether Jackson was at my parents' house or not.

But even as I told myself that, I checked my phone to see if any of my sisters had checked in.

To see if anyone mentioned Jackson being there.

But of course, this was one day when my phone was radio silent.

I'd find out myself in less than two hours.

38

JACKSON

On Sunday afternoon, I stood in Noah Worthington's backyard, a beer in one hand.

This was something I could never have predicted happening.

Not in a million years.

But Noah was grilling hamburgers and veggie burgers.

The Worthington's house was everything I would have expected.

On Memorial Drive, the house itself took up several lots. Then there was the backyard, replete with a centerpiece pool.

That was the best way I knew to describe the multilevel swimming pool. On one side, there was a lap pool. On the other, there were wide steps going into the water— with four lounge chairs in the water.

But to me, the most interesting part of the pool was on this side where Noah had his barbeque pit and what could only be called a dining area.

Looking back toward the three-story house, the pool wall was above-ground. And the wall was perfectly clear. With a waterfall.

So it gave the illusion of a wall of water spilling over the sides.

Although Noah was obviously in charge of the grill, Kade was there and Ainsley's fiancé, Wyatt.

The women were inside, doing whatever it was that women did.

I hadn't seen Brianna yet.

"So," Kade said. "I heard Noah roped you into coming to work for us."

"Yes," I said. "You heard right."

I found it interesting that Kade took ownership in Skye Travels and Noah didn't correct him.

Of course, Kade was part of the family now.

Kade held up his bottle of beer. "Welcome aboard," he said. "May you have smooth sailing."

Wyatt looked at me and rolled his eyes.

"If you like flying airplanes, you're in the right place," he said.

"Thank you," I said to Kade, then turned to Wyatt. "I understand you do some flying yourself."

Wyatt grinned. "Not sure you can be in this family and not have something to do with airplanes."

"That's not true," Noah said, flipping hamburger meat, then picking up a different spatula to flip the veggie burgers.

"Okay," Kade said. "You've got two, soon to be three son-in-laws who are pilots."

My stomach dropped as I did some quick calculations.

"Three?" I asked. That meant either Brianna or Noah's youngest daughter was also married.

Noah glanced in my direction. "I have another daughter, Danielle, from my first marriage. And Kade's right. She's married to a pilot."

And once again, I found myself wondering what I was doing here at the family's Sunday get-together.

I wasn't part of the family and I wasn't dating one of Noah's daughters.

At least not yet.

But no one other than me seemed to be concerned about this.

"Makes sense," I said, hopefully hiding my relief that Brianna didn't already have a serious man in her life that she'd somehow failed to tell me about. Obviously it hadn't registered with me in that split second that she'd already told me that.

"Another beer?" Kade asked, opening a refrigerator beneath the grill.

"No," I said, "I'm good."

And despite my efforts not to, I found my gaze straying toward the house, again, looking for Brianna.

This time, I was rewarded.

I knew her, even from here, across the expansive yard.

Brianna came out the back door, her long hair, smooth and bouncy all at once.

She was wearing a slinky red dress and as she walked toward us, I saw that she was wearing white sneakers.

White sneakers and a red cocktail dress.

At a barbeque.

And she pulled it off like nobody's business.

My throat was suddenly dry.

I hadn't even noticed that she was carrying a platter of something.

She looked at me and smiled as she handed the platter to Noah.

"Momma said you'd be wanting these," she said, her voice holding a Texas southern drawl I had not heard her use before. Not even in her YouTube videos.

Not even when we'd had dinner together.

I was already smitten by her and now I was utterly charmed.

Kade looked over at me and grinned.

I took a quick sip of my beer, but it was too late.

Kade and Wyatt exchanged a look that told me I wasn't doing a very good job of hiding my attraction to Noah's daughter.

"Thank you," Noah said. "We're about to eat, but why don't you show Jackson around afterwards?"

"Sure," she said, smiling at me. "What would you like to see?"

"I 'um…" I could not put two words together in my head, much less out loud.

Wyatt and Kade burst out laughing.

Noah thrust a plate of cooked hamburgers at Kade.

"Take that to the table," he said, then turned to Wyatt. "Let Savannah know that dinner is ready."

As the two other men left to do Noah's bidding, Noah looked at me.

"Don't worry about them," he said.

My gaze flicked briefly to Noah, then back to Brianna's emerald green eyes.

"I think I missed something," I said.

Brianna just smiled, took my hand, and led me toward the outdoor seating area.

"Like Daddy said, don't worry about them."

39

BRIANNA

I couldn't explain why I was so happy to see Jackson.

When I'd seen him standing with Daddy and Kade and Wyatt, my heart had skittered with feelings I normally kept at bay.

I'd grabbed up the plate of potatoes that Daddy was supposed to put on the grill and headed out toward the men.

Lightly holding his hand, I led him over to one of the outdoor tables and sat down.

I was overdressed, but I didn't feel overdressed.

The red bottomed canvas sneakers gave the silky red dress the exact look I was going for.

Breezy. Rich. Sexy.

I was most definitely going to be You Tubing about this look.

As I slid onto the bench, Jackson sat down next to me and set what was nearly a full bottle of beer on the table.

"Hi," he said.

"Hi." I put my elbows on the table and rested my chin on my hands. "I'm a little surprised to see you here."

"You knew I'd be here," he said.

I just shrugged. "Not really."

The rest of my family was spilling out the back door. My mother, Madison, Ainsley, Wynter, and our one brother Quinn.

I often felt sorry for Quinn.

He seemed so out of place sometimes.

It didn't even matter that he often did it to himself.

He could have been outside having a beer with the boys, but instead, he'd chosen to stay inside and hang out with his sisters.

"It was kind of him," I said. "But when Noah invited me, I hadn't realized I'd be crashing a family gathering."

"Daddy likes to share his family with people," I said, dismissing any insecurities he might be having about being here in Worthington territory.

"It's almost like he thinks we're dating," he said.

I shot him a serious look.

"Didn't you know that Daddy likes to play Cupid sometimes? And he's really good at it."

For the first time since I'd met him, Jackson looked shocked.

"I'm just kidding," I said bumping him with my shoulder and giving him a smile.

But he was looking at me with obvious skepticism.

"I don't think you are," he said, looking over his shoulder at Daddy as Momma stepped up to him and gave him a kiss on the cheek.

"He's been treating me like I'm one of the family since… well… since I got to Houston."

"That just means he likes you."

"Should I be worried?" he asked. "Is there something you're not telling me?"

I decided to cut him a break.

"You're the newest hire," I said. "He wants you to feel comfortable."

It was only a half truth. Daddy did go out of his way to

make his pilots feel like family. And he did occasionally have people over for Sunday dinners.

But he was going a bit overboard with Jackson.

"Do you eat meat?" I asked. "Or are you a vegetarian?"

"I eat meat," he said. "But I can eat anything."

I stretched out my hands.

"Good. Then I suggest you try a veggie burger. Momma makes them from scratch and they're the best you'll ever eat."

"Okay," he said, looking around. "Do we make it ourselves?"

"We will," I said. "But I think Madison has an announcement to make first."

He nodded and leaned back in the chair, seeming to relax a bit.

"How have you been?" he asked. "I haven't heard from you since…"

"Good," I said. "Busy."

I didn't want to talk about why I'd run out on him. Then I'd have to tell him about Madison. And that wasn't my place to talk about.

I also didn't mention that even though I'd run out on him—for good reason—I hadn't heard from him either.

No call. No text.

Not that I blamed him.

Not only was he starting a new job in a new city, he didn't know what was up with me.

He had every reason to be wary.

And now Daddy had invited him here, basically feeding him to the wolves.

But I was here now and I would make sure he was guarded.

40

JACKSON

Now that Brianna was here, I felt much more comfortable.

Everyone, including Brianna, acted like we were dating.

Or maybe it was my own wishful thinking.

After coming out of a broken home, to me, the Worthingtons seemed to have the perfect family.

Noah and Savannah had all five of their children together on just a regular Sunday afternoon. It wasn't even a holiday.

And apparently this was a weekly occurrence. Except for Madison, of course, because she lived in Denver. Though from what I understood, it wasn't unusual for her to jump on a plane with Kade and show up at random.

As everyone took a seat, Madison stood up, with Kade at her side.

"Before we get started," she said. "we have an announcement to make."

I knew, of course, what she was going to say.

She was absolutely beaming.

"We're going to have a baby," she said.

At first, there was nothing more than stunned silence. Then

everyone was up, hugging her, congratulatory handshakes for Kade.

"We should go congratulate them," I said.

"Sure," Brianna said. "Lead the way."

After we walked over together, she whispered something to Madison while I gave Kade a handshake and a clap on the shoulder.

"Life keeps getting better and better," I said.

"Yeah," Kade said. "Things are definitely changing at the speed of light."

"You'll be great," I said, giving Kade reassurance, I wasn't sure he needed.

He was getting reassurance from all around.Kade and Madison most definitely had strong family support.

I was surprised to find that I actually envied them a little bit.

After all the congratulations, everyone made their hamburgers, all but Wyatt and Kade choosing veggie burgers, I noticed, and found themselves places to sit.

It was odd how they didn't sit at a table together like I expected. Instead they made themselves comfortable while staying within earshot of each other.

I'd expected something a lot more formal at the family gathering of the legendary Noah Worthington and his family.

"Is it always like this?" I asked Brianna who sat next to me, eating a veggie burger.

"Like what?" she asked with a glance around.

This would be normal for her, of course.

I shrugged and ate a roasted potato.

"I don't know. Informal?"

"Oh God, no," she said, glancing up at the sky. "This is one of those rare Texas days where the weather outside is tolerable. Normally we usually stay inside the house."

I nodded. But I still didn't think she'd answered my question.

"But everyone seems so comfortable."

"Oh, that," she said. "That part doesn't change. I mean sometimes Momma and Daddy have formal dinner parties with guests over. That's different from this. This is just family."

I picked up a napkin and wiped my hands. "I guess I'm not a guest then."

She looked at me sideways. "I guess not." She straightened the lettuce on her sandwich. "Daddy seems to have designated me as your... for lack of a better word... tour guide."

"What does that mean?"

"It means he's taken you under his wing, but he can't always watch you. So he wants me to do it."

"That seems a bit... unusual." I almost said *odd*, but then I remembered who I was talking to.

A daughter did not want to hear that someone thought her father was odd. Even if he was.

"I guess," she said, sipping from a bottle of water.

"I don't have to have a guardian," I said.

Brianna pushed her plate away and rested her elbows on the table.

"Okay," she said. "Are you saying you'd rather be on your own? That you'll turn down having someone to help you find a place to live? To have people," she gestured around her. "who'll have your back if you need something while you transition?"

"Of course not," I said. "I guess I was just hoping for something a little more personal than just a tour guide."

She smiled at me from beneath her lashes. "Is that so?"

"Well," I said. "It's true that I am moving here of my own accord. But your father was quite convincing."

She shrugged. "I'm pretty sure you could have said no."

I grinned. "Maybe. It happened pretty fast."

"Maybe," she said. "that means you were ready for a change and didn't even know it."

I looked at her a moment.

"I guess you don't have two psychologists in the family without picking up some of the insights that come with it."

"I guess not," she said. "We're a family of pilots and psychologists."

"But not you," I said. "How do you fit in?"

She looked at me, her emerald green eyes serious now.

"Sometimes I'm not so sure I do."

41

———

BRIANNA

*I*t was a perfect day to be outside. I was more of an inside girl, but a little fresh air never hurt anyone.

The humidity didn't do much for my hair, but all things considered, I wasn't minding being outside.

The mood was more festive than usual.

With Madison announcing that she and Kade were going to have a baby, there was an excitement and anticipation in the air.

I hadn't meant to spill my guts to Jackson.

I blamed it on Madison and her happy announcement.

My guard was down and he was being attentive and charming.

Besides, despite what he said, he'd been looking a little lost when I'd found him outside with the guys.

As we sat on a lounge sofa next to the pool, I wondered what he would be doing if he hadn't been here spending the day with my family.

I also wondered how much pressure Daddy had put on him to be here today.

Jackson was obviously confused about why he'd been invited.

All things considered, I didn't blame him.

This had turned out to be a rather intimate family gathering.

Madison was home and she'd had a life-changing announcement.

And… although no one said anything, it was a special day for another reason.

Daddy's prostate cancer had just been declared to be in remission.

So we were not only celebrating Madison's news, there was a relief in the air that our little family hadn't had in months.

When Daddy had gotten the diagnosis, the whole family had pulled together, but it had shown us just how delicate life really was.

Daddy and Momma were the ones who held this family together.

Without them, we'd be just like all the other families out there who sometimes talked and rarely got together.

But this.

This was who we were and the way everything was right now—at this moment—the core of who we were was intact.

If Daddy wanted to share this time with Jackson, then he should do just that.

It helped, of course, that I liked Jackson.

And if I had to make a guess, I'd say that Daddy knew that.

Daddy had an uncanny sense about these things.

He'd seen a lot of his pilots fall in love under his watch. It wasn't even anything unusual for him anymore.

And he always did what he could to accommodate his people.

Just like he'd opened a small office in Denver for Kade when Madison moved there to teach at the university.

Daddy hadn't had to do that.

Madison and Kade would have figured something out.

But Daddy had made it so much easier for them.

And truth was, because of it, Madison got to come home more often.

It was kind of funny.

Both Madison and Ainsley had a running thing about which one of them was Daddy's favorite daughter. They both claimed the right to it, but from my vantage point, I'd say that Daddy loved us all equally.

As he should.

Just like Momma did.

Though everyone knew that Madison was her favorite. She had to be since Madison had followed in her footsteps to become a psychologist.

Momma's other favorite was Quinn, but only because Quinn was a boy and the youngest of her children.

"I'll be right back," Jackson said.

I watched as he made his way over to where Daddy was standing with Kade.

Whatever Jackson was, however uncertain he might be about his role, he didn't appear to be afraid of anything.

My father included.

And that made him all the more interesting.

42

JACKSON

"There you are," Noah said as I stepped up to the table where Ainsley was cutting cake and placing little pieces on little plates.

"Looking for me?" I asked.

"Nope," Noah said. "Just making sure you're having a good time."

"Couldn't be better," I said, picking up two plates of cake.

"Let me know if you need anything," Noah said.

"Sure thing," I said with a nod in their general direction.

"I think he's doing just fine on his own," I heard Kade say as I took the cake and walked back toward Brianna.

I hadn't asked her if she wanted cake and I frankly didn't care if she ate it or not.

But she'd opened up to me about herself and her family and I wanted to do something for her. And right now the most obviously thing I could do was to bring her cake.

"Thank you," she said with a smile as I set the plates on the little table in front of us.

That smile was worth whatever I'd gone through to get it.

It was worth the conversation that was no doubt going on about me right now.

It was pretty obvious at this point that I was interested in Noah's daughter Brianna.

So maybe that meant I didn't have to worry about telling Noah after all. Even if he didn't notice, Kade and Wyatt had noticed. And they would make sure to tell him.

They weren't going to cut me a break on this and I didn't blame them.

But it was Noah's fault. He was the one who'd thrown us together.

More than once he'd asked Brianna to show me around. Whatever that meant.

The way I figured it, at the moment at least, it meant bringing her cake.

To my surprise, she picked up a fork and took a big bite of the cake.

That simple gesture gave me another reason to like her.

A lot of the women I knew wouldn't go near a piece of cake.

They didn't eat sugar or they were watching their weight. So many excuses.

But not Brianna. Granted it was a tiny piece of cake, but she ate the whole thing.

I ate mine, too, and could have eaten another piece, put I didn't want to face Noah and Kade and now Quinn who seemed to be guarding the cake table.

"What happens next?" I asked, stacking our plates.

"A lot of options," she said. "The boys will probably have a beer and talk sports for awhile. Momma and the girls will go inside and start cleaning up. Then I don't know. But I suspect there will be internet shopping for baby things."

"A little early for that?" I asked and instantly bit my tongue. It wasn't my business to pass judgment on how another family celebrated a life moment.

"It doesn't matter," she said. "It's an excuse to look at things that Madison might need, but also to talk about the baby."

"Is that something you get into?"

"Not likely," she said. "I'm a minimalist, so I only buy what I really need when I need it."

"Not like the rest of your family?"

"Not hardly. Ever since I adopted a minimalist lifestyle, they don't understand me. Sometimes my sisters offer me money. They think I don't go shopping because I don't have the money."

"That tells me they don't understand subsidization."

She blew out a breath and looked at me with such relief that I understood what she did for a living.

"No," she said. "they don't have a clue."

"I'm sorry," I said. "They don't know what they're missing out on."

"How do you know?"

I shrugged. "I have a sister in college. Her brain works different from people over twenty-one."

Brianna laughed. "I understand completely what you mean. Even if I am over twenty-one."

I smiled to myself. She might be over twenty-one, but not much more.

"It's not easy being an entrepreneur," I said.

She studied me a moment.

"Your family doesn't understand you either?" she asked.

"I don't think my family gives *me* a thought, much less what I do."

"I'm sorry to hear that," she said, giving me that look that people gave me when they found out my family wasn't close.

"Nah, it's okay," I said. "I have the freedom to do what I want to do without family pressure."

She looked at me sideways for a moment.

"You must be very lonely," she said.

I didn't say anything because she was right. I was lonely.

But it wasn't something I admitted.

Not to anyone.

"We should get out of here," Brianna said, suddenly.

What? WTF?

"It's your family," I said. "You can't just leave."

"They've got their things they do," she said. "And like I said, I don't always fit in."

"What is it you'd rather be doing?" I asked.

"Well, I can think of about fifty other things."

I had to admit I was surprised.

It seemed like everyone was having a good time.

And it appeared to me as though Brianna was close enough to her family to tolerate them for a Sunday afternoon and evening.

"No one else is leaving," I pointed out.

"No one else has a video schedule to keep," she said.

"Ah," I said. "You'd rather be working." I understood the concept.

It was part of the reason why I was here and not already back in Denver. I needed to establish some work boundaries.

Getting a call in the middle of the night to fly someone somewhere wasn't exactly the kind of schedule that led to having a fulfilling life.

Sure. I liked flying. I ate, slept, and breathed it.

But lately I'd been feeling like there was something missing.

So I'd taken a job where I wasn't always on call.

"Not exactly," she said. "I was thinking more along the lines of doing some research."

43

BRIANNA

My family was used to me not being around.

It was strange in a funny kind of way. I wasn't the black sheep. I just had my own things.

I wasn't a pilot or a psychologist.

Actually Wyatt, Ainsley's fiancé, was more like me than anyone in my family, but he was a pilot, too, so he didn't count.

My younger sister was a college student, so I didn't count her either. Didn't count my brother either because he ran the Skye Travels office.

Actually, he wasn't like the rest of the family either.

He was a salesman. He was so good at business and getting people to do what he wanted, he could be in politics.

So, no, he didn't count. I could go days without talking to another human. I doubted he could go more than a couple of hours.

My family seemed more interested in the fact that I was leaving with Jackson than the fact that I was leaving early.

Well, technically, Jackson was leaving with me since he'd come here with Daddy.

We settled into my car and I headed toward downtown.

Jackson adjusted his vents and looked over at me curiously, with a little smile.

"So where are you taking me?" he asked.

"Minute Maid Park," I said as I merged onto the interstate.

"Minute Maid Park?" he asked.

I shrugged. "You might have gone to the Astrodome."

He looked at me sideways.

"I'm not *that* old," he said.

I laughed. "But," I said. "I'm betting you did go to a baseball game in the Astrodome."

"Yes," he said. "But you should know I was very young."

"I don't doubt that," I said, slowing down with the traffic.

"So what's going on in Minute Maid Park on this Sunday afternoon."

She grinned.

"The Astros are playing."

He looked blankly at me. "You're toying with me, aren't you?"

"What?" I turned on my blinker and merged over toward the exit. "Why would I do that?"

"So you're taking me to a baseball game?"

"Yes," I said. "That is, unless you mind."

"Trying to talk you into going to a game had crossed my mind," he said.

"Well," I said. "Problem solved. You don't have to talk me into it."

"Do you go often? To baseball games?"

"It's actually my first one this year."

"We should probably just go ahead and get married."

The car's automatic breaking system kept me from slamming into the car in front of me as I looked at Jackson.

But he was just grinning.

"Just saying," he said. "It would cut through the red tape. Since you're obviously the perfect girl."

"You're silly," I said, but my heart was pounding dangerously in my chest and I was having trouble paying attention to the road. Thank God for auto drive.

He just shrugged.

"Don't say I didn't warn you."

44

———

JACKSON

What Brianna considered research was what I considered a treat.

I rarely took the time to do anything I enjoyed. Like go to a baseball game.

Noah's suggestion that I work less was already in play.

And I had not been kidding when I'd told her she was the perfect girl.

Probably should have kept that to myself though, especially the getting married part.

But, damn, if she wasn't just perfect for me.

She understood pilots. Better than just about anyone I'd met, including some pilots.

And she understood working for herself.

She had a big family, but she wasn't so immersed in them that she couldn't get away and do her own thing.

And she was taking me to a baseball game.

And I hadn't even had to bargain or otherwise try to talk her into going.

She was taking *me.*

This was a most interesting and unexpected turn of events.

She found a parking place and we took off walking.

There was an excitement in the air that was unique to sporting events.

There was a line waiting to get inside, but she didn't mind.

Instead of complaining, she smiled at me.

"So how long since you've been to a game?" she asked.

"College," I said. "Early college, actually."

"You don't like baseball?"

"I'm actually a fan," I said. "But… you know… I was caught up in work."

"Daddy was right," she said. "Daddy's always right about these things."

"What things in particular?"

"Didn't he suggest that you work less?"

"That's not something a new boss usually encourages."

She just shrugged. "Daddy's not normal."

"And you're definitely his daughter," I said.

She grinned.

"Thank you."

We reached the counter and she reached for her handbag.

I put a hand over hers.

"Ground rule number one," I said. "The lady never pays."

"I'm the one who brought you," she said, but let her handbag drop back against her side.

I scanned my credit card and took the two tickets.

"Doesn't matter," I said, handing her the tickets.

She grinned at me as we stepped through the doors.

There were vendors everywhere. T-shirts. Hats.

"Want a soda or some water?" I asked.

"Water would be good," she said and we got back in line.

"So tell me something," I said.

She grinned. "Sure."

"What does a minimalist buy at a baseball game?"

"Anything," she said. "Might not keep it, but that's a different story."

"I understand," I said.

"I'll be right back," she said, nodding toward the ladies' room.

"I'll be right here," I said.

Keeping one eye on her as she stepped into the restroom, I ordered two bottles of water and two t-shirts.

If I was going to an Astros game, I wanted the whole experience.

If she didn't want her shirt, she could donate it.

According to her videos, that's what minimalists did.

After I swiped my card again, I went to wait for her outside the ladies' room.

45

BRIANNA

Standing at the mirror in the stadium restroom, I took a minute to regroup.

I liked going to baseball games. It was something I'd done with one of my college boyfriends and I'd discovered an affinity for it.

I had the Astro's schedule programed in my phone and had gotten an alert while we were having our family gathering.

When Jackson and I had started talking about getting out of there, I'd gone with a whim and driven us to the game.

He'd seemed willing to do whatever, but still, it had been a risk. It had been possible that he didn't even like baseball. Or that he had something else he'd rather be doing.

But turned out he did like baseball and he seemed quite content to spend the day with me.

But he'd said I was the perfect girl. That we should get married.

No one had ever said that to me before.

I'd laughed it off. Told him he was silly and moved on to something else.

But the truth was, I couldn't stop thinking about it.

I took a tube of lip gloss out of my handbag and smoothed it over my lips. It was the plumping kind that burned as it supposedly plumped up my lips.

I wasn't sure if it actually worked or not, but I liked the idea of it. One of my sponsors had sent it to me and I was still testing it out.

I was trying to act normal.

To pretend that he hadn't actually said that he wanted to marry me.

I'd known guys like that before. Guys who said things like that. They didn't mean it. They just threw the words out there. Like *we should get a beer sometime since we have so much in common.*

I squared my shoulders and determined that I should just ignore comments like that.

Any girl who fell for a line like that had some issues.

I was so not that girl.

I had my act together. I didn't need a guy to come along and play games with me.

We'd just enjoy the game. My father would be happy that I'd spent some time *showing him around* and we could go back to our lives.

Easy enough.

As I stepped out of the ladies' room, Jackson was standing there waiting for me.

My heart skipped a little beat in spite of my attempt to stay calm and not fall for Jackson's charming ways.

I was just entertaining him for the day. To help him feel welcome here in Houston and more importantly Skye Travels.

He might need help finding an apartment, but I knew some real estate agents who were great at that sort of thing.

He opened my water bottle and handed it to me, then he held up two t-shirts.

"What do you think?" he asked.

He looked quite pleased with himself that he'd bought us t-shirts.

I grinned and took mine from him.

"Hold this," I said, thrusting my water and handbag into his hands.

I pulled the t-shirt on over my dress and took my things back.

It was a look I happened to know worked on me, especially since I was wearing white canvas sneakers and we were at a baseball game.

He laughed and, handing me his water bottle to hold, pulled his own t-shirt over his head.

Well, now that we were wearing matching t-shirts, so much for being cool and detached.

I distracted myself by pulling our tickets out of my pocket and going about the business of finding our seats.

46

JACKSON

*B*rianna was absolutely charming.

She hadn't even hesitated to put on the t-shirt I'd bought her. Furthermore, when she put it on, she'd covered up her dress.

And now that we had on matching t-shirts, I felt even more connected to her than I had before.

And that was saying a lot.

A girl who liked baseball was enough to begin with. Then a girl who would put a heather gray t-shirt on over a gorgeous red cocktail dress was an anomaly to be sure.

We took our seats next to a man and his son who were already having beer and pretzels.

"Are you hungry?" I asked.

"Not really," she said. "But we could get some peanuts."

Damn. This girl was after my heart.

Peanuts to nibble on during a pro baseball game. The vender was coming our way, so I took some cash out of my money clip. It was fortuitous that I had cash since I rarely carried it.

The guy took credit cards, but it didn't seem right paying for snacks with a credit card.

I took two bags of peanuts and handed one to Brianna.

She smiled.

The game was just about to start, so we'd made it just in time.

The cameras panned around the audience for a few minutes until they spotted a teenage couple sitting high in the seats.

The two of them most definitely weren't watching the game.

It took a minute for them to realize they were on the screen for all to see.

The girl tried to duck away, but the boy grinned and kissed her on the lips.

The audience cheered and they both turned and beamed at the cameras.

Now this was a good way to spend a Sunday evening.

With a pretty girl who liked baseball and knew to order roasted peanuts.

The same girl who was wearing the t-shirt I'd bought her.

The first player hit a home run.

Now how often did that happen?

This day could not get any better.

The music started and we had to stand up to watch the player as he made his way around the bases.

"This is a good start," I said.

"It's a good day for a game," she said.

Indeed it was.

It was a good day to be on a date with Brianna Worthington.

And I didn't care what anybody else tried to call it, it was most definitely a date.

After the player made his way around the bases and everyone cheered, we settled back to watch the game.

I liked baseball just fine. No problem.

But I found myself watching Brianna more than I watched the game.

I'd watched her plenty on her You Tube channel, but she was even prettier in person.

While the players on our team left the field, she caught me looking at her.

"What?" she asked with a little smile.

"You're pretty," I said.

She laughed out loud.

"You're silly," she said.

And I just grinned.

I was learning that was her response when I said something that caught her off guard, especially something that she secretly didn't mind hearing.

47

BRIANNA

*J*ackson had me off-balance.

So much so that I could hardly pay attention to the game I was pretending to watch.

He was watching me more than he was the game.

I was actually quite flattered.

And although I knew that I put myself out there. That people watched me on my You Tube channel every day, they weren't watching the edited me.

There was something a little bit unsettling about just how intimate it seemed.

Or maybe it seemed that way because it was Jackson.

I'd been crushing on the guy since the moment I'd seen him from Daddy's office window.

I was quite content to stay at home in my own little world and often spent days doing just that.

But Jackson made me want to get out and do things.

To share things with him.

I wasn't an impulsive person.

The last time I'd gone to a game, I'd planned it months in

advance. I'd put it in my phone and even bought my tickets ahead of time.

They'd been good tickets, too. Behind the catcher.

Not the only seats left at the last minute that were in the nosebleed section behind first base.

But today I didn't even care where we sat.

I was just enjoying Jackson's company.

"How old were you when you went to your first baseball game?" he asked as the pitcher huddled with the catcher.

"I don't know. I was pretty young. Daddy used to do things with us every week. Individually. He didn't consider dealing with five kids at one time to be quality time."

"I'd say he was right," Jackson said, shelling a peanut and popping it in his mouth. "Sounds like your family was really close."

"It still is," I said, looking over at him, my gaze snagging on his sky blue eyes. "What about you?"

"No," he said. "We were anything but close. It was me and my sister against the world."

"What about now?" I asked.

"My parents are happily divorced. My sister had a rough time of it, but she's in college now and somehow she turned out to be well-adjusted."

"You must have had a lot to do with that."

"I did spend a lot of time with her. I think it helped."

He smiled at me, keeping his gaze locked on mine.

The crowd started cheering and yelling "Kiss. Kiss."

It was the kiss cam again.

One of those things to keep the audience entertained during the slow parts of the game.

I jumped when the guy sitting behind us tapped me on the shoulder. He tapped Jackson, too.

We both looked back at him.

He grinned and pointed toward the screen.

And there we were. Me and Jackson with a little heart drawn around us.

I just stared at the screen, frozen.

But Jackson didn't freeze. As I watched us on the screen, he wrapped his arms around me and kissed me on the cheek.

The crowd, however, wasn't satisfied.

They kept calling out "Kiss. Kiss. Kiss."

I pulled my gaze away from the screen and looked over at Jackson.

He was obviously enjoying this.

He shrugged and then before I had time to react, he placed his lips on mine.

Something inside me shifted and turned upside down.

The crowd clapped and cheered loudly.

And together Jackson and I turned and smiled at the camera.

This was most definitely not what I had expected when I'd impulsively driven up to the baseball game.

And I had no doubt that someone in my family, probably Kade or Wyatt or even Daddy was watching and saw it.

And I wondered how many of my You Tube followers would see this.

Then it occurred to me that I should get the footage so I could use it myself.

Showing Jackson around had just become being on a date with him.

No matter how much I'd tried to deny it.

48

JACKSON

I'd been wondering just when I was going to steal a kiss from Brianna when the Kiss Cam had speeded things up quite a bit.

There was nothing like a public kiss in a public place to let a girl know that you liked her.

The way I saw it, we didn't have to play games anymore.

We had that awkward first kiss out of the way, so now I could start kissing her on a regular basis.

She hadn't seemed to mind, once she got past the whole deer in the headlight response.

It was surprising to me just how much a girl who made her living talking to strangers could be so reserved and shy in person.

It shouldn't be surprising though. Some of the best performers had stage fright.

Brianna was no doubt used to being able to edit her videos before they went out for public consumption.

There was no editing the Kiss Cam.

Personally, I liked it that way.

Love and sex could get messy. Not something that had any order to it or if it did have order to it, it probably wasn't worth fooling with.

And I wanted to fool around with Brianna. As much as she'd let me.

I was smitten.

After I'd given up trying to deny it and just embraced it, I felt one hundred percent better.

We weren't teenagers. Her daddy wasn't going to try to keep us apart.

He actually seemed to like me well enough. He'd recruited me away from a perfectly good job. A job where I was in control of my schedule.

Actually my schedule was in control of me, but that was a whole different story.

Now I actually qualified for benefits for the first time in my life.

Coming back to Houston had been a game changer for me in more ways than one.

I had a new job in a new city and if I played my cards right, I was going to have a new girlfriend.

She was the reason I'd taken the job.

My therapist would have a blast with that one.

Probably throw out some label like attachment issues.

How did a sane man meet a girl and, just like that, turn his life completely upside down for her?

I hadn't even told my sister.

She was expecting me home next week.

I could only imagine what kind of shock she'd have that I'd decided to up and move to Houston.

It wasn't like she ever saw me anyway.

In fact, she often complained that I worked too much. That it wasn't good for me to work that much.

So there.

I'd taken care of all that.

I now had a job where I didn't have to work so much. And I could fly up and see her whenever I wanted.

If, of course, she had time for me.

But it was looking like she needed me less and less.

I was ok with that. As much as I loved my sister, it had been a huge responsibility to get through those troubled teen years. Those years when our parents seemed to forget that they'd had children together.

But we'd made it through.

And now we were both free to live our own lives as we saw fit.

And I saw fit to move to Houston so I could kiss the lovely Brianna Worthington whenever she'd let me.

Yes, I was most definitely smitten.

And instead of getting better, it was just getting worse and worse.

I couldn't get enough of her. And I had a feeling there would never be enough of her.

It was baffling how a beautiful, charming young lady like her had remained single for so long.

Perhaps her family intimidated them. Well… her family had pulled me in and thrown us together. So if anything, it was their fault.

It was Noah's fault for pushing his daughter on me.

He'd had to know that she was the kind of girl a guy like me would fall for.

I'd taken the bait, alright. Hook. Line. And sinker.

Now all I had to do was to convince Brianna that we should be a couple.

I was certainly convinced.

Outside of aviation, nothing had ever felt so right.

Of course, right now, she was ignoring me and pretending to watch the game.

It was okay. I knew that if she was ignoring me, she was probably trying not to think about me and that kiss we'd shared.

49

BRIANNA

$\mathcal{M}$y lips still tingled from Jackson's kiss.

I tried to distract myself by thinking about ways I could use it on my channel.

My channel wasn't really spontaneous or anything like that, but I was collecting more and more footage that I needed to find a way to use.

Like Ainsley's wedding dress try-on day.

That was an event that should have a use. I just hadn't figured out what it was yet.

Then there was the Kiss Cam with me and Jackson.

Completely spontaneous and unexpected.

But most certainly pleasant.

We'd been cute on the camera, wearing our matching t-shirts.

It hadn't been five minutes when the first text message came in.

AINSLEY: *Having fun at the baseball game?*

Ainsley said what she meant and meant what she said.

She definitely didn't hold back her opinions about things.

My face still flushed from Jackson's kiss and the attention we'd gotten, I texted her back.

ME: *Yes. Thank you for asking.*

AINSLEY: *Be careful.*

ME: *Always.*

I sighed and slipped my phone back into my pocket.

I knew exactly what she meant.

Ainsley didn't date pilots. At least not directly. Wyatt was her way around that rule she'd made for herself. Wyatt was a pilot, but not by profession.

She'd dated a pilot once and although she'd never said much to me about it, I was pretty sure she'd gotten her heart broken.

Fortunately Ainsley wasn't one to try to tell other people what to do. And she wasn't judgmental.

But she was caring, so it made sense that she'd caution me against something she'd gone through herself.

It didn't help that Ainsley was a pilot, too, and she was on the inside where she heard way too much about how some of the pilots lived. A girl in every port and that sort of thing.

But on the flip side of that, Daddy was a pilot and he was ridiculously in love with and devoted to Momma.

So my view of pilots was a different from Ainsley's.

And, yes, I was always careful. Too careful, probably.

"I'll be right back," Jackson said. "Do you want anything?"

"No," I said. "I'm good."

I watched Jackson as he headed down the stairs toward the door.

He was a handsome man and I wasn't the only female who noticed. A lot of heads turned in his direction.

A couple of people looked from him to me.

The Kiss Cam had made us look like we were a couple.

And I was surprisingly okay with that.

I liked Jackson and I even kinda liked it that people saw us as a couple.

Ainsley, it seemed, was a little late with her warning. I was already in over my head.

50

JACKSON

As I stood in line for a bathroom break, one of the other guys grinned at me.

"Saw you up on the screen," he said. "How long have you two been together?"

The question caught me off guard for a moment. I'd been deep in my own head, thinking about Brianna and how now that I'd kissed her, I wanted to keep kissing her.

"Not long," I said.

"You better hold on to that one," he said.

"You bet."

That was my intention, alright, even though I hadn't thought about it quite that way. Brianna was definitely a girl to hold onto. Had to get her, first, though.

And that was the real challenge. A girl like Brianna would have a lot of experience in warding off men.

A girl like her didn't stay single any other way.

I just had to nudge my way beneath that cool exterior of hers.

I was willing to take my time and do the work needed.

My grandmother would have called it courtship. She was

the one who'd taught me the importance of courting a woman.

I'd toyed with it a few times, but I'd never followed through.

Like Brianna, I had enough experience in warding off, in my case, women. Though the most successful way for me was to just have my sister tagging along.

Unlike Brianna, my sister didn't carry an approachable air about her. She was better now, but during the worst of her late teenage years, she been prickly enough that people rarely gave us more than cursory glances.

Being with Brianna, besides, obviously not being my sister, was completely different.

People wanted to be around her. To talk to her and get to know her.

That quality was what had made her You Tube channel so successful.

And yet she kept herself a little bit aloof.

Except… when I'd kissed her, there was no aloofness.

There had been nothing but warmth.

Ten minutes later, I headed back up the stairs to our seats.

And Brianna was having a conversation with the older fellow who'd been sitting next to us.

I just smiled.

Yep. People were attracted to her. Nothing she could do about that.

I'd no more than sat back down in my seat when the older fellow leaned over and spoke to me.

"I was telling your girlfriend that I met my wife at a baseball game. We'd never even met before that camera put us up on the big screen. For some reason she let me kiss her and something clicked."

"Wow," I said. "That must have been strange."

"It was," he said. "but I wouldn't take a thing for it. God rest her soul. She passed away two years ago. I still come to these games because she loved telling that story about how we met to anyone who'd listen."

I wasn't sure what to say. It wasn't exactly a sad story. More bittersweet.

"That's a wonderful memory you have," Brianna said.

"Yes," the older man said. "don't ever discount the little things in life. They can make all the difference. Any little thing we do can change the direction our lives take. Sort of like that butterfly thing they talk about."

The old fellow was right. My being available to bring Madison to Houston when her husband was running late had led me to meet Brianna. A woman I never would have had the chance to meet otherwise.

And I had every intention of making the most of this unexpected experience.

"You okay?" I asked, noticing that Brianna's eyes were moist.

"Of course," she said, leaning close. "It's just such a sad story, don't you think?"

"Like you said, it's a good memory, even if it is bittersweet. Think about all the good years they had together."

She nodded.

I had just learned something else about Brianna. Something I'd already suspected. She had a kind heart.

A heart that deserved to be protected and cherished.

51

BRIANNA

After the Kiss Cam and the conversation I'd had with the man sitting on my left, I'd sort of lost interest in the baseball game.

I couldn't stop thinking about kissing Jackson.

He seemed to be enjoying it, though.

Quite frankly, I was ready to go.

"You have a flight tomorrow?" I asked Jackson during one of the many quiet spells in the game.

"No," he said. "But Quinn wants me in the office early. There's a computer program I need to learn."

I was familiar with the computer program. It had a steep learning curve and I often wondered if Daddy kept it around as a way to weed out people who weren't committed to learning everything about Skye Travels.

It was one of those programs that was hard to learn, but then it was simple once a person got the hang of it.

At least that's what Madison told me. Kade had gone through it.

And Kade was one of the smartest men I knew.

I only knew of one new hire who had left because he didn't take the effort to learn the computer program.

"I don't want to keep you out too late," I said. Even as I said it, I knew I was being nonassertive. I was trying to get Jackson to be the one who wanted to leave.

"It's not late," he said, cheering when our team made another home run.

It was obvious that Houston was winning, though I hated to point out the obvious.

I sat for a few more minutes. Checked my phone. No messages. Had a couple of comments on my You Tube channel. I quickly responded to them.

Then I saw it. Someone had actually recorded the Kiss Cam and posted it on my social media.

So there I was, kissing Jackson, and it was going viral.

I should be happy about that. But something about it made me feel ill. Maybe it was the surprise and loss of control over it that I had.

I'd thought to use it intentionally. Maybe use it. Maybe not. But someone else had made that choice for me.

I closed my phone and tapped it against my knee.

"Jackson," I said. "I'm ready to go."

"Okay," he said. "Sure. Why didn't you say so?"

"I did."

"Alright, let's go."

We said goodbye to the nice man sitting beside us and made our way down the stairs and eventually out the front gates.

It was a bit of a walk to my car, but fortunately, I had on comfortable shoes.

We walked in silence, the loudness of the baseball game still ringing in my ears.

It had been fun, but it had been a long day. First the family gathering, then the baseball game.

And on top of that, there was kissing Jackson.

For a girl who spent most of her days at home, in a quiet environment, I had met my threshold.

I just needed to go home and recharge my batteries.

We got into my car and I pulled out of the parking space.

"Thank you," Jackson said. "Really enjoyed getting out. Going to the baseball game. I wouldn't have done it without you."

"You would have gotten around to it," I said.

If I had to identify my feelings, I'd say not only was I tired, but I was worried about Jackson. Mostly about my feelings for Jackson.

I kept hearing Ainsley's words in my head.

Be careful, she'd said. Translated from Ainsley speak into my language, *Guard your heart.*

Unfortunately it might be too late for that. But I might could salvage a bit of myself if I moved quickly.

Neither of us saying much, I drove straight to his hotel, put the car in park, and smiled at him.

"Thanks for going to the game," I said. "I'll see you around."

I didn't even give the guy half a chance.

He had no choice but to jump out of my car.

He stood there, watching me as I drove off. I knew because I watched him in my rearview mirror.

I just really needed to get to my condo and get some perspective on things.

My outing with Jackson had quickly turned into a date.

And I wasn't in the market for dating. Especially not one of Daddy's pilots. That was so not a smart thing to do.

If things went south, I'd still have to see him around on occasion.

That never worked for me.

When a relationship was over, I needed it to be completely over. Vanished from sight.

Seeing the person around wasn't something I could do. It tore me apart emotionally.

It didn't matter that I knew I was projecting an old college boyfriend onto Jackson.

The college boyfriend and I had been taking several classes together when we'd broken up.

Every time I saw him, it tore my heart out.

In fact, I'd gone so far as to drop one of the smaller classes. I was able to sit away from him in the other, larger, classes, but it didn't keep me from seeing him.

And no matter how hard I tried not to, I looked for him. Every. Single. Day.

I'd learned. Don't date where you work.

I didn't work at Skye Travels, but for all intents and purposes, I may as well. I'd see Jackson when I went to visit Daddy at work. At company Christmas parties and other random social events.

And since Daddy apparently liked Jackson, I never knew where he was going to show up.

It was better to nip this in the bud and not get too attached.

As I pulled into my reserved parking space, I found myself replaying the Kiss Cam in my head. Doing that thing where I analyze everything.

He hadn't seemed to mind.

But I had to be careful. If I took that kiss to heart, then I could get hurt.

And hurt could kill my creativity.

Which could kill my You Tube channel.

Which would kill my career.

Madison would say I was spiraling into a bottomless abyss for no reason.

I called for my elevator and waited impatiently.

I didn't know what Jackson's intentions were.

And that was the thing. He didn't have to have any intentions. I was the one who had taken him to the game.

And we'd had great fun until the old guy had told us that depressing story.

Geez. That was enough to tip anybody over the edge.

52

JACKSON

stepped into my hotel room, kicked off my shoes, and changed into my new t-shirt and long pajama pants.

It had been a long day.

My phone chimed. A text message from Noah. He'd put me down for a quick flight.

Imagine that.

After quickly washing up and getting ready for bed, I climbed in and stared at the ceiling.

I didn't even turn on the television. I didn't need distraction.

I couldn't think about anything other than Brianna and didn't even try.

Sure, I had lots to think about, but all that other stuff would just have to wait.

Right now, my main concern was Brianna.

She had changed after the old guy sitting next to her had told us the story about his wife.

I'd seen it the moment it happened.

She'd just dropped an invisible wall around herself and shut me out.

Normally, when I encountered a girl like that, I walked away. I just let them go.

Not worth the effort.

But I couldn't do that with Brianna.

Even as I'd watched her drive away, giving her the space she needed, I knew that I would have to chip away at that wall.

A woman that beautiful didn't deserve to have that many defenses.

She could learn to trust again.

I knew that in my heart.

In a lot of ways she reminded me of my sister during those troubled years.

Everything could be going along great, then something would remind her of what she was going through and she would shut down.

I'd learned how to break the defense of a troubled teen. I could break through the defenses of a beautiful woman.

Besides, Brianna was not only not my sister. I'd kissed her.

Right there in broad daylight in front of thousands of people and who knew how many other people had seen it on live broadcast.

We'd just skipped right to the part where we announced our relationship to the world.

If the old man hadn't told us that story about his long lost wife, I think we would have been ok.

But something about that story had obviously triggered something in Brianna.

Well, there wasn't anything I could do about it tonight.

And I had a flight tomorrow.

I'd figure it out then.

I always figured things out when I was in the air.

And as far as I knew, Noah wouldn't be flying with me, so I'd have time alone to think.

It didn't help that I was beginning to think of Noah as a friend and I liked Brianna's family.

I wasn't so sure I liked her sisters' men, but then I didn't know them either. Noah obviously thought they were good men.

I'd give them a chance.

It was the kind of guy I was. I gave everyone a chance.

I'd figure out this thing with Brianna.

In the meantime, I had memory of that kiss to keep me occupied.

My thoughts wound their way back to it.

The way her lips were soft and parted beneath mine.

There was no distance in that kiss.

That was part of how I knew that her walls were made of breakable glass, not concrete or stone.

53

BRIANNA

*E*verything always looked brighter the next day.

Waking with the morning sun in my eyes, I stretched and allowed myself to wake up slowly.

That was one of the best benefits of working from home.

Waking without the alarm clock. Nobody liked to wake up to an alarm clock.

I think they should be outlawed. There had to be a better, more pleasant way to wake up. But, then again, there was no good way to wake up in the middle of the night when it was still dark outside.

My mother had always told me that things would look better the next morning, especially when I'd been going through my teenage angst years.

I wasn't a teenager anymore, but sometimes even adults had those same overwhelming emotions.

And Momma was right. Momma was always right.

Things did look better in the light of day.

In fact, I woke up thinking about Jackson's kiss.

It had been gentle and possessive at the same time.

He'd staked his claim on me right there in front of

thousands of people—both live and broadcast live across the country. The city anyway.

The odd thing was, I didn't even mind.

It was just a sign of how far gone I was. Talking about a major crush.

He had the potential to be my next boyfriend.

And as my next boyfriend, I didn't know if he was going to break the heart that I'd meticulously glued back together or if he'd make me stronger.

Perhaps he'd make me stronger.

It had been a long time since I'd let a man into my life.

I wasn't saying I was going to let him into my life. I was just saying I was going to think about it.

Of course, it might all be for naught.

After the way I'd blown him off last night, he might not want to even talk to me anymore.

If he didn't, he wasn't the right man for me anyway.

I needed a man who would stand by me through thick and thin. Just not hang around for the good times, then disappear when things got rough.

I'd give him some space and we would see.

But today I had some work to do.

I'd probably just do some outlining of my next couple of videos.

Wasn't sure I wanted to actually get on camera today.

Being on camera required a certain amount of energy to make it work.

I never understood people who got on camera and vented. Nobody wanted to hear about a person's innermost problems. It was a good way to lose followers, if you asked me. I know I'd unfollowed some people after they went on some kind of rant or tearful disclosure.

People had enough trouble dealing with their own problems.

I stepped into my minimalist office that always brought me a sense of calm.

Just by stepping through the door to my office put me in the mindset of sitting down and creating something.

I didn't have to worry about anything else.

Everything I needed was right here, just the way I needed it to be.

I pulled out my chair, sat down, and lifted the lid of my laptop computer. I put my phone on do not disturb.

Today was going to be a good day.

I didn't have any appointments. Didn't even have to leave the condo.

To me, those were perfect days.

Within seconds I was lost in my own little world.

54

JACKSON

My flight the next day was to Alabama and back. Noah had a lot of contacts all over the country, especially Texas and Alabama.

My job was to fly to Dallas, pick up two businessmen and fly them out to a construction site. Wait while they looked it over. Then fly them back to Dallas before returning to Houston myself.

It sounded like a lot of flying, but really it wasn't.

Was probably going to be more waiting than anything else. But that's what I got paid for.

And as we liked to say as pilots. Flying is flying.

After a smooth takeoff, I flew up to Dallas. I didn't have much time to think during that part of the flight.

There was a storm north of Dallas and there were a lot of contingency plans being put in place. Just in case the weather models got it wrong.

Weather was one thing a pilot didn't play around with. Bad weather was the one thing that could for sure take a plane down.

But I landed in Dallas with no problem, picked up the two men, and headed toward Alabama.

I put the plane on autopilot, sat back, and let my thoughts wander a bit.

They, of course, found their way straight to Brianna.

I'd found the footage of the Kiss Cam on the Internet and saved it as a clip.

We actually looked like we belonged together.

I knew it was too soon to be making those kinds of judgment calls.

It wasn't the kind of conclusion a logical man would jump to.

But I'd never been considered a completely logical man.

I'd also never made impulsive decisions. Not until I'd gotten to Houston. Maybe there was something in the air that brought out a different side to me.

Impulsivity had become my middle name.

New job.

New girlfriend.

At least according to the Kiss Cam, she was my girlfriend.

All was not smooth sailing, though. I had to convince her that I was boyfriend worthy.

I wondered what she thought about me going to work for her father. The act of taking a job with Noah wasn't unusual. The part that was unusual was that I had never applied to Skye Travels.

Noah had recruited me.

I hadn't been looking for a job when he made the offer.

My logical self would have turned it down.

I had plenty of work to do and relocating to Houston on a whim was going to give me that much more I had to do. Taking a job for less work was going to give me more work to do. At least for awhile.

Find an apartment. Close out my old apartment and have my things sent here.

Not that I had all that much.

I was a minimalist at heart.

That and I'd always seen Denver as a temporary stopping place.

That temporary stopping place had turned into seven years.

Then I had a flash of inspiration.

I could sell my business.

That would give my clients a seamless transition. In fact, if I did that, they would hardly even notice that I was gone.

That was the thing about businesses. If done right, they could practically run themselves.

But back to Brianna.

Something had frightened her pretty bad.

No doubt something from her past.

But all I could do was to keep moving forward. I couldn't change her past, but I could change her future.

If she would let me.

55

BRIANNA

*B*y the time evening fell, I had accomplished quite a bit.

I'd even recorded a video. And I had to admit. Pretending that all was well had left me feeling like it might actually be.

Work was the balm that soothed.

I'd learned that a long time ago.

As I powered off my computer, I accepted that I had been rude to Jackson. But I'd needed to get away. To take some breathing room until I had time to sort things out in my head.

The first thing I needed to do was to meet with Momma.

I sent her a message.

ME: *Hi Momma. Can you meet for breakfast or lunch tomorrow?*

MOMMA: *Of course. Just tell me when and where.*

Momma was getting better at text messages. Or maybe it was because I'd contacted her first.

I decided on breakfast. The sooner I talked with Momma, the sooner I'd have an idea about what I was supposed to do to fix this thing with Jackson.

Momma wouldn't tell me what to do, but she could guide

me toward the right answer. At least the right answer for the moment.

I ran hot water in the bathtub, added some jasmine scented bubble bath, and slipped into the water.

Tomorrow was going to be a lot busier than today, at least as far as getting out and interacting with the humans.

Hopefully I wouldn't screw things up this time.

Normally I would have talked to Madison, but she was already headed back to Denver with Kade.

Ainsley was too biased and would tell me what to do.

So that left Momma.

After my bath, I poured a glass of pinot noir into a glass and curled up on my sofa with a good book.

A relaxing evening was exactly what I needed after the chaos of yesterday.

Then I turned on the local news, like I always did before going to sleep.

At first it was just normal stuff. Politics. Robberies. The weather.

Then they flashed the Breaking News image on the screen.

I stared in total disbelief as they showed an image of the Houston airport. Blinking lights. Lots of blinking lights.

And a plane on its side.

I couldn't tell whose plane it was.

I shot three quick texts.

Daddy. Ainsley. Madison.

My heart was in my throat.

ME: *Are you ok?*

I stood up. Paced across the length of the condo and back.

DADDY: *Yes. What's wrong?*

I went to one of the floor to ceiling windows and looked out. My hands were shaking so bad, I didn't even try to answer Daddy's text.

AINSLEY: *Why are you still up?*

I walked back to the sofa, sat down, then stood right back up. I tried to remember. What time was Madison's flight?

She should be back in Denver by now.

There wasn't any bad weather to delay her flight.

I paced some more.

Then went to stand in front of the television.

They'd gone to something else. A commercial.

They just flashed that up there. Then moved on. Like it was nothing.

MADISON: *Just landed. Why?*

I dropped onto my sofa and took deep calming breaths.

All the pilots in my family were ok.

Then on second thought, I answered Ainsley.

ME: *Is Wyatt with you?*

AINSLEY: *Yes.*

Wyatt sometimes flew his own plane.

But he was ok, too.

That just left one person for me to worry about.

DADDY: *On my way to the airport.*

If Daddy had been contacted, that could mean only one thing. It was a Skye Travels plane.

And that meant that it could be Jackson.

56

JACKSON

After my flight, I'd logged all my paperwork on the computer and walked through the office. The lights in the lobby were already off.

They were controlled by a main switch I didn't have access to. But there was enough light coming through from outside that I didn't need the lights on.

I was waiting for the elevator when I heard the first siren.

Could be anything. Probably a car. People drove like wild idiots on these interstates.

I stepped onto the elevator and rode down to the first floor.

As I stepped out of the elevator I realized that the sirens and lights were headed this way. There was one police car, sirens and lights blaring, already sitting on the tarmac.

Thinking I might be of some assistance, I went toward the noise.

I didn't know anyone's schedule other than my own. But a crash right here—and as I neared the tarmac, I could tell it was close—could be Noah or Kade or Ainsley or even Wyatt.

And any one of them would affect Brianna.

I used my pass to slip through the gate and was able to get

close enough to see that it was indeed a small aircraft. It was lying on its side. At least it hadn't exploded.

"Sir," someone called from near the plane. "Can you help us?"

"Of course," I said, jogging toward the plane.

"There's a woman in a wheelchair," he said. "Can you get her away from here?"

"Where is she?"

"She's still in the plane and her chair isn't operable anymore. It got pretty beat up in the crash."

I went to the door of the airplane and looked inside.

"Who needs the wheelchair?" I asked.

"My mother," a young lady said. "Did you find it?"

"Can't use it," I said. "Ma'am, can you walk at all?"

"Not really," she said.

"She has Parkinson's. Her legs are really weak."

"Don't worry," I said, stepping into the plane. "I'm gonna help you stand up and get to the door," I said.

She nodded and put her frail hands in mine.

"What's your name?" I asked as I carefully led her toward the door.

"Margaret," she said.

"Alright, Margaret," I said. "You don't look like you weigh too much."

"I don't," she said.

I smiled and glanced back at her daughter.

"Let's go," I said. "Can you get out of the plane by yourself?"

"I think so," she said.

"Ok then," I said. "You can follow us."

I slid out of the plane. Since it was on its side, it was only a foot or so to the ground.

I put an arm beneath Margaret's knees and another behind her shoulders and picked her up.

She barely weighed anything at all and she held onto me like a lifeline.

"No one has carried me like this since my wedding night," she said.

"I'm sorry," I said. "I just need to get you away from the airplane.

"I'm not complaining," she said. "Who needs a wheelchair when they have a handsome man like you?"

Walking carefully so as not to drop her, I took her toward the Skye Travels office building. I had instructions to get her away from the airplane, so that's what I did.

Her daughter followed along, jogging to keep up. I must have been walking faster than I thought.

"Which airline were you on?" I asked, afraid of the answer.

"Metro Commuters," the daughter answered.

Thank God. That meant it wasn't one of Noah's planes or Noah's people.

"I need to get you inside," I said, then spoke over my shoulder. "I need you to key in a code."

The daughter nodded and hurried to the keypad on the door.

There was no time to waste. The older woman wasn't heavy, but she was getting there.

"5. 3. 5. 9. 2. 4."

The door unlocked and the girl pushed it open.

There was nowhere for them to sit down here. It was just wide open, unused space.

I had to get them to the third floor.

So up the elevator we went.

I gently lowered the woman onto one of the lobby chairs. The daughter came and sat next to her.

"Thank you so much," she said.

"My pleasure," I said. "They're going to want to talk to you so you might be here a minute."

They both nodded.

"Is there anything else I can do for you? Before I got back out there and let them know where you are?"

"Mom's diabetic. Do you have any orange juice?"

"I don't know," I said. "But I'll go find out. Just wait here."

I wasn't sure where I was going to find orange juice, but I got lucky.

The staff refrigerator had several small bottles. It was always good to have the basics on hand in case a customer had a request.

Saved at least a few last minute trips to the market.

Like today.

I took the bottle of juice back to Margaret and opened it for her.

"Do you need a glass?" I asked when she seemed to be having trouble drinking from the bottle.

"A glass would be nice," she said.

Remembering now why I'd never waited tables, I got her a glass and grabbed a straw just in case.

"Thank you," she said when I handed her the cup and straw.

The daughter took it from her and poured some of the juice in the glass.

"Will you be okay here?" I asked. "I should go back and see if anyone else needs help."

"We'll be fine," the daughter said. "Thank you so much."

As I rode back down the elevator, it occurred to me that the young lady was quite pretty.

But I had barely even noticed.

It was almost like I was a married man, not noticing the single ladies.

Brianna had done that to me.

She ruined me for other women.

I grinned as I stepped off the elevator and went out to see if anyone else needed help.

                                57
                          ───────────

                           BRIANNA

I practically flew, in my car, to the airport. I wheeled into the parking lot and parked.

There were flashing lights everywhere.

I felt sick to my stomach.

I couldn't even check to see if Jackson's car was here. He didn't have a car in Houston. Not yet, anyway.

I raced up to the gate and stopped.

That's when I saw the airplane lying on its side, just like they'd shown on the news. And I still couldn't tell if it was a Skye Travel plane or not. Not in the dark with all the flashing lights. Not this far away.

There was a code for the gate, but I didn't come here often enough to have it memorized.

The only thing I could do was to go through the Skye Travels building.

But then Daddy drove up and parked his truck.

"Why are you here?" he asked, but didn't wait for an answer as he opened the gate.

We'd taken no more than a dozen steps inside the gate when Daddy put a hand on my arm.

"We need to wait," he said. "They don't need us getting in the way."

"But…"

"No but. It's not safe. And I won't have you getting caught up in all that."

I acquiesced. There was nothing else I could do.

Daddy was right of course. But if Jackson was out there… if he was hurt…

I couldn't think about that right now.

Not after I'd been thinking about his kiss all day long.

It had most definitely affected me in ways I hadn't expected.

We watched as firemen hosed down the place. Everyone seemed to have been gotten out by the time we got here.

I didn't see any activity around the ambulance. That had to be a good thing, right?

Then a man stepped away from the activity and started walking toward us.

Was it Jackson?

It was so hard to see in this shadowy light with the flashing lights.

But I was hopeful.

And as he came closer, I could see that it was him.

Leaving Daddy's side, I ran forward and threw myself into his arms.

He hugged me back, picking me up and twirling me off my feet in a circle.

He sat me on the ground and looked at me with a smug expression.

"I wasn't sure you cared," he said.

"I was just worried," I said, stepping back and clearing my throat, but he kept his arms around me.

By then Daddy was standing next to us.

Jackson let me loose then.

Daddy looked from Jackson to me and back to Jackson.

"Is that one of ours?" he asked.

"No," Jackson said. "Metro Commuters."

"How did you get involved?"

"I was here. Doing paperwork when it happened. They asked me to help," he said. "By the way, there's a lady and her daughter in your—our—lobby. The lady's wheelchair got damaged in the crash."

"Easy enough to replace," Daddy said.

Then he looked at us again.

"Why don't you two get out of here? I'll take care of this."

Both Jackson and I protested.

"Nope," he said. "I insist."

I just shrugged. Once Daddy made up his mind, there was no arguing.

"Do you need a ride?" I looked at Jackson.

"I was just about to call for transportation."

"I guess you don't have to do that," I said. "Daddy. Call us if you need anything at all."

"I've got this," he said.

I knew Daddy would be okay, especially since it wasn't one of his planes, but I was still feeling protective.

I looked back over my shoulder as we reached my car.

"Can I buy you a drink at the Skyhouse across the street?" he asked. "It'll keep us close a little longer."

"Good idea," I said, unlocking my doors. "Sure." The relief made my voice trembly.

I liked the way Jackson thought.

I also liked that he understood me.

He understood the importance of family.

One of the many reasons I liked him.

We were quiet once we were inside my car.

There was more traffic than usual. People driving up to the airport to get a look at the airplane that had crash landed.

"Was anyone hurt?" I thought to ask Jackson as I pulled out of the parking lot.

"No," he said. The only casualty was that little old lady's wheelchair."

"Fortunately," I said. "Could have been a whole lot worse."

And I'd been terrified that Jackson had been hurt.

58

JACKSON

We ordered drinks and found a table next to the window. The diner smelled like a mixture of apple pie and fried food. Typical.

But nothing was typical tonight.

We could see the flashing lights from the emergency vehicles from here even.

Everyone inside the restaurant/bar was speculating about what had happened to the plane.

No one knew for sure and no one had seen it happen, so there were a lot of ideas that didn't add up.

Brianna and I kept our mouths closed.

If anyone even suspected that we knew what had happened, they'd bombard us for information. Neither one of us wanted that.

"You're protective of your father," I said, once we got our drinks.

"Of course," she said. "he's my father."

I took a sip of the martini that the place was famous for and put my attention on Brianna.

"Maybe," I said. "But seems like there's a bit more to it."

She blew out a sigh and sat back.

"I guess you don't know," she said.

"I guess I don't."

She kept her gaze on the flashing lights out the window.

"Daddy had prostate cancer a few months ago."

"I'm so sorry. I didn't know."

She flicked a gaze toward me, then back to the airport across the street.

"I'm surprised he didn't tell you. Seems like he tells everyone. But he's the only one who tells it. Yet everyone tells everyone, so everyone probably knows."

"He seems to be doing well now."

"He's doing great," she said. "But he doesn't need stress. We… my sisters and I try to keep the stress off of him as much as we can."

"I'm sure you know how impossible that is," I said.

She nodded. "it's something we have to do."

"I understand." Even though I said I understood, I was pretty sure I only had a vague idea of what she was going through.

If she'd said her parents were going through a nasty divorce, then I really would have understood.

In truth, her whole close family was a mystery to me.

One that I liked very much.

I'd do everything I could to try to help her navigate things.

"What can I do to help?" I asked. "Just tell me and I'll do it."

"You're doing it," she said, twirling the stem of her glass.

Noah Worthington probably had no idea how lucky he was.

He had daughters who doted on him. Daughters who would do anything to keep him happy and safe.

She needed me to be supportive and that much I could do. Pretty much the only thing.

She hadn't even touched her drink.

59

BRIANNA

I sat at the table, the ice melting in my drink.

It was the least of my problems.

Somehow I'd ended up back in Jackson's company.

The good thing about that was that he distracted me. The bad part was that he distracted me.

I didn't like leaving Daddy over there in the chaos alone.

He should have someone with him as he tried to sort out the mess.

It wasn't one of his planes, but he had passengers from that flight in his building.

"I should be there to help him," I said, tapping my fingers against the table.

I didn't expect Jackson to understand.

I hadn't dated a lot of men, but I'd dated enough to know that mostly they put themselves ahead of a girl's family.

Once they found out how close our family was, they usually excused themselves.

It wasn't just me. My sisters had encountered the same thing.

It wasn't coincidence that both of the men they ended up with melded into the family and could appreciate the tight-knittedness.

"Alright," Jackson said. "Let's get out of here. Get back over there."

"Really?" I asked, some of the tension draining off.

"Yep," he said. "There's no point in us sitting over here not doing anything to help."

I agreed with him wholeheartedly.

I had a feeling that Daddy had sent us away not because he didn't want help, but because he had the idea that we wanted to be alone.

Surely he didn't really think that.

That wasn't how our family operated.

We were there for each other.

Granted, I had a propensity to watch from the sidelines, but that was just because I had nothing to do with the whole aviation side of things.

But now that I was here, I felt I needed to do something. It might not be much, but it needed to be something. I was a part of this family, after all.

"I'll go pay for our drinks," Jackson said.

I didn't protest.

I hadn't even touched my drink and he didn't seem to be the least bit concerned about that.

That was a relief.

As I watched Jackson standing at the bar waiting to pay, I was overcome with feelings of affection.

He was a good guy.

I truly believed his heart was in the right place.

I didn't know a whole lot about him and I certainly didn't know why he'd suddenly taken a job with my family's company, but when I was with him, I felt like I could trust him.

I got up and wandered over to the door.

The flashing lights had attracted the reporters. So instead of just the one reporter who'd broken the story, there was whole mess of them.

I took a deep breath.

I knew what to do.

60

———

JACKSON

As I paid for our drinks, Brianna waited next to the door.

That's when she was spotted by a reporter.

"You're Brianna Worthington," the reported said.

Brianna didn't say anything. She didn't have to.

"Was that one of your father's planes?" she asked.

"No," Brianna said.

"That must be a relief."

Brianna was cornered. And she no doubt wanted to get out gracefully.

"Come on," I said, taking her hand. "We have to go."

"Is this the new boyfriend?" the astute reporter asked.

Brianna didn't answer. For a woman who stayed in the spotlight, she didn't seem to care much for it.

I wanted her to say yes. To admit to the world that I was her boyfriend. But, it seemed, I was the only one who was ready to make that admission.

I understood. She made her living by being in the spotlight. Everything she did had to be thought out and planned.

This was unscripted.

And Brianna wasn't good at unscripted.

Knowing that actually made me feel better about her.

She may be an heiress, but she was just one of us. Trying to make her way.

"Do you want me to drive?" I asked.

She shot me a look that left no doubt that she was the one who was going to be driving.

Although the airport was right across the street, it was an ordeal to get across the traffic.

Brianna obviously knew what she was doing and got us back to the Skye Travels parking lot with ease.

"I guess we should check on the passengers in our lobby first," she said.

"I'm just following your lead," I said.

And truly I was just there to support her. I'd already done my duty by rescuing the old woman who'd lost her chair.

As we waited for the elevator, Brianna was silent.

So that was how she dealt with stress. By being silent.

Being silent was a whole lot better than being chatty.

I liked her more by the minute.

The elevator ride was quick and we stepped out into the Skye Travels spacious lobby.

"Where are they?" she asked.

"Gone, I guess, "I said.

"Were we gone that long?"

"I guess so," I said, but I heard Noah talking on the phone in the back.

Could be he had friends in high places. Friends who could take care of things quickly.

Brianna heard him, too, and we headed back to Noah's office.

He was sitting behind his desk, phone receiver glued to his ear.

61

BRIANNA

It was late when I dropped my keys into my key basket next to the door.

Another late night.

This was getting to be a pattern.

First there was my sister and her scare with the pregnancy.

Then tonight there was the plane crash and Jackson.

I'd been so afraid for him when I'd first heard the news.

In retrospect, it was almost like we'd been together for years.

But we weren't even dating.

And yet, when I'd thought he might be hurt, I'd been terrified.

I'd checked on my family first and when I knew they were okay, I circled around to Jackson.

We'd become rather close in a short period of time.

Fortunately, Skye Travels had no dating rules. In fact, I couldn't begin to name the pilots who'd married passengers or Skye Travels staff.

Sometimes it seemed like Cupid might have an affinity for Skye Travels.

It would make sense. My mother and father were madly in love and Daddy had started this company when he and Momma had first gotten together. So it was built off of love.

It was too soon for me to think about Jackson like that.

I'd only just met him.

Still. I was a firm believer in love at first sight.

Jackson had certainly charmed me at first sight.

The handsome pilot from Denver.

It was a good thing I was immune to the whole pilot in uniform phenomenon.

Or else I really would be throwing myself at his head.

I kicked off my shoes and went into my closet to change.

It seemed like I had something I was supposed to do in the morning, but I couldn't remember what it might be.

All I wanted to do was to get some sleep.

To wake up naturally and have a peaceful day to myself.

It was hard to make videos when I was all over the place.

I needed to just block out the rest of the week and focus on catching up.

Now was not the time for me to slack off on all that I was doing.

I'd caught a wave of momentum and the only way to stay on top of that wave was to keep going.

It didn't matter that people were telling me that I was working too hard. They didn't understand the process.

A lot of what I did was creative. And a lot of it was technical.

I liked the combination of the two things. If I got stuck on something creative, I could work on some rote work. The rote work freed up my energy and I often came up with my best creative ideas when I was doing something else. Something that didn't allow me to have to focus too much. Sort of like driving a car or taking a shower.

I actually got my best ideas in the shower so often that taking two a day really didn't seem like a bad idea.

My thoughts circled back around to Jackson.

I'd driven him back to his hotel.

It was becoming quite the habit for me to drive him around.

Well, he would just have to use an Uber the rest of the week because I was taking the rest of the week off to just work.

The irony of that sentiment was not lost on me.

But I loved my work. So much so that it didn't feel like work at all.

I put on my pajamas and climbed into bed, but I was too keyed up to sleep.

Instead, I pulled my computer over and turned it on.

I'd just check some of my You Tube posts before I tried to go to sleep.

By the time I looked up again, an hour had passed by.

With a sigh, I closed my computer.

My schedule was all twisted up.

I was usually asleep by ten. And here I was still up after Midnight.

Ever since Jackson had come into my life, everything had been different.

62

JACKSON

I had a habit of putting my phone on do not disturb during the night. I'd gotten tired of clients calling me when I was trying to sleep.

Since I hadn't set an alarm for this morning, I slept until half past seven. Later than usual.

I woke up bleary eyes and a little bit sore.

Then I remembered. I had carried a woman quite a long distance last night after the plane had crashed.

Maybe with my extra time I should start going to the gym more often. Couldn't hurt.

The only bad thing about using do not disturb was that I didn't get text message alerts.

My sister could call me, but that was it.

And my sister, being college age, would text than call any time of the day.

So when I woke up, I had ten text messages.

One was from a client practically begging for me to come back to Denver.

That didn't do anything to help my guilt about suddenly leaving all my Denver customers. But in my defense, I had given them all good referrals. I had also given them the Skye Travels Denver number.

Wyatt was one of only two pilots, so me leaving Denver was most likely going to overwhelm the system up there, but systems adjusted themselves as needed.

The other nine were from my sister.

TIFFANY: *Are you busy?*

TIFFANY: *If you aren't busy, I need to talk.*

TIFFANY: *Are you okay?*

TIFFANY: *Saw on the Internet that a plane landed sideways in Houston.*

TIFFANY: *Worried now.*

TIFFANY: *They said no one was hurt.*

TIFFANY: *Please text me back.*

TIFFANY: *Ok. Maybe you're asleep.*

TIFFANY: *Call me when you get up.*

Damn it. I already felt guilty about leaving Tiffany alone in Denver and now she needed me and I wasn't there.

I dialed her number and it went straight to voicemail.

ME: *Phone was turned off. Up late.*

I tapped my fingers against the phone, feeling helpless.

ME: *Are you okay?*

Now I sounded like my sister.

We were most definitely siblings.

I stared at the phone. Then let out a huge sigh of relief when the little response bubbles appeared.

TIFFANY: *Can you come home?*

Okay. Maybe not so much relief.

ME: *What's wrong? What happened?*

Forget this. I dialed her number, but it went straight to voicemail again. Why wasn't she answering the phone. She had to be right there holding it.

All sorts of thought shot through my mind.

Maybe it wasn't really her texting me. Maybe someone was holding her hostage.

TIFFANY: *Roommate is asleep.*

Thank God. I was going to be a nervous wreck.

TIFFANY: *Will get dressed and go outside to call.*

I got up and paced the length of the hotel room. And back again.

I needed to take a shower myself, but I didn't want to be in the shower when she called.

TIFFANY: *Heading outside now.*

Five minutes later the phone rang.

"What's wrong?" I asked, answering the phone.

"Ian broke up with me," she said, her voice breaking.

"Ian? The one with the earring?"

"Yes," she said. "He had an earring. But it was tasteful."

And, of course, she would defend him even now.

"Why?" I asked.

She didn't answer right away.

Probably wondering why she bothered to talk to me.

"I don't know," she said. "he saw me talking to this other guy in my practicum class. We were just exchanging notes. But he got all jealous about it."

I wanted to tell her that she was better off without Ian who had an earring and got jealous.

But obviously, she wasn't in a place to hear that.

"What do I need to do?" I asked.

"Can you come home?"

I mentally reviewed my schedule.

I didn't have any flights scheduled for today.

"I have to see if I can get a plane."

"Okay," she said. She was crying.

Damn. My protective brotherly instincts were in overdrive.

"Give me a few minutes to make some calls, okay?"

"Okay."

"Will you be okay for a few minutes?"

"I'm just going to lie down and wait for you to call back."

"Good," I said. "Let me see what I can do."

What had I been thinking? I couldn't move here and leave my sister in Denver.

Just when I did, something like this happened.

Maybe I needed to rethink some things.

But first I had to find an airplane.

63

BRIANNA

I took my time waking up the next morning.

After I made myself some hot tea, I went out on my balcony and sat on one of my two chairs.

It was a small balcony, but it felt sturdy with thick walls around the edges.

From here I could see downtown Houston in the distance, but the freeway was close enough that it was anything but quiet. The roar of car sounds could be loud at times.

I didn't mind though. It reminded me that I wasn't alone.

I loved my view and I couldn't imagine why anyone would want to live on the ground when they could live in the sky.

Maybe I wasn't so different from Daddy after all.

Daddy stayed in the sky as much as he could.

I shrugged and watched the city wake up.

Finished with my tea, I went back inside.

I had two missed calls from Momma.

My heart in my throat, I called her back.

"You called?" I asked when she answered.

"Are you okay?" Momma sounded worried. Momma rarely sounded anything but calm.

I sat on my sofa, taking deep breaths to get my heart rate under control.

"I was just sitting on the balcony drinking some hot tea. Why? What's wrong?"

"Nothing." I heard the relief in Momma's voice. "We were supposed to have breakfast."

"Oh da—." I stopped myself. Momma didn't tolerate curse language.

I stood up and walked into my kitchen.

"I am so sorry. I didn't see it on my calendar."

"It's okay," Momma said. "I was just concerned about you."

"Can we have lunch?" I asked. "If that's still an option."

"Yes," Momma said. "We can have lunch."

"Good. I'll go shower right now."

"Brianna," she said, stopping me.

"Yes?"

"Use a paper calendar."

As I ended the call and headed to the shower, I wondered what it must be like to always be right.

Maybe after lunch I'd go online and order a paper calendar.

As I showered and got dressed, I wondered what Jackson was doing.

We'd left without any plans to stay in touch.

I'd see him again.

He worked for my father now, so it was inevitable.

It was a good thing, I told myself.

I didn't have time for a man in my life.

Already, I was behind in my work.

Geez.

Even I was having trouble keeping the *work* in work from home.

64

JACKSON

I landed in Denver five hours later.

If this had truly been an emergency, I probably could have gotten here sooner, but I hated to call it urgent when I might need to use that chip later.

Even though I'd used the flight time alone to think, my thoughts had only gotten more tangled up.

My sister was an adult. A college student enjoying her life.

Unfortunately, it had become second nature for me to feel like I needed to take care of her.

If I hadn't been there for her, Tiffany could have gotten into so much trouble.

My parents had done her wrong.

I'd been old enough that their divorce didn't affect me like it did her.

But not Tiffany. Tiffany had been at that vulnerable, impressionable age when she could have gotten pregnant or even gotten herself arrested.

She did have an attitude.

But all that had smoothed out for the most part. From what

I'd read, she'd always have some issues, but after all, who didn't?

She wasn't my child and I didn't have to take care of her any more.

I'd already done more than most people would have done.

Even as I told myself all these things, I had a visceral response to her being upset.

It was easy to look at Tiffany's life from the outside and see that her boyfriend hadn't been right for her.

But I'd told her that I would be there for her. I couldn't tell her that, then not follow through.

That was more like what my parents had done.

They had put themselves ahead of their children.

After securing the plane, I borrowed one of the cars they kept for pilots and headed toward my sister's apartment near the university campus.

Of course, I ended up sitting in traffic.

I sent Tiffany a text letting her know.

ME: *Stuck in traffic.*

TIFFANY: *It's ok. My friend came over and we're hanging out.*

Her friend?

I dialed her number, but it went straight to voicemail.

Why did she do that?

She just sent me a text.

I'd pictured my sister sitting alone in her university apartment. Crying her eyes out.

Alone and devastated.

I'd rushed up here.

And now she didn't have time to talk to me because her friend was there?

I would be there shortly and find out for myself just what was going on with Tiffany.

As I sat there in traffic, my thoughts wandered back to Brianna.

After she'd dropped me off at my hotel last night, I'd fallen asleep thinking about her.

I'd woke up thinking about her, too, but my morning had been interrupted.

And actually my whole day.

The only good thing about today so far was that I'd gotten to spend some time in the air.

But even then, I'd worried about my sister the whole way up here.

My sister who was now hanging out with her friend.

I hadn't set up any future plans with Brianna, but I had her phone number.

After I got finished with Tiffany, I could focus again on Brianna.

65

———

BRIANNA

The little café, Momma's favorite, was crowded. She liked it that way.

Our mother liked to be around people. It was a trait that served her well in both her profession as a psychologist and as a mother of five children.

Not to mention the wife of a successful entrepreneur.

The server brought out mimosas for both of us. Since I was running late, Momma had ordered for us.

"How's it going with Jackson?" she asked.

I took a sip of my orange juice and champagne drink to give myself a moment to catch up.

"There's nothing going," I said.

Momma narrowed her eyes at me in a way that told me she didn't believe me.

"You've got that look," she said.

"Momma," I said. "There's nothing going on with Jackson."

"Okay," she said.

Momma was dressed in a tight red pencil skirt and matching jacket. She'd switched to flats instead of the heels she wore when we were growing up.

Fashion had always been one of her passions, but she'd become a bit more practical now that she had hit sixty.

She hadn't slowed down, though. Not even a little bit.

She had an active social life while maintaining a busy work schedule.

And all that on top of having a solid, loving marriage and five adult children.

I admired my mother and I strove to keep her approval.

I knew that she'd love me no matter what I did, but I wanted her to be proud of me.

"Did you see Ainsley's dress?" I asked, changing the subject.

She always knew when anyone did that, but she let it slide.

"I'm going to see it tonight," she said.

"It's lovely," I said. "and it suits her perfectly."

"I'm glad the two of you got to spend that time together."

Momma believed that it was important for her children to spend time together, not just as a group, but one on one.

Just as both she and Daddy made it a point to spend time with each of us.

She had some kind of schedule that she kept up with, making sure her time was spaced out fairly between us children, but I just met her whenever she asked.

It wasn't up to me anyway, so I focused on my own schedule, not my mother's.

My phone chimed indicating a text message.

I turned it over.

JACKSON: *Can I see you this weekend?*

I turned my phone back over, but Momma hadn't missed a beat.

"Jackson?" she asked.

"Yes," I said. She would find out eventually anyway. None of us could keep anything from her for very long.

"So when are you going to see him again?"

"I don't know," I said.

"Should we order?" Momma looked down at her menu.

"Sure," I said, looking blankly at my own menu, but I didn't actually see it. It was just a blur in front of me.

"Momma?" I asked. "How did you know that Daddy was the one?"

"Good heavens," Momma said. "I knew it the moment I saw him. But…" she held up a finger. "I didn't know that I knew."

Damn. That was exactly what I was afraid of.

I was afraid that I already knew that Jackson was the one, but I wasn't ready to admit it to myself.

Sometimes I thought too much.

66

JACKSON

I taxied toward the Skye Travels hangar.

There was a storm coming in and Noah wanted all his planes in the hangar.

I'd made it back from Denver just in time.

The trip to see my distraught sister had turned out much differently than I'd expected.

Tiffany had made friends.

In fact, she had a really good support system now.

I understood why she'd called me.

I had always been the one she'd called when she was upset. But now, even though she called me like she always had, she didn't actually need me.

A sobering realization.

But one that I already knew. I knew it when I took Noah up on his offer, even though I hadn't realized I'd known it.

I'd known for some time that I needed to take control of my life and do something I wanted to do instead of always doing what someone else needed.

My sister was going to be fine on her own with her own friends.

I knew that now.

The next time she called and asked me to come home, I'd make sure it was important, like her needing a lung or maybe for a birthday or holiday.

But not like today.

Not when she was just feeling sad. Especially not when she had friends to console her for things like that.

I'd sent her a text before my flight left from Denver, thinking she'd have plenty of time to respond before I got back to Houston.

I'd taken the leap and just asked her out plain. No excuses about needing a ride or looking around town or anything other than the actual truth. I wanted to see her again.

But with the airplane secure in the hangar, I scrolled back to the message I'd sent her.

It said delivered.

But there was no response.

My thoughts went through the whole process from she doesn't want to see me to maybe she was the one needing a lung, not my sister.

She wouldn't have to ask twice.

But as I rode up the elevator to the Skye Travels office, I realized that if she didn't respond to my text or my phone call, if I decided to call her, I couldn't do anything about it.

Even if I did manage to get her address, I couldn't just show up at her home.

That would be too much like stalking.

No. I'd put the ball in her court.

Now I had to just sit back and wait.

Unfortunately waiting was not something I was good at.

I was horrible at it.

I stepped off the elevator into an empty lobby. Even the receptionist had left early.

At any rate, the way I saw it, there was no point in waiting for something when you knew that you wanted it.

I pretty much tried to live my life that way.

Within reason, of course, my goal was to live like there was no tomorrow.

I blamed my parents' divorce. My sister and I blamed all our flaws on the divorce. It's what adult children did.

I went to my office, turned on the computer, and started filling out paperwork.

Keeping my phone next to me, I tapped it anytime it went dark, but Brianna wasn't responding.

I thought about asking Noah about her, but quickly dismissed that idea.

It was already bad enough that he thought I wanted to date her. He didn't need confirmation.

Maybe I needed to send another text.

Sometimes texts got lost, right?

Maybe she'd accidentally deleted my number.

It could happen.

Or maybe she just didn't want to talk to me.

Before I gave up, though, I was going to, first, send her another text, then second, I would call her.

After that if she didn't answer, there was nothing I could do.

I would just have to wait until I happened to see her again.

That could be anytime at all. Tomorrow. Or next year.

Not the best plan for me, especially since part of the reason I'd moved to Houston was so I can spend time with her.

But I could not tell anyone that.

And I had no choice but to wait.

67

BRIANNA

I needed to answer Jackson's text, but I just didn't know how to respond yet.

I had heard it from a reliable source that he had flown to Denver. Something about his sister, but that was all I knew.

So I figured I had plenty of time to respond before he made it back.

I didn't know who I was fooling. Even my mother could see that I was crushing on him.

Of course, she was a psychologist and I swore she could read minds sometimes.

After I left the café, I drove around a bit.

Driving helped to clear my head.

And this time of the day, the traffic wasn't unbearable.

Instead of heading to my condo, I found myself driving toward Daddy's office.

Technically the Skye Travels office.

By now the parking lot was empty.

I pulled in and sat in my car.

I looked up to the third floor and saw that someone had left the lights on.

I didn't see Daddy's truck, so I was pretty sure he wasn't the one who was working late.

Turning off the motor, I got out of the car and walked to the main door.

It was unlocked, so I went inside and pressed the elevator button.

As I rode up to the third floor, I suggested to myself that this was a bad idea.

There was a strong possibility that Jackson had returned from Denver and was the one in the offices.

Ignoring my own suggestion, I walked through the lobby and went straight toward Jackson's office.

I hadn't responded to his text, but perhaps this was my response.

Some things were better in person.

Like kissing him.

Ever since he'd kissed me on the Kiss Cam, I'd replayed it in my head a thousand times.

And the truth was I wanted more. One kiss was not enough.

My flat ankle boots were quiet on the floor as I walked down the hall.

When I reached his door, I stopped and just looked at him.

He was scowling at the computer screen. There was something about the Skye Travels computer program that did that to people.

I'd never personally used it, but I didn't know anyone who actually liked using it, especially not at first.

I could tell he hadn't shaved today. His face had a sexy scruffiness to it.

His pilot's cap lay on the desk and his white shirt was unbuttoned at the collar.

Jackson had obviously finished working for the day.

He looked up and blinked at me.

I smiled and went to sit on the edge of his desk.

"Hi," I said, picking up his cap and turning it over.

"You didn't answer my text," he said.

I set his cap on my head.

"You sent me a text?" I asked, innocently.

He turned his attention back to the computer and continued doing what he was doing.

For about five seconds.

Then he closed the computer and stood up.

"You shouldn't walk into strangers' offices," he said. "and put on their hats."

"What's wrong with wearing a stranger's hat?" I asked, laughter bubbling in my voice.

He moved to stand in front of me and put one hand on the desk on either side of me.

I was trapped.

"Because…" he said. "It makes you look sexy."

"Is that so?" I asked, but the laughter had dropped from my voice.

"That is so," he said, leaning closer.

I adjusted the cap.

"Then I suppose I should do it more often."

"I don't think you realize how dangerous it is," he said, his breath warm against my left ear.

"Maybe not," I said, but I was quickly losing the thread of the conversation with him this close.

"Or…" He moved to speak close to my right ear. "Maybe you don't care."

"I care," I breathed.

Right now what I cared about was kissing him.

Anything else flew right out of my brain.

He leaned forward again, his lips hovering closer to mine.

"How much do you care?" he asked.

I licked my lips. "A lot," I said, but I wasn't even sure what we were talking about now.

Then he placed his lips against mine and my eyes fluttered closed.

It was surprisingly erotic with me sitting on his desk wearing his cap and him standing with me captive in front of him.

And the only place we were touching were our lips.

I wanted more. More of everything. More of his lips. I wanted more of his body touching mine.

But I didn't move a muscle.

I just soaked in the feel of his lips against mine.

After what seemed like an eternity, he leaned back just enough to look into my eyes.

He gently stroked my cheek with his thumb, sending shivers through me and making me want him all the more.

When I went put my arms around him, he took my wrists and held them behind my back with one hand.

Then he gently placed his other hand on my cheek and kissed me again.

This time the kiss was more. More everything. More urgent. More passionate.

He kissed me thoroughly to the point that I thought I might come undone.

When he finally released my hands, he put his hand on my butt and slid me forward against him.

Now there was nothing between us other than his slacks and mine.

He shifted me again, this time finding himself a home between my legs that had somehow gotten parted.

I put my arms around his shoulders and pressed my body against his.

Now, it seemed, we were touching everywhere.

And yet I couldn't get close enough to him.

His lips were both urgent and gentle against mine.

I met him kiss for kiss, all the attraction of the past few days pouring out of me.

He moved me again and now I was pressed against his hard shaft.

I moved against him, my body aflame now.

Oh. My. God. He was doing things to me that were…

I fisted my fingers in the soft cloth of his shirt as my hips ground against him.

I opened my mouth and whimpered as I came for him.

He held me to him as my body shuddered with waves of pleasure.

Then I went limp against him.

He just held me until I settled.

"See," he whispered against me. "this is what happens when you put on a stranger's hat."

68

JACKSON

J did what any gentleman would do.

I walked Brianna to her car.

"Can I drive you to your hotel?" she asked.

And that way danger lay. Even knowing that, I barely stopped myself from agreeing.

"I need to finish up here," I said. "I'll get an Uber."

"I thought you only used taxis."

"Bad experience with taxis," I said.

Brianna looked at me with a curious expression.

I just shrugged and opened her car door.

After she got behind the wheel, I leaned against the door.

"I don't think you ever answered my question," I said.

"What question is that?" she asking, turning on the motor.

"I believe it was something about this weekend," I said.

"Right," she said.

"Isn't that why you showed up here? To give me an answer in person."

She looked at bit confused.

"I guess," she said. "I don't really remember."

I laughed.

I think I actually had Brianna Worthington flustered.

And thanks to me, her cheeks were flushed.

She looked quite fetching, if I did have to say so myself.

I grinned at her.

"I think the least you can do is let me take you out to dinner. On a real date."

Either her cheeks were flushing even more or the glow from the dashboard was reflecting onto her cheeks.

No. She was definitely blushing.

"Okay," she said. "you can text me."

She reached for the door, so I stepped back and closed it.

I watched as she drove away, until I could no longer see the rear lights of her car.

I really could have used that ride, but I couldn't risk having her go near my hotel right now.

Brianna was a lady and deserved to be treated like one.

If I managed to get her alone in my room right now, there was no way I was going to be able to keep my hands off of her.

That one kiss at the baseball game hadn't been enough.

I'd wanted more.

And now that I'd had more, I still couldn't get enough.

And there was no way that I would ever get enough of Brianna Worthington.

It was unfortunate that I now worked for her father.

But that wasn't enough to keep me away from her.

Hell. If it was a problem, Noah could fire me.

I could pick up where I'd left off in Denver or even start my own company here in Houston.

Either way, the only thing that could keep me away from Brianna was Brianna herself.

69

BRIANNA

As I drove from the airport to my condo, I turned up the music on my Apple play list to try to keep my thoughts focused on something other than Jackson.

It didn't work, though. The music only made me think about him more.

Skipping around through my songs didn't work either.

Even the ones who used to remind me of other people now made me think of Jackson.

It was like he'd wiped my brain clear of everything except for him.

I couldn't get him out of my head.

And I didn't want to.

It was probably a good thing I wasn't driving him back to his hotel.

It was hard enough leaving him standing there in the parking lot.

Leaving him at his hotel would be hard also.

But he was taking me on a date this weekend.

I'd agreed to go out with Jackson. And we hadn't even established which day.

He'd essentially locked in my schedule for the whole weekend.

I pulled into my private parking space and got on my private elevator.

If he wanted to take me on a date, then I'd let him.

I'd send him my address and he could pick me up here.

That way we'd be on my turf.

As I rode up the elevator, I replayed every moment of that action we'd had on his desk.

I was feeling oddly satisfied.

And at the same time, he'd given me something to look forward to.

A date this weekend.

I had videos to make. And now I was going to have to go shopping.

Jackson was a bad influence on my capsule wardrobe.

Maybe, I thought with sudden inspiration, as I stepped off the elevator into my condo, I'd borrow something from Ainsley. Madison's clothes were more in line with my style, but since she lived in Denver, I didn't have access to her closet anymore.

Ainsley would have something I could borrow. I knew because I helped her pick out most of her dress-up clothes. And that way, I wouldn't clutter up my own closet.

Feeling rather pleased with my options, I put on my pajamas and climbed into bed.

Like I did every night, I checked the comments on my You Tube channel to see if there was anything I needed to respond to.

Everything looked routine enough. Nothing to worry about.

Then I noticed a comment on one of my latest videos.

I was used to negative comments on occasion, but I'd never had anything really hateful posted on my account.

Tonight, it turned out, was different.

The comment had been posted on my last video.

GABE: *I think you're my neighbor. Looks like we have practically the same view from our apartments.*

I just stared at the comment.

I had known better than to film from my own balcony with the city behind me, but I honestly hadn't expected anyone to pay attention. There were so many millions of people in Houston, what were the odds that someone would bother trying to pinpoint where I lived?

After seeing his comment, I went back and checked some of my other videos.

And there he was. He'd posted stray comments on six of my previous videos. After I found six, I stopped counting.

By themselves they were innocuous.

But taken together, they totally creeped me out.

I climbed out of bed and double-checked my door locks. I rarely worried too much since I had a private elevator.

But whoever this Gabe fellow was seemed to be paying far too much personal attention to my channel.

Trying to put it out of my head, I set my phone on the charger on my nightstand and allowed my thoughts to drift back to Jackson.

Jackson was a much more pleasant thing to think about than a fellow named Gabe who seemed to think it was okay to let me know that he lived nearby.

Fortunately, I was a quick learner and I wouldn't be filming on my balcony again.

In fact… I climbed out of bed and pulled down the video that showed my location.

It was the first time I'd ever pulled down a video. The damage may have been done, but I could put a stop to any further damage.

70

JACKSON

The rest of the week went by quickly.

I had two more flights to Dallas and one to Alabama.

By Thursday, I'd decided that I wanted to see Brianna earlier rather than later.

It took all I had to wait until the weekend.

So on Thursday, while I waited for takeoff, I sent her a text.

ME: *Want to have dinner tomorrow?*

BRIANNA: *Ok.*

I smiled to myself. She must have been looking at her phone when I texted her to write back that quickly.

ME: *Want me to pick you up at your place?*

BRIANNA: *Sounds good.*

ME: *Send me your address.*

I got the go ahead for takeoff, so I put my phone aside.

As the airplane achieved ground effect, I whistled to myself.

I was alone in the plane at the moment, on my way to pick up a passenger in Dallas.

So today was a good day.

I put the plane on autopilot and settled in for the flight.

I was looking forward to Friday. And if I played my cards right, I might get a second date on Saturday. Even a daytime Saturday date would be great with me.

I wanted to spend as much time as I could with Brianna.

I'd take her to a nice dinner. Since I didn't know Houston all that well, I'd ask the concierge for a recommendation.

Maybe I'd take her a single red rose.

Not too much. Just enough to be romantic.

I didn't care about playing games.

I wanted to date her and I wanted her to know that I wanted to date her.

I wasn't going to pretend that I didn't like her. Or any of that silly stuff that a lot of guys did before they decided to commit.

I was all in.

Hell, I'd moved here and left my business behind to be closer to her.

Maybe it was something I wanted to do anyway, but she'd been the impetus. Just like my friend had gotten me to Denver with him.

I had a tendency to get somewhere and stay until something happened to motivate me to make a change.

Some would probably call that stability. Me? I just called it getting comfortable and not wanting to go to the trouble to move around for no reason.

I flew through a puff of clouds.

I was the luckiest man I knew.

Not only did I get to do what I loved for a living, but I had found the woman of my dreams.

And now that I'd found her, I wasn't going to let her go.

BRIANNA

J'd been filming when the text had come in from Jackson.

I had to edit out that part.

In fact, I might have to film the whole thing over again.

As I sat at my Apple computer working on the edits, even I could see that I was different after I got his simple text.

My eyes were brighter and my smile was more genuine.

Maybe no one else would notice.

I'd put it all together, then decide later.

After I had a good draft, I checked my email. I had two letters from sponsors and one from a potential sponsor.

I had no more than gotten finished with those responses, when I got a text from Ainsley.

AINSLEY: *Hey. Wyatt is in Wyoming. Want to get a pizza and binge on Netflix tonight?*

It kind of surprised me. Ainsley and I had never been the best of friends, but since Madison had moved to Colorado, Ainsley seemed to have turned to me for friendship.

ME: *Tonight?*

AINSLEY: *Yes. He'll be back tomorrow.*

ME: *Okay. Sounds like fun.*

I definitely couldn't hang out with her tomorrow night, but I didn't tell her that.

AINSLEY: Awesome. I'll come over after I finish up some paperwork.

ME: *Okay.*

Who would have thought that pilots had so much paperwork?

It didn't surprise me that she didn't ask what time I stopped working.

Even my own sister didn't seem to comprehend that I had things to do.

Maybe I'd show her my sponsor letters.

Then she would at least, maybe, start to understand that I really did have a paying job.

At any rate, I turned off my computer and called it a day.

I took me all of fifteen minutes to straighten and clean my condo. And that included putting a load of towels in the washer.

Ever since I'd become a minimalist, I was able to keep my condo up so much easier.

There just wasn't so much to do.

And I loved it that all my things had a home.

I went out on the balcony overlooking the city and sat in one of my two chairs.

ME: *Bring Beau.*

Ainsley sent me a thumbs up. Beau was the dog she'd adopted after she'd met Wyatt. If I remembered correctly, the dog had been the reason she'd met Wyatt.

It was all a romantic story, but I was sketchy on the details.

Normally sitting on my balcony brought me peace and tranquility.

But I found myself looking around. It was crazy because the

way the condos were laid out, none of the other tenants could see my balcony. And I couldn't see theirs.

It was a really nice design.

But somewhere nearby there was a guy named Gabe who seemed to think that we were neighbors. And he didn't mind announcing it to the world.

That was actually probably a good thing.

If anything were to happen to me, they could look back at the comments on my channel and a good detective would spot his posts.

I logged in on my phone and took some screenshots of his comments.

Just for extra insurance.

Just in case.

I knowingly put myself out there in the public eye and some attention was to be expected.

But in this strange world we lived in, a girl could never be too safe.

72

JACKSON

I stepped off the elevator into the living room of Brianna's twenty-seventh floor condo.

Her living room, as big as my entire apartment, had floor-to-ceiling windows that provided an extraordinary view of downtown Houston.

Brianna, wearing a little black dress and high heels stood waiting for me. Her hair swirled around her shoulders like a mermaid.

"Hi," she said.

"Hi." I immediately wished I had gone with my first instinct to bring her a red rose. Instead, I'd shown up empty handed.

"You look beautiful," I said, pressing a kiss on her forehead.

"You look pretty good yourself," she said.

I stepped back and took her hands in mine.

"You're trembling," I said, turning her hands over, palms up.

I placed a gentle kiss on one palm, then the other.

She shook her head.

"No," she said. "I'm okay."

"You're not a very good liar," I took her hand and walked toward the window. "But you do have the best view in town."

"It is nice, isn't it?" She took a deep breath, then blew it out slowly.

There was something she wasn't telling me, but I'd let her slide for now. Whatever it was, I didn't want it to ruin our date.

"I have a very important question for you," I said.

She turned and looked into my eyes. I could just fall into those green eyes of hers and lose myself.

"What's that?"

"Do you prefer Mexican food or Italian?"

"I like both," she said.

My lighthearted question had the desired effect of releasing some of the tension from her features.

I lifted her hands and lightly kissed the backs of her fingers.

"Mexican it is, then," I said. "But first… You have to tell me what's bothering you."

Shaking her head, she smiled and looked away. But I didn't miss the fact that her smile was a little wobbly.

I could push her on it.

But she'd tell me when she was ready.

"Are you ready to go then?" I asked.

She smiled then and locked her gaze onto mine.

We stepped into her private elevator. When it stopped on the nineteenth floor, she held her breath and watched as the door slowly slid open.

I took her hand.

A middle-aged woman stepped inside.

I thought she had a private elevator, but apparently a private elevator was only just so private.

The women greeted each other as any two people would in this situation. They'd seen each other before, I surmised, but didn't actually know each other.

Wasn't my business. The only thing about it that was my business was how wary Brianna had been when the elevator had come to a stop.

I hope she'd tell me if something happened.

But then we didn't seem to know each other well enough for her to tell me. Not just yet anyway.

73

BRIANNA

I hadn't told anyone about the messages I'd gotten from Gabe. Not even Ainsley.

This was the first time I'd left the condo in two days.

Instead of borrowing clothes from Ainsley or going shopping, I'd just decided to wear a pair of jeans and a sweater.

Whoever Gabe was had really shaken me.

Now I found that I wanted to tell Jackson, but I didn't want it to ruin our evening. So I pushed it to the back of my mind as I settled into the driver's seat of my car and backed out of my parking space.

As I drove out of the parking garage, I felt some of confidence returning. Gabe didn't know who he was messing with.

I could have blocked him, but I hadn't just yet. I wanted to wait. To see what else he posted. If I had to, I could even delete his comments.

But in the meantime, I didn't want to tip my hand that I was aware of him. And I certainly did not want him to know that I was alarmed by him.

Jackson gave me the address to the restaurant and I put it in my GPS. It wasn't far. Just ten minutes. I hadn't been there before, but I was up for something new.

He took my lead and we rode in silence.

I dropped the car off with the valet and Jackson took my hand as we walked toward the restaurant door.

We were seated at a secluded table in no time.

We both ordered water. After the server walked away, Jackson caught my gaze.

"You'll tell me if there's something I need to know about, right?"

I nodded, swallowing the lump in my throat. I hated this feeling of helplessness.

Everything had been going so well. I'd been so happy with my YouTube channel. With my life.

Now I was wondering if I needed to move.

I could move into Ainsley's high-rise building, but I'd just gotten my place perfected. I loved everything about it.

"Did I do something?" Jackson asked, his brow furrowed.

"No," I closed my eyes and shook my head. I was going to have to tell him. This was going to be bothering me and he deserved to know what was going on with me. It just wasn't fair to him.

The server dropped off a margarita for each of us. I took a sip of the bitter drink and made a face. I really didn't like margaritas, but they were part of the Mexican food experience.

Then I searched Jackson's eyes.

"I made a mistake," I said.

"What kind of mistake?" he asked, showing immediate concern.

"I… 'um… I recorded a video on my balcony."

He looked at me sideways.

"That's a mistake because…" he asked.

I picked up a chip and dipped it into the salsa, but I didn't eat it.

"Because I revealed where I lived."

"Has someone hurt you?" he asked, his expression going fierce.

He seemed like such a mild-mannered guy. I actually took comfort from his fierce look.

I shook my head. "No. But…" I tapped my fingers on the table. How much should I tell him anyway?

"You can tell me," he said. "maybe I can help."

I nodded. He was right, of course. I didn't have to shoulder this on my own. And if I told anyone in my family, it would certainly be blown out of proportion before it needed to be.

Maybe it would be easier if I showed him.

I pulled out my phone. Logged into my account.

And froze.

I had a new message from Gabe.

74

JACKSON

*H*aving a troubled younger sister, I was keenly in tune to knowing when something was bothering someone I cared about.

And something was definitely troubling Brianna.

She didn't seem like the kind of girl who was easily alarmed. She had a good family. Lots of support. Was successful. Confident.

But at the core, like the rest of us, she was vulnerable.

And something was definitely wrong.

She was being vague about answering me. So much so that she reminded me of Tiffany. If I'd learned one thing, it was patience.

I sipped my margarita. Not one of my favorite drinks, but I'd been the one to pick this place.

The server came back. Took our order.

Brianna was looking uncertain about what to do.

Then, as though she'd made a decision, she slid her cell phone over in front of me.

"This is the latest message from someone named Gabe," she said.

I read the message that had been posted on one of her YouTube videos.

It was from someone named Gabe.

GABE: *I really like your videos. Do you think we could meet?*

"So you think this person knows where you live?"

"Yes. There was another post. One that said…"

She took her phone back and scrolled up until she found what she was looking for.

"This one," she said, sliding it back to me.

GABE: *I think you're my neighbor. Looks like we have practically the same view from our apartments.*

I could see why she'd think that. Gabe stated it quite clearly.

I ran a hand through my hair. If I were Gabe, I wouldn't have posted that message on a public forum. I would have found a way to find her privately.

I could think of all sorts of possibilities. Gabe didn't appear to be very sophisticated.

This obviously concerned Brianna and since it concerned her, I was going to do something about it.

"Do you think you can get me Gabe's IP address?"

"I think so," she said. "When I get home, I can log in on my computer. See about it then."

"Okay," I said. "Look. Try not to worry. We'll figure out how to deal with this."

She smiled and this time her smile was a bit less wobbly.

"Okay," she said. "Thank you."

I reached over and squeezed her hand. "Thank you for telling me," I said.

"Thanks for listening. I know it's probably nothing, but it's been really bothering me."

"Does it help a little to tell someone?"

She smiled. "It does help."

I squeezed her hand again.

I had someone I could call about this. I didn't want her to

stress over it too much. But I also knew better than to minimize it. If something happened to her because I didn't take it seriously… I'd never forgive myself.

But right now I needed to do what I could to lighten her mood.

Life was hard enough without worrying about somebody who was being stupid.

75

BRIANNA

I felt a little bit silly after I told Jackson about Gabe. I knew that keeping something to myself was the worse way to handle anything.

I was surrounded by psychologists. That was just Psychology 101. Talking about something helped it seem less scary.

I probably could have told Ainsley or even Momma just as easily. But for some reason, I wanted to tell Jackson.

It was something I couldn't explain. I just trusted him. I trusted him not to freak out and to even know what to do.

And I hadn't been wrong.

He didn't freak out. And he knew what to do.

He knew to look for Gabe's IP address.

And I would have thought about that if I hadn't been so freaked out myself.

This was why it was important to have a person. Someone who could be trusted to be on our side.

I looked at Jackson from beneath my eyelashes.

He was handsome and attentive.

He seemed like he cared about me. About what I thought.

How I felt.

I'd cut myself off from having that kind of relationship for far too long.

"Can I change the subject?" he asked.

I grinned. "You're a quick learner."

He shrugged. "So I've been told."

"What's the new subject?"

He picked up a chip. Popped it in his mouth.

"I can't live in a hotel forever."

"You want help finding a place to live."

I'd told myself I could refer him to a realtor. But now I didn't think it was such a good idea to let someone else handle something so important as finding him a place to live.

"I can go online," he said. "But I'd feel so much better if I had someone who lives here to give me their opinion."

"I know some realtors," I said.

I was giving him an out. Just in case…

"I was hoping you could help me," he said.

I grinned. "I'd be happy to. Are you looking to rent or buy?"

"Rent," he said. "Give me time to get my bearings. Figure out my next direction."

"Good idea," I said. But there was something about the way he said it that brought a flush to my cheeks. Or maybe it was the way he looked at me.

Either way, I felt more excited about the future than I had in a really long time.

Other than Gabe clouding my horizons, I had so many good things going.

I had my YouTube channel, everything was good with my family, and now I just might have a new boyfriend.

A man I liked very much.

Jackson Fleming had quickly become more than just a pilot from Denver.

Jackson was a man after my heart.

76

JACKSON

Two weeks later

I could officially say that I'd checked out all of River Oaks and Uptown Houston looking for a house or an apartment to rent.

After another busy day of apartment touring, I was stretched out on Brianna's sofa, my feet on her ottoman.

The fire in the fireplace blazed with a perfect view of the Houston skyline behind it.

"Have you liked anything yet?" she asked, coming to plop down beside me.

We'd just gotten back from a walk down to a little shopping area behind her condo and were finishing up hot chocolate from a little gelato shop.

She'd promised me it was the best gelato. I'd been crazy not to believe her.

"You know what." I said. "This hot chocolate has me thinking about the Gray House. The Gray House was an apartment complex a block or two from Brianna's and the gelato shop was right behind it. There were also several good restaurants and nice shopping right there.

Since I'd decided to leave my car in Denver for my sister, I almost didn't need a car. Almost. But Houston was a driving town and since I had to get to work every day, I was definitely going to be car shopping soon. Now that was my least favorite thing to shop for.

"Seriously?" she asked. "After seeing the high-rises and spending time here with me I can't believe you'd even consider a low-rise apartment."

"It's a mid-rise," I said. "and it's nice. Remember, I'm just a pilot. Not a wealthy YouTuber like you."

Not to mention the heiress to a fortune.

Brianna and her four siblings stood to inherit one of the most successful private airlines in the country. Maybe even THE most successful.

"Right," she said, with a little pout before she hid behind her cup of hot chocolate.

I'd spent a lot of time here with her in her condo. When I wasn't flying, I was here. Mostly. I still had my hotel room. I didn't tell her, but having that room was starting to feel like an unnecessary drain on my finances.

I didn't tell her because I didn't want her pressuring me to make a hasty decision about where to live. It was bad enough me pressuring myself.

She pulled her feet up on the sofa and leaned against me, resting her cheek on my shoulder.

Besides, none of that mattered as long I had her and we could do this.

This was heaven on earth.

"There is one good thing about the Gray House," she said.

"What's that?" I asked, kissing her on the cheek."

"You're within walking distance of my condo."

She turned to press her lips against mine.

That was most definitely a good advantage of the Gray House.

Shifting her beneath me, I slid down as I put my hands on her knees and parted her legs.

Oh dear lord.

The woman wasn't wearing panties.

I glanced up at her. She was wearing a knowing, satisfied grin.

As much I enjoyed pulling her panties off of her, seeing her there all bare, in her full glory instantly made me hard as stone.

And I was about to lick that smug grin off her face.

I kissed her inner thighs first. She tugged lightly at my hair, urging me upwards toward her center.

But I took my time, working my way up. She tasted so good. Like honey.

A quick glance told me her grin had turned to an expression of longing. Hooded eyes. Lips parted. Quick breathing.

She was incredibly sensitive and I knew how to make her come, but I wasn't ready yet.

I slowly licked every part of her, enjoying her squirming and little whimpers.

She released my hair and stretched her arms back over her head.

I'd tortured her long enough.

Spreading her knees wide, I rubbed my tongue against her clit in little circular movements.

Her breath hitched and she came with a moan and a catch of her breath.

I moved to pull her into my lap, held her close, and kissed the top of her head as her body pulsed in the aftermath of her climax.

There was nothing more satisfying than making my girl come.

77

BRIANNA

I tapped play and watched the video I'd just made about summer skincare.

I'd taken a moment to endorse a face cream that a sponsor had sent me. I'd tried it out for two weeks now.

And if I did have to say so myself, it was making a difference. Or… it could possibly be coincidental.

I'd been with Jackson for that same two weeks. And to say it nicely, my blood had been flowing to every corner of my body. Corners I didn't even know needed blood.

Jackson was attentive. It hadn't taken him any time at all to figure out my body's secrets.

And it wasn't just the sex. He was also attentive to other things. He quickly learned how I liked my coffee and he brought me coffee on several mornings.

I enjoyed spending time with him. So much so that the only time I was getting any work done was when he was flying.

There would come a time when I would have work in front of him.

But I wasn't there yet.

Leaning into the mirror, I coated my lashes with mascara.

Today I was meeting Momma for brunch.

It just so happened that Jackson was on a flight, so the timing was good.

A quick glance at the clock over my vanity had me speeding things up.

It was time for me to head out the door.

The one thing Momma didn't tolerate was tardiness.

She was always on time and she expected us to be also.

The elevator stopped on the twenty-fifth floor and a man I hadn't seen before stepped on.

He was older than me, maybe mid-thirties, and was clean-shaven. He was tall and stocky. Not my type.

It was a little too late, but I pulled my shades of out my handbag and put them on.

That was really about the only thing that bothered me about my condo. The private elevators were only semi-private.

Sometimes I could go up and down all day and never see anyone else. But then, sometimes, like today, I wasn't so lucky.

I kept my eyes glued to my phone, but I could feel the fellow watching me. Until I'd started getting those strange posts on my YouTube channel, it wouldn't have bothered me, but I was wary now.

I'd made a mistake and even though I'd learned from it, I had to deal with the ramifications.

The elevator stopped at my garage floor and the doors slid open.

I could see my fire-engine red Maserati sitting there, waiting for me.

But I didn't move.

I kept my head down as though I hadn't noticed.

"Is this you?" the man asked.

"No," I said, punching the button for the lobby—the same button he'd already pushed.

The thought of getting off and walking through that

deserted garage, alone, with this man having the opportunity to follow me, made the hair on the back of my neck stand on end.

I always followed my instinct.

We rode in silence to the lobby. I got off and strode straight to the front doors.

The stranger from the twenty-fifth floor stopped off at the mailboxes.

With my heart still in my throat, I handed my keys to the valet.

"Ron," I said. "Would you be a dear and bring my car down?"

"Sure thing, Ms. Worthington," Ron said and dashed off to get my car.

The stranger from the twenty-fifth floor was nowhere to be seen as I hopped into the driver's seat of my car a few minutes later and merged into traffic.

78

JACKSON

I'd had better days for flying.

I was on my way back from a little airport in Louisiana to pick up a cat. From what I understood, Ainsley typically took the flights that involved animals, but she wasn't available today.

It was funny, really, how much some people would pay to get the perfect pet.

Something like a seeing-eye dog, I could understand. Those dogs were rare and well-trained. Worth top dollar. But the little cat I had strapped into the passenger seat watched me through the peep-hole of his carrier.

I didn't have anything against animals. I'd even tried talking to the little guy at one point, but he just looked at me with those huge blue eyes encased in a ball of fur.

I hit another pocket of turbulence.

"Sorry," I said, then rolled my eyes at myself. I was apologizing to a cat. The little fellow would probably claw my eyes out if he could get out of that carrier.

This particular airplane had WIFI, so I didn't have so much turbulence to contend with, I would have taken advantage of it.

Still, I was surprised when a text came in.

It was from my buddy on the police force in Denver.

ERIC: *Have some information for you*

ME: *Great. In flight right now.*

ERIC: *No problem. Give me a call tomorrow.*

Eric owed me a favor from way back and I'd never called it in. I'd flown to Florida and picked up his daughter after her boyfriend had slapped her around.

It had been a bad deal. That was one time when I was grateful I was a pilot with access to planes.

Of course, I'd had to get a plane from somewhere else. One of these days I was going to have my own airplane. I had the money set aside, earmarked. Just hadn't gotten around to it.

I'd gotten sidetracked. Right now I was apartment shopping. Then I'd be car shopping unless I wanted to continue using taxis and Ubers.

And… I might just be ring shopping soon, too.

The thought came out of nowhere and I dropped my water bottle, spilling water across my pants leg and over the leather seats.

I was normally pretty self-aware and I knew myself pretty well. I knew that I was easily distracted and put off changing things that required a lot of time and effort.

At least… that's how I'd been before I'd taken this job at Skye Travels.

Now I was changing everything. It suddenly occurred to me that the reason I'd been dragging my feet on renting an apartment was because I was thinking about marrying Brianna.

I grabbed a towel and wiped at the water I'd spilled all over the place.

I didn't have plans with Brianna tonight. It was like it was understood now.

79

BRIANNA

"What's wrong?" Momma asked after I took my seat across from her.

The table was covered with a pristine white tablecloth and a little white daisy in a white vase sat in the middle of the table.

The servers, all men, wore black tuxedos. I never asked, but I sometimes wondered if that was why this was one of Momma's favorite restaurants. It was very elegant and formal.

I found it interesting, too, after comparing notes with my sisters, that I was the only one of us four girls that Momma brought here.

The other restaurants appeared to be interchangeable, but not this one. I didn't know if it was by design or by accident.

Except that Momma never did anything by accident.

The little French restaurant was full, but not crowded.

"Nothing," I said, pulling the shades off my face and slipping them into my bag. I looked up and smiled at her.

Momma was looking at me sideways. She shook her head a little.

"Something," she said, but slid her menu forward and decided to let it go. For now.

She'd come back to it. Go at it a different way. Momma was nothing if not persistent. And she never forgot anything.

It made her an excellent psychologist. Both her fine-tuned memory and her uncanny sense of when to circle around and bring something back up.

For her children, it was merely annoying. The only way we ever got away with something was if Momma had absolutely no inkling whatsoever.

Very rare. Maybe one time.

"How's Daddy?" I asked as one of the servers set a mimosa in front of each of us.

Momma sat back, taking her glass with her. Daddy was Momma's kryptonite. Him being sick was the only thing I'd ever known to make her vulnerable.

"He's doing well," she said. "I'm having trouble getting him to get sufficient rest."

"Momma," I said. "If you put yourself in his shoes, you know you'd be the same way."

Momma smiled a little and took a sip of her drink.

"You're my perceptive one," she said.

"I'm not a psychologist," I said. "Madison—"

Momma interrupted me.

"Madison has had years and years of training to get where she is. You, on the other hand, have an innate sense about things. About people."

Momma lifted a hand and motioned ever so subtly to indicate the café.

"It's why you're so good at connecting with so many people on YouTube."

I sat back and fought to keep my jaw from dropping. This was the first time Momma had ever said anything to indicate she had any idea about my level of success.

But it was a fleeting compliment.

"You're right," she said, with a little smile. "I would never give up. It's how your Daddy and I roll."

I put a hand over my lips to keep from laughing out loud. Momma wasn't trying to be funny. But I'd never heard her say anything about rolling and it sounded strange coming out of her mouth.

She leaned forward. "So tell me about you and Jackson."

"There's nothing to tell," I said, but the blush across my cheeks said otherwise and I knew it.

"Your father tells me he's a good man."

"Right," I said, leaning back and running a finger along my glass. "Any idea why Daddy took such an interest in him?"

Momma shrugged. "Not really. Your father does what he does. He also has an innate sense about people."

"Hmm." I nodded, meeting my mother's gaze. "I guess. It just seems like he's been trying to hook us up from the beginning."

"And by hook up, you mean dating?"

I looked blankly at my mother for moment, then I laughed out loud. I couldn't help it.

"Yes," I said. "Of course."

But there was that heated blush again as I had a flashback to last night when Jackson had his mouth on me, making me come so hard I was turned on just from the memory.

"You are an adult," Momma said. "You can do what you want to do."

"Thank you," I said.

The server brought our tuna sandwiches that Momma had apparently already ordered.

"So if it's not Jackson, then tell me what's troubling you."

80

———

JACKSON

By the time I got to the Houston airport, the skies were clear and I made a perfect landing.

I still had water splashed across my pants leg, but hopefully it wouldn't be noticeable.

Things happened in the air. Couldn't be helped.

Happened all the time.

But the realization I'd had did not happen all the time.

I liked Brianna. A lot.

Over the past couple of weeks, I'd even found myself imagining a future with her.

One day.

To realize that I'd been dragging my feet in choosing an apartment because I was thinking about actually marrying her in the foreseeable future scared the living daylights out of me.

And the thought of buying a ring made the whole thing all that much more real.

It wasn't that I was opposed or a commitment phobic. I just wasn't ready yet. After being a confirmed bachelor all my life, it was a shock to my senses.

Something I needed to take some time to figure out.

To adapt to.

It wasn't a big deal.

After landing the plane and taxing over to the Skye Travels runway, I knew what I had to do.

I had to take an evening. Spend some time by myself.

Sit out on the hotel's balcony—which I only just discovered two days ago—and drink a beer.

I was caught up in Brianna Worthington's web and I needed some alone time to sort out what that meant, exactly, for me.

I needed to face this with my eyes wide open.

I'd known all along that she deserved the best. I just wasn't sure I was giving her that.

Wasn't sure that going along with the flow was considered giving her my best.

Bottom line was I needed a minute to just think.

So I did what any man would do. I sent Brianna a text.

ME: *Got in late. Going to turn in. Talk to you tomorrow.*

The little response bubbles showed up, then disappeared.

I sat in the plane, holding my phone. Waiting.

Finally, the bubbles showed up again and I got a response.

BRIANNA: *Okay.*

Okay. I knew her well enough to know what that meant. Loosely translated, it meant *what the hell?*

I couldn't really blame her. We'd been pretty much attached at the hip for a couple of weeks now. Since shortly after the baseball game.

One night wouldn't hurt.

Maybe I'd even take a minute and call my buddy in Denver. He might have information that could help her.

She would understand. Right?

81

BRIANNA

I stared at my phone. Waiting for another text message from Jackson. Some kind of explanation. Like *I have the flu. My sister needs to talk to me. I have to leave at 5:00 in the morning for another flight.*

Something, as flimsy as it might be, that it might explain what was happening.

I tapped my phone screen with a freshly manicured nail. I'd left the nail salon about three hours ago, with a new muted red color that I'd been wanting to try.

I had the same color on my toenails, too.

I was a little bit cross, as much as I hated to admit it, that I'd gotten my nails done and Jackson wasn't here to see.

And that awareness just served to make me cross with myself. I hated that I had gone to that kind of trouble to make myself pretty for a man… when I didn't even have a date with said man.

I'd made assumptions about him that maybe I shouldn't have.

Assumptions that we'd have plans when we didn't.

I went into the kitchen, poured myself a glass of pinot noir and went to sit on my couch that overlooked the city.

I sipped the wine. Let it burn the back of my throat.

The cars were backed up on 610 South. Nothing new.

People were always going somewhere. Yet so many of us had nowhere to go.

I could have somewhere to go if I wanted to. I could go to Ainsley's condo. Or I could go to Momma and Daddy's house.

But I wasn't in the mood.

I set the wine aside. I wasn't in the mood for that either. I got up and went to my computer. Work. Work was my retreat. My safe place.

Whenever I was troubled, I could lose myself in work.

I wouldn't make a video though. I didn't trust myself to be my best positive self.

Instead, I did a little research. A little outlining for future videos.

People really had no idea how much work went into making a video. In fact, it seemed that the easier and spontaneous looking the video looked, the harder it was to make.

I tapped my pen on my pad of blue paper. Momma would be proud. I still outlined on paper. Close enough.

Flipping back, I looked over some of the notes I'd written earlier in the week.

I had more ideas than I could get to and then by the time I got to them, I'd already changed the idea into something different.

I may not keep a paper calendar, but I outlined on paper.

My phone chimed. I had new messages on YouTube.

I signed in and scrolled down to the new messages. There were only a handful and I dashed off a couple of quick replies.

My breath caught in my throat.

I had a new message from Gabe.

82

JACKSON

eeling like a heel, I called my buddy Eric to distract myself.

I stood out on the balcony, the wind whipping through my hair.

I could see Brianna's high-rise condo building from here, but, of course, I couldn't tell which place was hers.

"Hey, Buddy," Eric said. "You didn't have to call tonight."

"It's okay," I said. "I had a few minutes."

"The wife and I are just sitting down to dinner," he said. "I can text you the information."

"No," I said. "Don't worry about it. We'll talk tomorrow. Go. Enjoy."

After I disconnected the call I went back inside and sat down on the chair by the window.

Something was wrong with me.

I knew Eric was married. And I tried not to call married couples after work hours.

From my experience watching my parents, marriage was hard enough without somebody calling and interrupting their private evenings.

I loosened my tie and stretched out my legs.

Truth was, I didn't know what to do with myself without Brianna.

Somehow over the last couple of weeks, we'd become a couple.

We were supposed to be together tonight.

We didn't have plans, but couples didn't have to have plans.

I kicked off my shoes. Tugged off my socks. And ran a hand through my hair.

I was an idiot.

With no flight scheduled for tomorrow, I didn't have to get up early. A good night to spend with Brianna.

I probably even could have slept over at her place. Again.

We always stayed at her place, not mine, because I didn't have a place.

I couldn't expect her to spend the night in my hotel room when she had a perfectly good condo right there.

Maybe that was the answer.

I straightened my shoes and tucked my socks inside them.

Since I didn't have to fly tomorrow, I'd go by the Gray House and get an apartment. It was past time for me to make a decision.

It was walking distance to both Brianna's place and shopping and restaurants. She and I could do things without having to drive around in the traffic. It was a good decision.

I felt a little bit better having made it, but it didn't alleviate my overall feeling that I'd made a mess of the evening.

I just hoped that tomorrow I could make it up to Brianna.

Damn it.

This wasn't going to happen again.

I was not going to let myself get into that pattern where I had things to make up to Brianna for.

I was going to get my act together.

This was the turning point.

Right now.

I either got my head right or I cut her loose.

I was doing good to get through one evening with her.

I wasn't dumb enough to think I could get through the rest of my life without her.

Hell. Who did I think I was kidding?

I wasn't going to make it through this one night.

I pulled my socks out of my shoes and put them back on. Then I put my shoes back on and straightened my tie while I scheduled an Uber.

I didn't even want to take the time to change out of my work clothes.

Ten minutes later I knocked on her door.

But Brianna wasn't the one who opened the door.

It was a police officer.

83

BRIANNA

"*D*o you have identification, Sir?" Officer Brandt asked after she opened the door.

I was standing in the kitchen, filling two mugs with hot peppermint green tea while Officer Sidney Brandt answered the door.

I wasn't expecting anyone and when she offered to get the door, I figured it was another officer.

Or worse, Daddy. I hadn't told anyone in my family, but the police were loyal to Daddy. If one of his girls was in trouble, damn right they'd let him know.

But apparently, it was neither since she was asking for identification.

Surely Gabe wouldn't be so bold as to show up at my door.

My heart pounding a hundred miles an hour, I took a step toward the door, trying to see who it was.

"Sure." The man at the door peaked around, looking for me as he pulled his identification out of his back pocket.

It wasn't Gabe.

It was Jackson.

Flooded with relief, I forgot all about the tea and jogged to the door.

I threw my arms around Jackson and just held on.

I'd been so strong.

But now that he was here, the tears welled and spilled over, soaking his shirt.

"I take it you know this man," Officer Brandt said.

I took a deep breath and pulled myself together.

Wiping my eyes, I disengaged myself from Jackson's hold and turned around, holding his hand.

"This is my boyfriend," I said. "Jackson Fleming."

Officer Brandt looked a bit skeptical, but stepped aside to let Jackson inside.

"I'm still gonna need his license," she said. "for the record."

After he handed over his license, I pulled him toward the sofa.

"What's going on?" he asked. "Are you okay?"

"I'm fine." I sat down on the sofa, then remembered my tea. "I'll be right back."

I bounced back up and, retrieving the tea, handed one to Officer Brandt.

She thanked me, but set it down on the end table while she logged Jackson's information.

Wrapping my hands around the warm mug and breathing in the peppermint, I went back to sit next to Jackson.

It occurred to me that I should offer Jackson some tea, so I just held out my mug toward him. Any energy I had was suddenly wiped out of my.

"Tea?"

He shook his head.

"Do I get to know what's happened?"

I glanced at Officer Brandt, but she didn't seem concerned with us at the moment.

"I got another message from Gabe," I said, keeping my voice low.

"Gabe?"

I nodded, not sure why I was whispering. I'd just told Officer Brandt about it.

"There's really nothing we can do." Officer Brandt returned Jackson's license. "I'll get this filed. You can come down to the office and file a restraining order if you want to, though to be honest, I don't think it'll do any good. The message didn't hold an actual threat. And we'd have to get a warrant to find out who Gabe is and where he lives."

"I understand," I said.

"Just watch your back. This happens all the time with social media."

"I know."

"Any questions?" Officer Brandt flicked a glance over at Jackson, but she seemed to have decided that he was okay.

"Not right now," I said. "I'll walk you out."

Using the last of my energy, I walked Officer Brandt to the door and locked it behind her.

Everything would be okay now.

Jackson was here.

And truth was, if Jackson had been here when I got the last message from Gabe, I probably wouldn't have called the police.

I'd been alone and after Momma had dragged it out of me, she'd suggested I report it.

So that's what I had done, knowing it wasn't going to do any good.

I propped on the edge arm of my sofa.

"What are you doing here?" I asked.

84

JACKSON

I hadn't been able to stay away from her. And this was what happened the one time I did try it.

I get to the door and she has a police officer at her condo.

I should have been here.

For a man who didn't play games, I wasn't doing a very good job at being transparent.

"I had some things to think through," I said. "But turns out I didn't want to be away from you."

There. That was about as truthful as I could get.

She looked at me sideways, then nodded, and slid onto the sofa next to me.

"Gonna tell me what happened?" I picked up her mug of tea and handed it to her.

She took a sip and made a face before handing it back.

I hid a smile. Brianna did not like cold tea.

"I got another message from Gabe," she said. "And it… scared me."

"What did it say?"

She opened her phone and scrolled through her account.

"I don't see it," she said.

"It's okay," I said, leaning back. "Take your time."

She laid her head in my lap and scrolled through her messages. I ran my fingers through her hair. I was enjoying just being here with her. Enjoying the unexpected moment.

"It's gone," she announced after about five minutes of scrolling.

"What do you mean?"

"None of the messages are here anymore."

"None of them?" I asked, looking over her shoulders.

"I think…" She looked up at me. "I think Gabe deleted his account."

Gabe probably saw the police come in. That was a logical explanation. But I kept it to myself.

I didn't need to add to her worry and stress.

Besides, I was pretty sure my buddy, Eric, had some information that would help. Tomorrow I'd know for sure. Then we'd have more to go on.

In the meantime, both Brianna and I both needed some rest.

"I'm glad you're here" she said, resting her phone against her chin.

"I'm glad I'm here, too," I said.

"So really," she asked. "Why are you suddenly here?"

I ran a finger along her cheek. "Is it such a bad thing that I didn't want to be away from you?"

"No," she said. "but apparently it took you a minute to figure that out."

I bent down. Kissed her softly on the lips.

"I needed to think about my apartment situation. I can't keep living in a hotel."

"We've looked at a ton of apartments," she said.

It was only six different apartment complexes, but it did certainly seem like a lot more. Any more and I'd be too overwhelmed to keep them straight.

"And it's time I made a decision."

She tilted her head up to look at me.

"Have you?"

"Yes," I said, taking a deep breath. I knew there was no right or wrong answer, but it just felt…well…not quite right. Not wrong. Just not right.

85

BRIANNA

The Gray House.

It was a good choice. Walking distance from here. Close to restaurants and shopping.

Five. Ten. Minutes away, tops, on foot.

A nice area.

It wasn't a highrise, but it was a good place to live.

Close.

I took a deep, ragged breath. He wasn't trying to get away from me. Out of all the places we'd looked at, that was the closest one that suited him.

And he was right. He couldn't keep living in a hotel.

"The Gray House is nice," I said, ignoring the lump in my throat.

"Yeah," he said. "I liked it and I especially like that it's close to you."

I nodded and picked up my phone. Looked again, blankly, at the messages.

I didn't trust myself to say anything right now.

Somehow it seemed like everything was changing. Jackson was going to have his own apartment and there would be more nights like tonight. Night where he was tired and just wanted to go home and sleep. Or nights when he just wanted to have time to himself.

I knew. I was like that.

Except for these past two weeks, I hadn't been like that.

I'd come to look forward to our evenings together. I'd told Officer Brandt that he was my boyfriend, for God's sake.

"Do you think Gabe just pulled his account? That he just went away?"

"Maybe," Jackson said, twirling a strand of my hair around his fingers.

"Maybe he saw the officer come into the building," I said. "and it scared him."

"I thought of that," he said. "That would be a good resolution, don't you think?"

"Too easy," I said.

"Maybe." He pulled me into his lap and kissed the soft part of my neck just beneath my jaw.

I set my phone down and wrapped my arms around him.

"Do you think maybe we could try to forget about him until tomorrow?" He trailed kissed down my neck to the top of my t-shirt.

"I think…" I said. "I think he's taken up enough of our time and energy for one night."

"I agree."

Pressing his lips against mine, he stood up, taking me with him and carried me toward my bedroom.

What had started out as a terrible evening was turning into a pleasant one.

Much more pleasant than I had expected.

As he carried me through my bedroom door, I left all worries about Gabe behind and focused on this handsome man I just couldn't get enough of.

Moonlight streamed in through the windows overlooking the city.

Tomorrow I would have to sort out what was bothering me about Jackson moving to the Gray House.

Tomorrow. There would be plenty of time for thinking.

86

JACKSON

The next morning I stood outside the Skye Travels terminal waiting for a plane to be brought around. The soft breeze felt good to my skin, making me happy to be alive.

I'd woke with a message from Noah asking me to take last minute flight up to Dallas.

Seemed like he was going to Dallas a lot lately.

I didn't mind, since flying was flying.

And I rarely turned down the opportunity to get into the cockpit.

Besides, it had been a good night followed by a good morning.

I'd woke this morning to the sight of Brianna wearing my white button-down shirt. It was about five times too big for her, but was sexy as hell.

"You have a message," she'd said. "I think it's Daddy."

She'd known perfectly well that the message from Noah, but it didn't bother me that she knew.

"I guess you're gonna need your shirt back," she'd said as she started to unbutton it.

I'd tossed my phone aside and pulled her to me.

Just remembering how sexy she was wearing my shirt and how even sexier it was to get her out of it, made me hard.

"Mr. Fleming?"

I turned. One of the technicians was rushing toward me.

"The flight is going to be delayed."

"Something wrong with the plane?" I asked.

The technician shook his head. "Nah. A thunderstorm in Dallas."

"Right," I said. I'd seen the storm on the radar, but my calculations, I could go around it. "I'll just wait inside."

As I walked across the tarmac, my phone buzzed.

It was Eric.

"Hey," I said. "Sorry to call you last night."

"No worries," Eric said. "I have some information for you."

"Good," I said. I was hoping we could put this whole thing with Gabe to rest so we could get on with living our lives.

"It's not what I expected," Eric said. "Probably broke some rules getting this information."

I had no doubt about that.

Even the Houston police weren't willing to look into it for Brianna. And they knew who her father was.

As he talked, I stopped and stood right there on the tarmac.

This wasn't what I expected either.

Not at all.

I pressed my fingers against my forehead

"Thanks, Eric," I said. "This goes above and beyond what you had to do."

"Hey," he said. "It's what buddies do. We take of our own."

After we said goodbye, I turned to the technician.

"How long is the delay?" I asked.

"An hour maybe."

"I need to make it longer. There's something I have to take care of."

Noah could fire me if he wanted to, but this wasn't for me.

This was for Noah's daughter.

And the woman I was going to marry.

We take care of our own.

I couldn't have said it better.

87

BRIANNA

The next morning I sat in my office, flipping through the video footage I'd taken from Ainsley's wedding dress shopping day.

Unlike before, I was now aware of so many little things. Like in one of the better clips of Ainsley stepping out of the limo, a lovely silver bag over her arm, there was a view of the Skye Travels logo splashed across the tail of the airplane.

There was a time when I would have seen that as good advertising for Skye Travels.

But now I saw it as an identifier. Ainsley was also wearing her Skye Travels uniform.

Skye Travels on the cap. Skye Travels on her shirt.

I absolutely hated that this was now the lens through which I worked.

Any identifying information had to be left out of my videos.

Officer Brandt had said it. Momma had said it.

And I knew it.

Gabe, though he had suddenly disappeared, knew it.

He may have disappeared, but I had screenshots of his

posts. And his IP. Houston police may not want to do anything with the IP address, but I had it.

His latest post was burned into my mind.

Can I buy you a coffee? Let me know.

That meant so many things to me.

It confirmed that Gabe lived in my building.

It also confirmed that Gabe was getting bold.

To publicly ask me for coffee like that was either incredibly bold or incredibly stupid or both.

Bold or stupid, it struck fear in my heart.

The only other time I'd had fear like this was when Daddy was diagnosed with cancer. That had been worse in many ways because it was someone I loved.

This was worse in that I felt not only helpless, but violated.

I was actually wondering if I should be the one looking for another place to live.

But I loved my condo and I was determined not to let someone run me off like this.

Unable to focus on work, I closed my computer and stood up to stretch.

It was a beautiful day outside. Wispy white clouds swirled across the blue sky like the foam on the top of a cappuccino.

According to my phone, it was 72 degrees outside and sunny. Perfect weather.

I went into my closet and put on my running shoes. I wasn't going running, but they would do for walking.

I put my shades on top of my head and headed toward the elevator.

It was a good time for a walk. Get some fresh air and clear my head.

When I got on the elevator, it stopped on the twenty-fifth floor. My heart pounding in my throat, I quickly pulled my shades down over my eyes.

The same man who'd ridden down from this floor a couple of days ago stepped into the elevator.

"Heading out?" he asked as the elevator doors closed.

I nodded and made some unintelligible sound.

"It's a beautiful day outside."

I kept my eyes pinned on the numbers above the door as they slowly ticked downward and wondered if gripping my phone too tight could break it.

The elevator stopped on the fifth floor and a young lady with a little solid white puppy in her arms stepped inside.

"Morning," the man said to her.

"Good morning," the girl said brightly.

I was screaming in my head. *No. Don't talk to him.*

"What kind of dog is that?" the man asked.

"He's a miniature American Eskimo dog."

"Cute," the man said, reaching over to scratch the dog's ears. "What's his name?"

"Snowball," the girl said with a shrug.

"An apt name." The man put his hands in his pockets. "My wife and I had a husky for eighteen years. Her name was Frosty." He stared into space. "We had a painting done of her and it hangs in on living room wall."

Alarms bells were going off in my head at a deafening rate.

This was like a bad movie playing out in my head.

I could see the whole thing unfolding right before my eyes.

The man had connected with the young lady. They both had white dogs. Hers was named Snowball and his was named Frosty.

He would invite her to his apartment—where he lived alone —no wife—under the guise of showing her the painting of his dog, Frosty.

Then he would rape her and kill her. The girl would never be seen again.

The elevator dinged and the doors slid open.

The man held the door for the girl to step through, then glanced over at me.

I shook my head, ever so slightly, and held my ground.

The man shrugged and stepped out of the elevator, leaving me there.

I followed.

The young lady went toward the door to the dog park.

The man went to the mailboxes. The same place he'd gone before.

I went to the front desk.

"Hi Melvin," I said to the concierge. "Can I just hang out here for a minute?"

"Miss Worthington," Melvin said. "You can hang out here all day if you have a mind to."

I rested my chin on my hands and watched the man as he checked his mail.

If I was a good sleuth, which I'd never had an inclination to be, I would have checked out his box number. I already knew he lived on the twenty-fifth floor.

"Melvin," I said, keeping my eyes on the man. "Do you know who that man is?"

Melvin glanced up from his keyboard. Followed my gaze.

"Oh yeah," Melvin said. "That's Judge Kronbach. He's a good guy. Lonely, though, since he retired last month."

"Oh."

"His wife runs a business out of their home, so she probably doesn't have much time for him. Poor guy."

I wasn't sure if I was disappointed that my sleuthing instincts were a mile off or if I was just relieved. Whatever it was, my knees went weak.

"Just curious," I said. "He said something about losing his dog."

"A husky named Frosty. A bit before your time. Everyone loved that dog."

Damn.

"Alright, Melvin," I said. "I think I'm gonna go take a walk."

"Sure thing," Melvin said with a smile. "It's a beautiful day."

My thoughts exactly.

It was a beautiful day. And I was a mess.

88

JACKSON

Brianna didn't answer her text messages. So naturally I couldn't get up the elevator.

It was a great security measure. But it was terribly inconvenient for the guy who wanted to see her and couldn't get to her door.

I paced around the lobby for a bit, glaring at my phone.

I even went old-school and rang her number.

I had to confess that I was getting worried.

Not that I had anything to worry about. But it wasn't like her to vanish like this.

Maybe she was working. Maybe she had her headphones on.

She wasn't mad at me. We'd had a good morning and had parted ways after a thoroughly good kissing.

I paced back through the lobby and stopped near the concierge desk.

Melvin was sitting there, watching me surreptitiously.

It was ironic that I knew all the concierges, but I couldn't get up the elevator to my girlfriend's condo.

Melvin caught me looking at him and smiled.

"Good morning, Mr. Fleming."

"Good morning," I said, shoving my hands in my pockets. I knew the rules. And I knew the rules were there to keep Brianna safe.

But what if the very rules that were there to protect her were preventing me from keeping her safe?

I stepped up to the counter.

"I know you can't tell me," I said, scrubbing a hand over my chin. "But have you seen Brianna this morning? She isn't answering her phone."

Melvin was a consummate professional. I had to give him that.

"Did you have an appointment?" he asked, tapping on his screen.

Was there a list of people he was allowed to let up to her condo?

Was I on it?

"No," I said. "I just needed to tell her something. And she isn't answering her phone."

"Doesn't sound like her," Melvin said.

"No," I said, relieved that Melvin understood my concern.

"Did you contact her family?" he asked.

"No," I said, taking out my phone and scrolling until I found Noah's number. I didn't have anybody else's numbers. Not Madison's. Not Ainsley's.

"I don't want to alarm her father."

"No. Wouldn't want to falsely alarm anyone. Especially not Noah Worthington." Melvin widened his eyes with a little shake of the head.

If I hadn't been so worried about Brianna, I would have laughed. Melvin obviously knew Noah.

Melvin pushed back in his chair and looked past me, outside to where the valets were helping a middle-aged woman out of her car.

"It's a beautiful day," Melvin said. "If I were an energetic young lady, I'd consider taking a walk down to the little park." He nodded his head to the left.

I looked at him blankly for a moment.

Then it occurred to me what he was saying. He was saying that Brianna had gone for a walk.

"Right," I said. "I think I'll do the same."

Before he could say anything else, I took off out the door and headed around to the sidewalk that led to the park.

89

BRIANNA

A butterfly fluttered from one pale yellow daisy to another.

I sat on a wooden bench in the little park that was only five minutes from my condo.

There were flowers everywhere. It reminded me of my grandmother's house over in Alabama. She'd always had a yard full of flowers. All colors scattered about, no rhyme or reason.

The weather was perfect. The sun was warm on the top of my head and a light breeze brushed lightly against my skin.

From where I was sitting, I could see the rooftop of my building off to my right and I had a good view of the three-story Gray House apartment complex in front of me.

Jackson was right. The Gray House was a good choice for him.

The only problem was I saw a better option.

My place.

In spite of this problem with Gabe, I didn't want to move.

I had a bird's eye view of the Thanksgiving Day fireworks on the west and the Christmas Day fireworks on the east.

I could see in all directions.

It was perfect.

I didn't want to ever give it up.

But I also didn't want to give up Jackson.

He was perfect for me.

What was the point in him moving into another apartment when we were going to spend all our time at my place anyway?

My sister, Madison had lived together in Denver with her husband before they got married. Ainsley and Wyatt lived together now.

My parents hadn't said a word about it.

So living with Jackson wouldn't be breaking any kind of rules, stated or otherwise.

But Jackson seemed determined to get his own place.

Maybe he didn't want to live with me. I didn't even know if he saw us being in a long-term relationship. It was probably too soon for him to know.

It should probably be too soon for me to tell.

I had no choice, as far as I could see.

I had to let him move into the Gray House. Let him come around at his own pace.

It was risky to rush him.

Besides, it was possible I was wrong.

I could be the one coming to my senses by the time his lease was up.

A movement off to my left caught my attention.

I looked up and saw Jackson standing there. Watching me with a little smile.

My heart did a little flip backwards.

I wasn't wrong.

Jackson was the man for me. The only man.

But what was he doing here?

He was supposed to be on his way to Dallas.

I stood up and he closed the distance between us, wrapping his arms around me.

We just stood that way for however long it was. The little butterflies fluttering around us.

90

JACKSON

I wasn't much of a fighter, but I could hold my own.

If there was any chance Eric was wrong, I was ready to tear this whole town apart.

But, fortunately, I didn't have to. Brianna had been sitting calmly in the park, butterflies fluttering around her.

She was stunningly beautiful.

"Where's your phone?" I asked.

She patted her jeans. "I guess I left it at home."

And a bit scatterbrained at times.

I laughed, letting the tension drain out of me.

"Come here," I said, taking her hand and pulling her toward the bench. "I have something to tell you."

"Okay. What is it?"

She sat beside me, searched my eyes.

"I heard from my buddy in Denver. He went around some red tape… probably broke a few rules… and looked into that IP address you gave me."

"And?"

I laced my fingers with hers. The Gray House was in front

of us. Her high rise building off to our right. This should have felt perfect. But it didn't.

"I think it's actually good news," I said. I'd have to think about this housing thing later.

"Are you going to tell me?" she asked, tapping on my fingers.

"The IP address belongs to a woman who lives in your building."

"A woman? That is not what I expected." She looked up, her gaze following a bird as it landed on a tree limb.

"Her name is Maria Gabriella Sinclair."

"Maria Gabriella?" Brianna looked at me with disbelief.

"Yeah. Looks like your admirer is a woman."

She dropped her head onto my shoulder.

"Oh my God. I thought I had a psycho stalker."

"I don't think so."

She looked up at me again. "Are you sure? You trust your guy?"

"With my life and those I love."

She smiled a slow smile.

"Then I guess I don't have to worry," she said, laying her head back on my shoulder.

"No," I said. "I guess you don't."

And she didn't have to worry. Because if anything happened to Brianna, I would tear this city apart, piece by piece.

There was nothing more important to me than family.

"Hey," I said. "I was wondering—"

My phone chimed.

It was Noah.

NOAH: *Where are you?*

Noah didn't actually care where I was. He just cared where I wasn't.

ME: *Storm in Dallas. Flight was delayed.*

I stared at my phone. Waiting for Noah's next message. He never contacted me unless he had a reason.

NOAH: *Come to the office while you wait. Want to talk to you about something.*

ME: *On my way.*

"My love," I said. "your father summons."

She sighed. "Then you have to go."

Maybe that was a weird benefit of working for the girl's daddy.

She understood.

91

BRIANNA

I felt even less like working than I had before I'd headed out for my walk.

Somehow Jackson had found me.

I slowly walked backed toward my building. On a whim, I stopped at the little gelato shop and bought a hot chocolate. It was a weirdly perfect mixture of hot and cold.

There weren't a lot of people out this time of day. It was a refreshing reminder of the benefits of being an entrepreneur. I didn't have to punch a clock or work on someone else's timeline.

If I wanted to take a walk in the park and get a hot chocolate in the middle of the day, I could do just that.

So Gabe was Gabriella.

Not a stalker at all, but a fan.

I wish I had some way to contact her, but she'd deleted her messages. Maybe me calling the police had frightened her away.

I hated that. I hated that I had assumed the worst.

I'd learned a couple of valuable lessons though. I'd learned to be careful with my not giving away details that could give away my actual location.

And, it was odd because I'd never been mistrustful of others.

Maybe it was just a reminder that I was human.

Jackson had really gone above and beyond to find out who Gabe was. He'd probably even put his friend in a compromised position.

And… I smiled to myself. He'd called me *my love*.

I'd fallen hook, line, and sinker for Jackson.

By the time I got back to my condo, I'd finished my hot chocolate.

My cell phone was right there on my desk where I'd left it.

I had two messages. Both from Ainsley.

AINSLEY: *Are you busy?*

AINSLEY: *Can you meet for a drink tonight?*

The messages had come in an hour ago.

ME: *Sure. Everything ok?*

Ainsley must not be flying today because she wrote right back.

AINSLEY: *All good. Just wanted to talk.*

ME: *Skyhouse?*

AINSLEY: *I'll be there at 5:00*

Five o'clock then.

Ainsley kept herself busy. Meeting out of the blue for a drink wasn't in her nature.

I sighed. Something else to worry about. Probably something to do with her wedding.

It was clear I wasn't going to get any work done today.

So I picked out some clothes to wear tonight and turned on the water for a bath.

I hummed to myself as I stepped into the hot water.

It was a relief that I didn't have to worry any more about Gabe.

I felt bad that Gabriella had decided to pull her messages, but it was for the best.

And I wasn't going to worry about Jackson.

I was just going to enjoy the moment.

Live in the moment. Words my grandmother had taught me when I was a girl.

Words to live by.

Today is all we have. Don't wish away today for a tomorrow that may never come.

92

JACKSON

When I walked into Noah's office. He was pacing. I'd never Noah pace before.

As a grandfather, he still made a fine figure of a man. Could be on the cover of a men's magazine. Handsome. Successful.

Five children with his current wife Savannah and another daughter with his first wife.

He had quite a legacy to leave them.

So far his daughters had married well. Ainsley, in particular, was marrying an entrepreneur, a billionaire in his own right.

Noah would expect no less for Brianna. I had my own business, but my scale was small potatoes compared to Skye Travels. And even that I'd given up to come to work for Noah. As merely a pilot. Bottom of the totem pole.

"Have a seat," he said.

I sat down in one of the chairs in front of his desk.

"Mine?" I asked, indicating the bottle of water sitting on the table between the two chairs.

He nodded and brought his own bottle of water with him to sit in the other chair.

"Sorry about the flight," I said. "The tech said Dallas wasn't letting anyone land, so I used the time to take care of something."

Noah waved a hand in dismissal.

"I'm not concerned about that," he said.

That told me that he was concerned about something. Just not the flight that I hadn't completed today.

"Something wrong?" I asked.

I thought back over the past two weeks. I couldn't think of anything other than today's flight that he might have an issue with.

If this was about Brianna, then… I straightened. If it was about Brianna, then I'd just have to tell him that my intentions were honorable.

There was no way to know how he'd take the news that I planned to marry his daughter.

I'd hoped to wait awhile. Date longer than just two weeks.

I needed to introduce her to my sister.

Noah interrupted my thoughts.

"I need your help with something."

"Name it," I said, twisting the top off the water bottle.

"As you know, I have offices scattered in various places around the country."

"Yes, sir." Mackinac Island for one. A place I planned to take Brianna one day.

"What you may not know is that, with the exception of this one in Houston, I started them all so as to keep good pilots where they wanted to live."

"I'd heard rumor, yes," I said.

"Same thing with the one in Denver," he said.

I had a sinking feeling in the pit of my stomach. Denver. This was what I'd been worried about since the first day Noah had summoned me into his office.

"You have Kade Johnson up there," I said. Kade was Madison's husband and they seemed to have established a good life for themselves up there. But things changed. With Madison expected a baby, they might be thinking about moving closer to home.

"That's right," Noah said. "I'd planned on Kade taking over running the office, but with the baby on the way, he wants to take a step back. Not forward."

"So you don't have anyone to run the office," I said, hoping the resignation wasn't evident in my voice.

"No," Noah said. "And damned if business isn't booming up there." He grinned. "A lot of it is probably because you left."

"Probably." I finished off the bottle of water.

For a day that had started off so well, this day was just going downhill fast.

"I know you just moved here," Noah said. "But…"

"You want me to move back," I said. I'd known this was going to happen. I'd known it in my gut.

"I can make it worth your while," Noah said. "Make up for the inconvenience."

I took a deep breath. Blew it out.

There was no way Noah could make up for the disruption he was causing in my life.

Or… maybe this was his backhanded way of telling me I wasn't good enough for his daughter.

If I moved back to Denver, took the promotion, maybe I'd be on my way to becoming good enough for Brianna.

Or maybe he was just getting me as far away from her as possible.

And Denver would do it. I'd heard Brianna say she wasn't moving from here. She was Houstonian through and through.

I watched Noah out of the corner of my eye. Why couldn't he just tell me straight? Or was I supposed to just get it?

At any rate, he was getting me out of his daughter's life once and for all.

Maybe that was the real reason I'd dragged my feet on

taking out a lease on my own apartment. I'd been waiting for the other shoe to drop.

I couldn't fight Noah Worthington.

If he wanted me out of Houston, even under the guise of running the Denver office, then I had no choice.

Either that or I could leave Skye Travels and go back to working for myself.

Noah had put me in a difficult spot.

93

BRIANNA

The Skyhouse Bar and Restaurant was busy tonight.

Ainsley was there when I got there, in her favorite booth in the back.

She was drinking a mimosa, looking at her phone.

I slid into the seat across from her.

"So where is Wyatt?" I asked.

"He had to fly up to Colorado," Ainsley said.

"And you're here… why?"

Ainsley shook her head. I have a flight in the morning.

"A seeing eye dog?"

"Yes." Ainsley smiled.

Ainsley had become the go-to pilot for transporting seeing eye dogs. It had evolved on accident, but now she was the one who always took those flights.

I'd heard her say that she liked flying animals more than she liked flying people. Animals didn't expect inane conversation.

"They're really busy today," I said, looking around for a server to bring me a drink.

"It's Friday," she said.

"Oh, right." I'd forgotten that it was the weekend. The days just blurred together and I didn't even keep up with the days of the week. The only thing that kept me somewhat focused was my production schedule.

Not seeing an available server, I reached across the table and slid Ainsley's mimosa toward me.

Her eyes widened and she reached to stop me, but it was too late.

I took a sip.

This was not champagne.

Ainsley was drinking ginger ale.

Holding the glass in front of me, I met Ainsley's troubled gaze.

"Ainsley?" I said.

She sat back against the booth.

"That's what I wanted to tell you," she said.

I slowly set down the glass and slid it back over to her.

"You're pregnant?" I asked, belatedly hoping she didn't mistake my surprise for judgment.

She nodded. "I just found out. I haven't even told Wyatt yet."

I fought to keep my jaw from dropping.

"You have to tell him," I said.

"I know," she said. "I'll tell him tomorrow night. But…" She looked at me, her eyes brimming with unshed tears.

"Ainsley," I said, reaching over to put a hand over hers. "It's okay."

"I know," she said, wiping her eyes. "It's just. We were planning to get married on Mackinac Island. And I have my dress."

She looked up at me. "What if I can't get into my dress?"

Putting a hand over my mouth, I looked at her.

"Is this about the dress?" I asked.

"It's the perfect dress," Ainsley said, tapping a finger against her glass.

"Ainsley," I said, a bubble of laughter spilling from my lips.

Ainsley, my sister who'd never cared anything about fashion was having a meltdown, not because she was unexpectedly pregnant, but because she might not be able to fit into her wedding dress.

Ainsley looked blanked at me.

"You're gonna have a baby," I said.

Ainsley smiled. Then she started laughing. Seconds later, we were both laughing like schoolgirls.

The server came to our table and looked at us with a raised brow.

I wiped my eyes and tried to order with a straight face.

"One cosmopolitan with olives coming up." He looked at Ainsley. "Want another?"

She shook her head. "No. I'm good."

As the server walked off, Ainsley sobered.

"But seriously? What am I supposed to do?"

"It's easy," I said. "Make the reservations and tell the fam. Trust me. We'll all find a way to get there."

She took another deep breath.

"You're right," she said, but she still looked skeptical.

"Don't worry, Ainsley," I said. "I'll help you."

"You have your own things to do," she said, but I was shaking my head.

"I'm not *that* busy," I said. "I work from home, remember?"

Ainsley rolled her eyes. "I know how you feel about that."

"But this is different," I said. "this is my sister's wedding."

Ainsley ran her hands along the edge of the table.

"How are you?" she asked. "What's going on with you and Jackson?"

"We're okay," I said with a shrug. "It's too soon to know."

Ainsley was looking at me sideways.

Then she nodded, with a little knowing smile.

Ainsley knew that I liked Jackson. A lot.

And she knew that I thought we might have something.
I just wasn't ready to talk about it yet.

94

JACKSON

Brianna had a bottle of champagne chilling when I got to her condo later that evening.

"What's the occasion?" I asked, following her into the kitchen and taking the corkscrew she put in my hand.

"Sometimes there doesn't have to be an occasion," she said. "sometimes we can just celebrate the moment."

Had Noah talked to her about transferring me to Denver?

She was acting a bit unusual.

She was dressed in a cute sundress with a short sweater over it. Her hair was smooth and straight. Like she'd been to the salon.

I poured champagne into the two glasses and after handing her one, picked up the other.

"To everyday moments," I said, holding up my glass in a toast.

She tipped her glass against mine and we both tasted the smooth bubbly champagne. I didn't normally drink champagne, but this was some of the best.

"Can we go out on the balcony? I need to talk to you about something," I asked, watching the bubbles in my glass.

"We need to talk," she said, with a little smile that did little to hide the hitch in her breath. "The most dreaded words in any relationship."

Relationship.

"Not like that," I said.

Rolling her eyes at me, she turned and swept toward the balcony.

The wind was light and the sun was warm. I spent hours most days in the air, but this view never got old.

She propped a hand on the railing and looked at me with big green eyes.

Damn. I was caught in between a rock and a hard place.

I needed to take the vice-president job in Denver to keep Noah happy and to perhaps make myself more worthy of her. But I wanted to stay here in my current position, working as a pilot with Noah, to be with her.

"I met with your father today," I said, leaning against the rail, then changing my mind and leaning against the side of the building instead.

"Oh," she said. "No wonder we need to talk."

"Yeah." I sipped the champagne and watched the strings of cars traveling along 610.

She squinted her eyes as she watched me.

"Well, I know he didn't fire you." She waited a beat. "Did he?"

I laughed. "No. He didn't fire me." Though that might have made things a lot more simple.

"What then?" she asked.

Running a hand through my hair, I looked back at her.

"Apparently with the baby coming, Kade doesn't want to be in charge of the Denver office."

"That doesn't surprise me," she said. "Then what?" Realization crossed her features. "Ohhh. He wants you to do it."

She turned away from me and tipped back her glass.

She hadn't been expecting this. So my conversation with her father wasn't the reason we were having champagne.

Good to know that she hadn't been lying about that.

Brianna truly was the perfect woman.

The seconds ticked past as we stood silently on the balcony. The wind whipped her hair across her face. I wanted to touch her. To hold her, but I didn't know what she was thinking.

Didn't know if she would be receptive.

When she turned, her eyes were bright and she wore an expression of resignation.

95

BRIANNA

A flock of black birds swooped together below us. It was unusual for most people to live above the path of the birds, but I was getting used to it.

It was a myth that it was quiet living in a high rise. I rarely heard neighbors, that much was true, but traffic noises funneled straight up to my condo.

Holding my empty champagne glass in my hands, I turned around and searched Jackson's clear blue eyes. A blue that rivaled the blue of the cloudless sky.

I didn't know what Daddy was doing, but whatever it was, I knew he had to have a reason. Daddy never did anything without a reason.

He wanted Jackson to move back to Denver. It had just been two weeks since he'd asked Jackson to move here. To work for him. To work less than Jackson had been working in Denver.

Maybe Daddy's shit was slipping.

He'd been through a lot and he was getting up in age.

It was a depressing thought and I chose to push it to the back of my mind. I'd talk to Madison about it. She was a psychologist. She'd know. Momma was a psychologist, too, but the last I was going to ask her about was Daddy's level of cognitive function. There would hell to pay if she even knew I was questioning his abilities.

There was only one thing to do.

I had to let him go.

He would want this. It was a good opportunity. A promotion. And he'd still be no more than a flight away. Just like Madison.

Madison whom I rarely saw anymore. If I never saw my own sister, how did I expect to see the man who would be running the Denver office of Skye Travels?

I tried to smile. Hoped the effort looked like the smile it was meant to be.

"You have to go, then," she said.

Jackson didn't respond. No expression. But his eyes seemed hooded.

"Okay," he said, turning to rest his elbows on the balcony railing. He stared into the distance. "Guess it's a good thing I didn't sign a lease."

"I guess so," I said, biting my tongue to keep from questioning my own father's motives and ultimately his competence.

"I should go then," he said, reaching for my hand.

I put my hand in his and he pulled me into a hug.

The wind swirled around us, seeming to wrap us together as one.

But it was an illusion.

There was one thing I'd learned from older sisters.

Long distance relationships never worked.

Jackson shifted and kissed me lightly on the lips.

"I should go pack a bag," he said, his breath soft against my cheek. "Flying up with Noah first thing in the morning."

"Of course," I said, forcing a smile.

I walked him to the door and after I locked it behind him, I went to my reading sofa in front of the window and dropped onto it.

Shards of pain from my broken heart made their way through my body. I put my head on my hands and took in deep ragged breaths.

Jackson hadn't even fought it. Not even a little. Maybe it was what he wanted.

The one thought that surfaced was simple.

Daddy giveth and Daddy took away.

96

JACKSON

We flew out at dawn the next morning. Noah was in the pilot's seat.

The sunrise glinted over the city as we circled around and headed west. It should have been beautiful. Instead, it was just another day and I'd barely slept at all last night.

The coffee I'd swallowed down sat heavy in my stomach and I wore more sunshades even though I didn't need them.

"You hung over?" Noah asked as the wheel came up.

I laughed without humor.

"No," I said. "Just… didn't sleep much." I turned and looked out the window.

Every mile took me that much further away from Brianna and the distance tugged on my heartstrings.

I didn't want to be here.

Today flying was not flying. Today flying was torture.

It was a new experience for me. Being in the air and wanting to be on the ground.

Noah and I hardly said anything to each other on the entire flight.

I'd never traveled with Noah this early, so I didn't know if he was just quiet in the mornings or if he was responding to my lack of interest in conversation.

Maybe taking an office job with infrequent flights was the best thing for me at this point in my life. If I was going to be feeling like this about being in the air, then it was time.

We sat in silence as we waited for the plane to be secured. Noah took off his headset and looked at me.

"We'll meet with the building manager first," he said.

"Okay," I said, watching a black SUV driving toward us. The vehicle that would be taking me to my new job.

The rest of the morning was much of the same. I went through the motions, but I felt like I was a robot, responding to comments, not adding anything unsolicited.

As we walked through the private terminal, heading out to lunch, I passed one of my buddies. Christopher.

I didn't even notice him until he called my name. I'd been too lost in my head, hiding behind my sunshades.

He clapped me on the shoulder.

"How have you been?" he asked.

I turned to Noah and some guy whose name I couldn't even remember.

"I'll catch up," I said. "I'll just be a minute."

They walked off, talking low to themselves.

I removed my shades and walked with Christopher over to a window overlooking the tarmac.

"You look like you've been rode hard and put up wet," Christopher said. "What's happened? Last I heard, you'd gone to work for Skye Travels."

Christopher looked toward Noah's retreating figure.

"Was that Noah Worthington?" he asked.

"Yeah," I said. "That's him."

"What are you two doing up here?" Christopher adjusted his tie and propped a foot on the bench.

"He wants me to run the office up here."

"That's great news," Christopher said. "Congratulations."

"Thank you."

"It'll be good for you," Christopher said. "You've been working too hard."

I nodded.

"Well," Christopher said. "Got a flight to catch. Be seeing you around. We'll get a drink."

"Sure thing," I said, as Christopher darted off to wherever he was heading.

I sat down on the bench and pulled out my phone.

Everyone said this was a good move for me. Everyone.

I quickly located the video of the Kiss Cam and replayed the whole clip.

Everyone said this was a good move.

Except me.

97

BRIANNA

Two days later

*I*t was the typical Sunday dinner.

The scent of Daddy's favorite pasta sauce filled the kitchen with hints of basil and garlic.

It was typical except that Madison and Kade weren't there. Ainsley and Wyatt were at Mackinac Island, doing some looking around. I was the only one who knew why they were there. Ainsley still hadn't told anyone that she was pregnant.

It had only been three days since she told me, but it seemed like forever ago.

It was cloudy with rain on the horizon, so we were inside.

Quinn was there, deep in conversation with Daddy, in the living room. A football game playing in the background.

Momma and Wynter were in the kitchen. Wynter was telling Momma about her upcoming internship.

Industrial Organizational psychology. Not a clinical

psychologist like Momma and Madison, but still in the same field.

So now there were three of them.

Momma, Madison, and Wynter in psychology. Daddy, Ainsley, and Quinn in aviation. I was the middle child in every possible way.

How had a YouTuber with a love of fashion evolved in the middle of such a family?

I sat on a bar stool, listening to Wynter's animated description of what she was going to do. She was going to be living in Austin for a year. Maybe I should have gone away for a time.

I dipped a broccoli floret in some kind of ranch dip and considered how that could have gone. It was an option, of course. I could do my work anywhere. I wasn't tied to here.

The problem was that here was the only place I wanted to be.

I'd visited Denver. The Rocky Mountains were magnificently lovely and I wouldn't mind the view. Madison's apartment definitely had a stunning view of the mountains.

But Denver wasn't Houston.

Houston was the only place I wanted to be. And I loved my condo. It was perfect for me.

The whole chain of thoughts made me sick to my stomach.

The only reason I was even thinking like this was because of Jackson. Jackson was going to be moving to Denver.

And since long distance relationships didn't work, that was going to be over. Maybe not at first. We could put forth some effort to continue dating, but it would be too much.

Our relationship would die a slow painful death. It was better to just rip off the band-aid.

Give the relationship a quick death. It would hurt like hell for a while, but then the healing could start.

I hadn't been looking for a relationship when I'd found Jackson and I wouldn't be looking for one again.

Picking up my glass, I stopped. Momma and Wynter were both staring at me.

"Are you okay?" Wynter asked.

"Sure," I said, with a shrug and a feeble attempt at a smile.

"Mamma, when do we—" Wynter started, but Momma interrupted her.

"Wynter," she said, thrusted a platter of vegetables in her hands. "Take these to Daddy and Quinn."

Wynter made a face, but took the platter and headed to the living room where Quinn was yelling at the television.

"I told your father to leave Jackson out of this," Momma said.

"What do you mean?" I sat forward, peering at my mother.

"I told him that he should find someone else for the job in Denver. That Jackson was here now. And he should let him be."

"But he didn't," I said. "Why?"

Momma shrugged and stirred the pasta sauce. "You and Jackson."

We hadn't tried to keep our relationship a secret. It had started out about as public as it could with the whole Kiss Cam thing. But I honestly didn't think anyone was paying any attention.

I ran a finger along my empty glass.

"If you knew," I said, slowly. "and you told Daddy." I looked at Momma with moist eyes. "Why did he do it?"

"I don't know why Daddy does what he does," she said.

My chin trembled as I looked at her.

"Come here," Momma said, wrapping me in a hug. I always felt safe when Momma was there. She knew how to hug. How to make someone feel loved.

I tried not to cry. I really did. But the tears started and once they did, I couldn't stop them.

My tears were soaking Momma's sweater, but I knew she didn't care.

As the television muted in the background, I took a deep breath. My crying was spent for the moment, at least.

Momma and I stepped apart and turned. Noah was standing there watching us.

I lowered my gaze and turned to escape to the powder room. I didn't want anyone to see me with puffy eyes and tear streaked cheeks.

I stepped into the powder room off the kitchen and looked at my puffy eyes. After running cool water over a wash cloth I pressed it against my eyes. Good thing I hadn't worn eye makeup today.

I took a minute to pull myself together then stepped back out to the kitchen.

Daddy held two beers and handed one to me.

"What's this?" I asked.

He shrugged. "A no occasion beer with your father." He opened the back door and we stepped out onto the patio. "No football required."

The wind whipped at the clear water of the pool and tousled my hair into my eyes. It was going to storm.

There would be no flights out of Houston tonight.

I took a swallow of beer. God. How long had it been since I drank a beer?

It was funny that the first thing I thought of with bad weather was that flights would be cancelled. There was no getting away from heritage.

"Have a seat," Noah said.

I sat on one of the marble benches next to the pool and he sat beside me.

We sat quietly for a few minutes, drinking in silence.

The beer was surprisingly good. Straight out of a frosty bottle.

"I think I need to apologize to you," Daddy said.

"Why? What did you do?"

He looked so guilty. He reminded me of a little boy who got caught with his hand in the cookie jar.

"First, you should know that I like Jackson."

"Okay," I said. This was a really weird conversation to have with my father.

"I'm going to tell you something and if you ever repeat it to anyone, even… especially… your mother, I'll deny it."

"What is it Daddy?" I asked. "Just tell me. Please."

He sat forward on the bench, adjusted the buttons on the cuff of his long-sleeved white shirt. Even at home, Daddy looked professional.

"So… I tested him."

"You tested him?" I turned and faced my father eye to eye.

Pieces of the puzzle started to slide into place.

"So…" I said. "How did he do?"

98

JACKSON

I paced from end of my hotel room to the other.

Holding my phone out in front of me, I stared at it as though it had done something to me.

It hadn't, of course.

But I needed to make a call. A call I did not want to make.

Maybe I'd just send a text.

I'd been taught that texts were unprofessional, but in today's world everyone used texts. For everything.

It was acceptable now, right?

At least if I texted him I wouldn't have to hear his voice. His disappointment.

I walked out on the balcony, slick with rain. The lull wouldn't last long. I looked over toward Brianna's condo building.

I had been an idiot.

I'd done exactly what I'd said I wasn't going to do anymore.

I'd put work first. And not just a little bit.

I couldn't have been more stupid if I'd just walked into a wall.

I didn't want to move back to Denver. I lived here now. Well, technically I didn't have an address… or a car. But I had mentally moved here.

And I hadn't even discussed it with the girl I wanted to marry. I'd just made assumptions about her.

I'd made assumptions that she'd want a man with a certain kind of job.

I unlocked my phone.

Why the hell not?

ME: *Noah. I'd like to decline the job offer.*

I backspaced. No. That wasn't what I wanted to say.

ME: *Noah. I don't want your job. I want your daughter.*

Nope. Backspacing again.

ME: *I've made a decision.*

There. That seemed okay. It was vague enough while being curious enough.

Before I could change my mind, I hit send.

I held my phone. Stared at it. Waiting.

Then I tossed it onto the bed. Noah was a busy man. He wasn't going to send back an immediate message.

The man had more important things to do.

Although… in my defense, he was going to have to go through the process of hiring someone to run the office in Denver.

That was significant for him.

But not what I needed to be focused on.

What I needed to be focused on was Brianna.

I'd been an idiot and I needed a way to convince her that I was more than just that.

That I was someone who could be her forever man.

I tried to think of something I could do to convince her that I'd stay around. That I wasn't going anywhere.

But I was coming up empty.

My phone chimed.

I dove for the phone. It was an answer from Noah.

"Meet me in my office in an hour?"

I reread the message. It was actually a question from Noah. Not a request, but a question.

I went onto the app and scheduled an Uber to pick me up.

99

BRIANNA

Two Days Later

It was a regular Tuesday morning. I sat in a little outside café just a short walk away from my condo.

A half-empty white coffee mug sat in front of me. Not the paper kind like the other places had, put a real ceramic mug.

Biting the end of my blue ink pen, I stared into the swirl of coffee and creamer.

The sunlight was warm on my back, but the air had a faint chill.

Autumn was my favorite time of year. That was rather unfortunate since Houston rarely had autumn days. Most years we went from scorching hot to less hot then scorching hot again. Two seasons.

I was the only one sitting outside. Everyone else who come to the café hurried inside, waited impatiently for their coffee and muffin or scone, then rushed out. All dressed in their work clothes.

This time of morning, I was usually sitting inside, drinking my morning coffee, planning my day.

But after my conversation with Daddy two days ago, I'd felt strangely disconcerted. And somehow being alone in my condo wasn't helping me sort out the feeling.

So I'd stuffed the paper calendar I'd ordered from Amazon into an oversized handbag and headed out.

At first, I was going to sit downstairs in the lobby, but it was such a pretty day, I'd walked toward the shopping area instead.

I sat with my back toward the Gray House. I didn't even want to think about that right now.

I tested him. Daddy's words play over and over in my head like a bad song.

Don't know yet.

He'd sworn me to secrecy. So I couldn't talk to anyone about this. So I stayed to myself, seeking solace in being around strangers who didn't ask questions.

I opened the calendar to this month and opened my phone calendar, too.

One by one, I began to transfer my schedule, self-imposed as it was, from my phone onto paper.

After just about five minutes, I sat back and smiled to myself.

Momma was right. There was something satisfying about seeing everything written out on the page. It was whole different way of looking at things.

I looked up when a young girl, wearing the black and white outfit of a server, stopped at my table.

"I brought you another coffee," the girl said.

"Oh…" I glanced in my cup, still half full.

"You don't have to pay for it or nothing," the girl said, shyly. "I just thought you might like a fresh cup. Hotter."

I bit my pen again, then realized that it was going to quickly become a habit, and laid it on the calendar.

The girl wasn't a day over nineteen. And she was blushing.

"Thank you," I said.

The girl smiled and set the cup down.

"Can I take this one?" she asked, nodding toward my old cup.

"Of course."

As she reached over to pick up my mug, I caught a glimpse of her name tag.

Gabriella.

Her hands shaking just a little, the girl smiled and turned away.

Something clicked and I went with it.

"Gabriella," I called after the girl.

She stopped and turned around.

"Can I get you something else?"

I pushed back the chair across from me with me foot.

"Come here," I said. "I need to talk to you a moment."

She glanced over her shoulder, but did as I asked.

She was a pretty girl. So young. So innocent.

I smiled in an attempt to set her at ease.

As I sat there, trying to decide how to approach her, she put her hands over her face.

"Please don't be mad at me," she said.

"Why would I be mad?" I asked.

The girl just shook her head.

"Gabriella? Are you Gabe?"

"Yes," she said, lowering her hands. "I admire you so much."

Having a lot of followers had never really translated in my head to being admired by someone. Not like this.

"We're neighbors," I said.

"Yes." Her words came out in a rush. "I wasn't thinking.

Then when Mother said the cops came to your floor, I took everything down. I didn't mean anything by it."

I just nodded. "Gabe?"

"Her middle name. My Mother… her name is Maria Gabriella… saw my posts I'd made with her account and I'm still grounded."

She looked back toward the shop.

"I'm so sorry," she said.

"Gabriella," I said, stretched a hand toward her, then pulling it back. "It's okay. I'm actually honored that you followed me."

My phone chimed and a text message popped up from Ainsley.

AINSLEY: *Can you give me a ride to the airport?*

"Seriously?" I muttered out loud.

"I should go," Gabriella said, taking the opportunity to stand up.

"Right," I said. "We'll talk later." I smiled.

Grinning Gabriella turned and went inside the café.

ME: *Car service?*

AINSLEY: *Nothing available.*

ME: *Why don't you call an Uber?*

AINSLEY: *Please don't make me do that.*

I sat back in my chair, running a hand over my new calendar. I'd been having such a good morning.

ME: Where's your car?

AINSLEY: *Getting serviced.*

I held back my snarky comments. Ainsley was usually much more organized.

With a sigh, I closed my calendar.

ME: *At café. I'll be a few minutes.*

I caught Gabriella's attention and asked for a to-go cup.

AINSLEY: *You're the best.*

I didn't know about that.

But there was one thing that I had figured out during my unplanned soul searching.

Family was everything. And without family we had nothing.

100

———

JACKSON

When they said it takes a village, *they* were undoubtedly talking about the Worthington family.

I'd been nervous as hell to tell Noah that I did not want to run the Skye Travels office in Denver. Not even if it came with the coveted vice-president title. Vice President of Skye Travels nonetheless.

But I'd manned up and done it anyway.

I told him I wanted to stay at Skye Travels. As a pilot. In Houston.

He'd looked at me sideways and, I swear, he grinned.

Looking back, the last two days had been a blur. I'd been sworn to secrecy though, especially when it came to Noah's wife Savannah.

Ainsley, however, quickly jumped into my business.

And that's how I ended up standing here, in my full Skye Travels uniform, pilot's cap and all, on the tarmac in front of one of Noah's planes.

The really odd thing was that I didn't have a flight scheduled, but Ainsley did.

The little plane was prepped and ready for Ainsley to take it… somewhere. Atlanta, I think.

When Brianna's fire-engine red Maserati drove slowly out onto the tarmac coming toward me and the plane, I knew that Noah and Ainsley had pulled off whatever it was they had planned.

I knew just enough to know that I was supposed to be standing right here. Right now.

Noah's words echoed in my head.

I'm giving you a chance to make it right.

I breathed in deep and let it out slowly.

Just tell her.

The car stopped and Ainsley stepped out of the passenger side. Like me, she was dressed in her pilot's uniform.

Walking past me, she clapped me on the shoulder.

"Good luck," she said and walked around the plane, checking the tires.

I slid my hat off my head and walked toward the driver's size of the Maserati.

Brianna rolled down the dark window and slid her sunshades up to the top of her head.

Blinking against the early morning light, she looked at me.

Her gaze darted toward Ainsley, then back to me.

I was as tongue-tied as a teenage boy standing in front of his first crush.

"Are you flying with Ainsley today?" she asked.

"No," I said, feeling a smile spread to my eyes.

She glanced around again.

"Are you just getting back?"

Brianna knew her way around the tarmac, but she was obviously baffled.

"No," I said, again.

She held up her hands and lifted a brow.

"What then?" she asked.

"May I?" Not waiting for an answer, I opened her door and held out a hand.

Still looking at me like I was insane, she put a hand in mine and stepped out of the car.

"I wanted to show you something," I said.

"Okay."

I swept a hand, encompassing the tarmac and the airport.

"This," I said. "This is where I'm going to be working."

She put her hands on her hips.

"What about Denver?"

"Your father is looking for someone else to run the Denver office."

She was looking at me with those green eyes that I loved so much.

"Why?" she asked.

Ainsley came back around the plane and looked at us.

"Brianna," she said.

"He's a pilot," she said.

"So am I," Ainsley said, then turned on her heel to board the plane.

It was an odd interaction that I hadn't anticipated, much less understood, but since I did understand sibling shorthand, it didn't particularly concern me.

"Brianna," I said. "I'm not leaving here. I'm doing exactly what I want to do. I don't want to sit at a desk." I shrugged. "I'm a pilot."

"What are you saying?" she asked.

I held out my arms.

She walked into them and I knew.

Whatever else may be, we'd figure this out.

101

BRIANNA

*H*and in hand, Jackson and I walked back toward the Skye Travels building.

The sun was warm on the top of my head. The wind soft on my skin.

"So… you gave up the chance to go back to Denver and be a vice-president of Skye Travels so you can stay in Houston and just be a pilot."

He looked at me with mock shock.

"What kind of profanity are you saying?" he asked. "There's no such thing as *just a pilot.*"

"Right," I said, grinning at him. "I forgot who I was talking to for a moment."

"Besides," he said, lifting my hand and kissing the backs of my fingers. "Why would I go there when you're here?"

"You're right," I said. "That would make no sense."

We stepped inside the building and stepped into the elevator.

Once the elevator started to move, he pulled me into his arms and kissed me.

I wrapped my arms around him and matched him kiss for kiss.

The elevator dinged and the doors opened.

I was pressed against the back wall and his hands were all in my hair.

I'd never felt to ravished in all my life.

The elevator door closed, but it didn't go anywhere.

A few minutes later, the elevator door opened again.

Someone stepped inside and cleared his throat.

Jackson released me and turned, shielding me from view.

"Hello Jackson," Quinn said. "Hello Brianna."

I stepped out from behind Jackson, the back of my hand against my swollen lips.

"How did you know it was me?"

"You seriously have to ask that?" Quinn asked. "If you only knew all the machinations that have been going on around here the past couple of days to get you two back together."

"Machinations weren't necessary," I said, as Jackson wrapped his arms around me again.

Quinn looked at Jackson. "Well, somebody had to do something."

I looked into Jackson's blue eyes.

"Is he right?" I asked.

Jackson kissed me on the tip of my nose.

"Sometimes I'm a little slow to get things going, but I always end up in the right place," he said. "at the right time."

"And this is the right place at the right time."

"Absolutely," he said.

The elevator door opened and Quinn stepped off.

"I'll be out for the rest of the day," he said over his shoulder. "If you want to use my office."

I frowned at Jackson.

"Use his office for what?"

Jackson pulled me back into his arms.

"I can think of quite a few things we can use his office for."

I smiled as he kissed me again.

Today was turning out to be a really good day.

Life was good.

EPILOGUE

BRIANNA

It was the first time I'd flown with Jackson.

He made a pass over the Grand Hotel as we headed toward the Mackinac Island airport.

It was a beautiful cloudless day and the hotel was surrounded by flowers in fall colors.

The longest porch in the world. A lovely place for a wedding.

Ainsley's wedding had come up quickly. I'd known it would since I helped plan it, but still, it came up faster than I'd anticipated.

Jackson reached over, squeezed my hand, and winked at me.

I smiled. In the three weeks since he'd met me on the tarmac and promised to stay in Houston as long as I wanted to, he'd done nothing to make me doubt him.

He'd been sweet and attentive.

Our routine had picked up where it had left off, but he hadn't said anything else about looking for an apartment.

When I tried to bring it up, he deftly changed the subject.

I didn't know what that was about, but I figured he had

something to work out for himself. He'd let me know when he was ready.

Jackson made a smooth as silk landing and taxied over to park next to the other Skye Travels planes. Three of them. The bold red Skye Travels logo splashed across them.

I felt a sense of pride to be part of this family.

And I was proud of Jackson. Like me, he was doing what he wanted to do.

Every day when he got into an airplane, he was doing the thing that he liked most to do.

Just as I was doing what I like to do when I was making You Tube videos.

As far as I could see, we were both happy doing what we liked to do and we were happy together.

Since there were no cars on Mackinac Island, there was a horse and carriage waiting for us.

"Welcome to Mackinac Island," the driver said after we were settled. Another driver would be along to get our luggage.

Jackson wrapped an arm around me and held me close as we traveled along the cobbled road toward the hotel.

"Would you mind driving us through town before dropping us off at the hotel?" Jackson asked.

"Not a problem," the driver said. "More than happy to oblige."

I looked sideways over at Jackson. We were already the last ones to arrive.

He just smiled and kissed me on the cheek.

A flock of birds fluttered from one tree decked out with leaves of golds and reds, made a loop through the air and landed on another tree, also decked out in colorful leaves.

We passed a few cottages where the people of Mackinac lived year round.

One had a clothes line in the back yard with white sheets pinned to it.

It was quaint. And I liked it.

The clip-clop of the horses lulled me into contentment. That and being snuggled up next to Jackson. He smelled like a heady combination of engine fuel, vanilla, and something that reminded me of a spruce tree.

We were on our way to Ainsley's wedding, but I was so head over heels in love with Jackson, I couldn't even give sufficient thought to my sister getting married.

As we reached downtown, the sun was starting to set, splashing the sky with pinks and yellows. A pink sunset.

The driver slowed the buggy as we reached the center of town to allow the tourists to flow safely around us.

Then we stopped right there in the middle of town. Buildings on one side, the lake on the other.

"Look," Jackson said, nudging me off his shoulder.

I straightened and looked around.

First I saw Daddy standing there with Momma at his side. Ainsley and Wyatt were there. Madison and Kade. My sister Brianna and my brother Quinn.

"Did we miss the wedding or something?" I asked, trying to make sense of why my entire family would be standing there like they were waiting for us.

"I don't think so," Jackson said.

He removed his arm from around me and slid to his knees.

"What are you doing?" I asked, swallowing a bubble of laughter born of confusion.

"Brianna," he said. "Our first kiss was in front of God and everybody, so I thought your family should be here."

He glanced over his shoulder.

"And anyone else who happens to be around."

We were getting some curious looks from the tourists walking around us.

A woman smiled at me as she passed.

My brow creased, I looked back to Jackson.

"Brianna," he said.

My breath hitched. There was something in his expression.

My gaze flicked toward my family, then back to Jackson.

"It's Ainsley's wedding tomorrow," I said.

Jackson just grinned.

"It was her idea."

I looked over at Ainsley. She grinned and tilted her face up to kiss Wyatt.

Jackson tugged on my hands to get my attention.

"But…"

Quinn stepped up to the buggy and handed Jackson his iPad.

"Show her this," he said.

Jackson held up the iPad.

"What?" I asked.

"Look," he said, pointing to the image on the iPad.

I squinted at the image.

Then looked up again.

It was us. We were on a webcam.

Right here. Right now.

I didn't know what to say. An image of us on the Kiss Cam flashed through my mind.

"Brianna," he said, setting the iPad aside and taking my hands.

I put my hands over my lips, my eyes wide.

"Will you marry me?"

It seemed like the world stopped. It turned upside down.

Then it settled back into place again. Only now it was even more right than it had been before.

Everything was perfectly in place.

"Yes!" I said, throwing my arms around him and kissing him right on the mouth.

Somewhere in the back of my mind, I heard people clapping. Cheering. My family. Strangers.

It was like the kiss cam kiss all over again.

Only this time it was the webcam kiss.

It suited me just fine.

I wanted the world to know that this was the man I was going to marry.

Are you ready for another Skye Travels romance? Turn the page for a preview of Three Broken Rules...

PREVIEW THREE BROKEN RULES
CHAPTER 1

Wynter Worthington

I slid my reading glasses off my nose to the top of my head and looked out the little oval window of the Lear jet taking me home.

As I took the air pods out of my ears, one, then the other, the familiar roar of the jet replaced the soft background music I'd been listening to.

My job took me all over the country. But each and every time I returned to Houston, I got butterflies in my stomach.

They were good butterflies, usually.

Born and bred in Houston, no matter where I traveled, Houston had my heart. It was home.

It was a warm cloudless May morning and even though the plane wasn't even on the ground yet, the air felt different than up north. Softer.

It made no sense, but when I could see the tops of the trees, I felt like I was practically on the ground.

I wasn't a nervous flyer, but only because I couldn't afford to be.

I was the youngest of the four daughters of Noah and Savannah Worthington.

THE Noah Worthington of Skye Travels.

I had earlier memories of flying in airplanes than I did of riding in automobiles.

But that was just the way the mind worked.

Memories were a funny thing.

Not always accurate, but quite powerful.

It didn't take much to send me down a rabbit hole when it came to thinking about thinking.

I'd done my dissertation on metacognition. And it had paid off enormously. I was one of the most sought after consultants in my field—industrial/organizational psychology.

I gathered up my wire-bound notebook and pencil and shoved them into my leather bookbag.

I liked to use the quiet flying time to brainstorm or just to think.

Momma would call it meditation. And it was. When I wanted to get technical, I called flying a positive addiction.

All the pilots in my family agreed with me. And we certainly had enough of them. Pilots in the family. Five to be exact.

That was a lot of pilots in one family.

I had nothing against pilots, specifically. But I had a lot of insights into their way of life. And I'd argue with anyone who said their way of life wasn't different.

And, yes, I would admit that my daddy was an exception. And my sister, Ainsley. Probably. She was older than me, though, and I couldn't say what she'd done before she met her husband, Wyatt.

And, Momma was Daddy's second wife. So for all I knew, Daddy had gone through a cad stage, too.

As much as I loved Daddy, it didn't change my opinion of the pilot lifestyle.

"Prepare for landing," Jackson said over the speaker.

Jackson was my sister Brianna's fiancé. A good pilot. More often than not, Daddy assigned him to my flight, either Jackson or Daddy flew me himself.

Personally, I didn't make any specific requests about pilots. I knew that as long as I was flying with Skye Travels, I was in good hands.

Daddy only hired the best in the field.

If something was going to happen on a flight, it was just going to happen.

I checked my seatbelt. I hadn't even bothered to unhook it on the flight from Chicago to Houston.

The airplane rocked gently as we passed over the top of the suburban mall just before Jackson took it in for a smooth, as always, landing.

It wasn't that there was anything wrong with pilots.

I liked them just fine.

It was their lifestyle. The uniform. The glamour of travel. The mystique.

As we taxied along the runway, I saw that my car was already there. Ready to take me to my parents' house.

Sure. It was uncommon for a twenty-five-year-old professional to live with her parents, but it saved me tons of money.

I'd commuted to the University of Houston and now I spent probably seventy-five percent of my time on the road.

It would make no sense to pay for a place of my own when I was never there.

As I waited for Jackson to secure the plane, I stared out the window.

The red Skye Travels logo was emblazoned across the building's new glass door.

The driver of my car came through that door and walked outside onto the tarmac.

I hadn't seen this driver before, but although I knew most of the drivers, I didn't know all of them. I didn't know all the pilots either for that matter.

The driver was wearing black pants and a solid white button-down shirt with a solid black tie. No jacket and no cap.

He had short dark hair and, even though he wore black sunshades, I could see that he wasn't a day over thirty.

His walk caught my attention. He actually walked with the familiar swagger of a pilot.

Stopping at the car, the usual black SUV, he looked in my direction.

My heart did a little flip and I noted a strong physical attraction to him. Stronger than usual.

I looked away. Checked my phone messages.

As a frequent traveler myself, I didn't date in my own back yard.

Perhaps being a frequent traveler myself was the very reason I knew so much about their lifestyle.

I lived it myself.

So that was how I came around to my first rule of dating.

Never crush on a pilot.

Cooper Abrams

IT WAS one of those clear, cloudless Texas mornings that smelled hot. It may be just the end of May, but I'd lived in Houston long enough to know that it didn't matter.

It was full on summer.

I'd left my jacket inside the office in the private terminal and as I stood with the sun beating down on the top of my head, I decided to hell with it and rolled up my shirt sleeves.

It was my first day on the job and my task for the day was to pick up the boss's daughter from someone else's flight and drive her home.

So much for thinking that I was going to start off this job doing what I loved most.

Flying.

I'd watched the pilot of the Lear jet make a smooth as silk landing then taxi over to the private terminal of Skye Travels.

Breathing in the heady scent of jet fuel, I stood next to the shiny black sedan.

The driver was in the restroom upstairs puking his guts out.

I was only in this situation because I'd had compassion for the guy.

The receptionist had been right in the middle of ordering my uniforms when we'd heard the guy in the bathroom. And, of course, I'd volunteered to check on him.

The poor guy had been distraught that he wouldn't be there to pick up someone named Wynter.

I'd done my homework on Skye Travels and in the process I'd learned that about half of the Worthington family was involved in this particular aviation business, many of them pilots.

It didn't bother me. I knew it was a family run business. That's how it worked.

What did bother me was that somehow I'd missed knowing that there was a fourth daughter named Wynter.

Apparently, she somehow managed to keep a low profile.

I adjusted my tie as the pilot opened the door. I was a hair's breath away from loosening my tie. Since I wasn't flying, there didn't seem to be much point in wearing the tie while I stood out in the heat.

But before I could loosen my tie, a young lady stepped out of the plane. She was a thousand times different from what I was expecting, though if someone had asked me what I was expecting, I wouldn't have had an answer for them.

I wasn't sure if I'd been expecting a hot party girl or a younger version of Mrs. Worthington—pretty, but serious. Part of that expectation came from the driver's obvious loyalty.

This girl was neither of those.

She was dressed all in black. A black pencil skirt and a matching short jacket over a black blouse.

Before going down the steps in her black high heels, she pulled a pair of black sunshades out of her bag and put them over her eyes.

Damn. I'd gotten no more than a glimpse, but from that simple glimpse, I saw that she was stunningly beautiful.

I'd seen pictures of her sisters and had been impressed by how pretty they all were. Noah's wife, too.

But even that didn't prepare me for this petite elfin girl with straight shoulder-length hair.

I usually went for the girls with long hair, so it was especially surprising that I felt that immediate gut kick of attraction to someone who wasn't my usual type.

The warm Texas wind blew her hair into her face and she pushed it impatiently away before putting one hand on the rail and starting to make her way down the steps.

She moved with a combination of caution and grace.

It occurred to me that this might not even be Wynter.

But when the pilot followed her down the steps, I knew it had to be her.

"I'll get your bags," the pilot said.

"Thank you, Jackson," she said. Her voice carried a slight huskiness to it that made her even more attractive.

As she came toward the Land Rover, I remembered that I was her driver.

The key was in the car and it was already running, so I opened the back door and stepped aside for her to climb inside.

"Thank you," she said with a little smile.

I wanted to see more of that smile, but without the sunshades hiding her eyes.

After closing the door behind her, I opened the trunk and helped Jackson load two suitcases.

"Take care of her," Jackson said, with a clap on my shoulder.

"Sure thing," I said. "Nice landing."

"Thanks," Jackson said. "See 'ya around." Then he turned and went inside.

He didn't know who I was. Didn't know that I was the newest Skye Travels pilot.

He didn't know. And neither did Wynter.

I climbed into the driver's seat and looked into the rearview mirror.

"Where can I take you, Miss Worthington?" I asked.

Wynter

I SETTLED into the back seat of the SUV and took off my sunglasses. The air conditioning was blowing at full force, keeping the oncoming outside heat at bay.

"Home please," I said, looking into the driver's eyes in the rearview mirror.

I sensed an air of patience about him.

He nodded once and tapped the GPS screen.

"Can I get the address?" he asked, then looked at me in the mirror. "just to confirm."

I rattled off my address and he tapped a line on the screen.

"You're new," I said, turning the vent off my face.

He grinned, looking at me again in the mirror.

"It's actually my first day," he said.

"Oh," I said. "Well. I hope it's going well."

He drove the car around the plane and took off toward the

gate. I pulled my phone out and checked it, mostly out of boredom.

"It's nothing like I expected," he said.

I set my phone down.

"How is it different?" I asked, finding the conversation much more interesting than scrolling through my messages.

He pulled out onto the freeway.

"I didn't expect to be driving, for one thing," he said.

"You thought you'd be shadowing," I said.

"Something like that," he said as he switched lanes.

The traffic was light right now. I estimated he'd have me home in about fifteen minutes.

"I didn't catch your name," I said, scooting over toward the middle of the bench seat, but the seatbelt had me locked in place.

"Cooper," he said.

And obviously Cooper was a man of few words.

"It's nice to meet you Cooper," I said, determined to get him talking. "Where are you from?"

"Originally Alabama," he said.

I smiled. "My mother is from Alabama."

"Small world," he said, holding the steering wheel loosely.

"How did you end up in Houston?"

He didn't answer at first. Seemed distracted by the GPS.

I could see why he didn't expect to drive today. He seemed unfamiliar with both the car and the roads.

He took the correct exit and headed toward Memorial Drive.

"Work," he said, looking back at me with an odd expression.

"What?" I asked, teasingly. "There's no need for drivers in Alabama?"

"I thought I'd like a change of scenery," he said.

I looked out the window as we drove though one of the most upscale residential areas of Houston.

I'd visited my grandmother in Alabama. She still lived in a modest, but comfortable house in a quiet neighborhood. Too quiet for my taste.

"Do you find it to be much different here?" I asked.

Cooper, too, looked around. "I'll let you know," he said, turning right at the stop sign.

A few minutes later we pulled up to my parents' house. It was unassuming, modest looking from the outside.

But on the other side of the front there was a house big enough to get lost in. There was a courtyard, for God's sake. Momma had said the courtyard was the selling point for her. Said it reminded her of a castle.

It had to be big to raise a family of five. And at least half the time, one of us had a friend over. Then there was the housekeeper and the nanny.

It was much quieter now that I was the only one of their children living at home.

I never heard either Momma or Daddy complain about me living there. To be honest, the way our busy schedules were, I rarely saw them.

Cooper put the car in park.

"Big place for a little girl," he said.

It took me a second to realize he didn't know that this was my parents' house. I wasn't offended by his statement in the least. Something about the way he said it actually sounded like a compliment.

"I like a lot of space," I said, putting my phone back in my handbag and unhooking my seatbelt.

"I'll get the door," he said, getting out of the car and stepping back to open my door.

With one hand on the door, he held out his other hand for me.

I put my hand in his to allow him to help me step out of the car. Anyone who said it was possible to get out of an SUV gracefully while wearing a straight skirt and heels was lying.

I found not being able to see Cooper's eyes behind his dark shades a little bit disconcerting, but mostly disappointing.

I wanted to see his eyes. To see if he was handsome with his shades off as he was with them on.

He closed the door behind me and tucked my hand in the crook of his arm.

It was a surprisingly old-fashioned move that caught me off guard.

I didn't tell him, but I thought that Cooper was going to do just fine as a driver. Or whatever else he decided to do for that matter.

He led me to the front door and released my hand.

"I'll wait for you to get inside," he said.

Instead of opening the door, I just looked at him. I appreciated him escorting me to the door and seeing me safely inside, but...

"Is there something else I can do?" he asked.

I lifted a brow.

"I'm going to need my luggage," I said.

My sense was that Cooper rarely forgot anything and even more, was rarely flustered.

But today was the exception.

Keep Reading Three Broken Rules...

Kathryn Kaleigh is the author of over seventy novels, over one hundred short stories, and many collections.

kathrynkaleigh.com

www.ingramcontent.com/pod-product-compliance
Lightning Source LLC
Chambersburg PA
CBHW020549120726
47903CB00001B/202